CIMARRÓN

CIMARRON

CIMARRÓN

ANDREW MCBRIDE

THORNDIKE PRESS
A part of Gale, a Cengage Company

LIBRARY OF CONGRESS CIP DATA ON FILE.
CATALOGUING IN PUBLICATION FOR THIS BOOK
IS AVAILABLE FROM THE LIBRARY OF CONGRESS.

ISBN-13: 978-1-4328-9402-3 (hardcover alk. paper)

Published in 2023 by arrangement with Anthony Dugdale

Printed in Mexico
Printed Number: 1   Print Year: 2024

ACKNOWLEDGMENTS

Thanks to Tiffany Schofield, Hazel Rumney, Erin Bealmear, and Kathy Heming at Five Star; and to The Scribblers, especially Liz.

The "hanging tree" mentioned in Chapters Two and Three is actually in Vulture City, Arizona. To suit my own purposes, I transported it fourteen miles to Wickenburg.

■ ■ ■ ■

PART ONE:
DECLAN FLYNN

■ ■ ■ ■

He was caught between two guns.

A man with a rifle behind him, and another on the slope above.

If either spotted him, he could be shot to doll rags trying to climb that slope, naked of cover, cruelly revealed in blue half-light, in the baleful eye of the moon. It didn't mean anything that the man above had once been his friend. A bullet from a former friend would kill just as easily as a bullet from an outright enemy.

Still, he had no choice. He willed himself to find the courage to move forward.

He began to climb the slope . . .

CHAPTER ONE

He came down from the Vulture Mountains. He was riding a buckskin horse and leading a pack mule.

His name was Calvin Taylor. But mostly he was known as Choctaw, a nickname he was trying to lose.

It was October 1873 and he was twenty years old.

He reined in the buckskin and studied what lay before him, his eyes narrowed against the glare of the late morning sun.

The mountains were at his back, and ahead, to the north, was desert, studded with saguaro. And beyond that the town, an untidy speckle of buildings sprawling over flat land.

Wickenburg, Arizona Territory.

There was supposed to be a sizable river — the Hassayampa — somewhere past this settlement, but he couldn't see it.

The buckskin shook his head and the rider

patted the side of the horse's neck with affection. Choctaw had shown absolutely no originality in naming the animal Buck. Buck was a powerful gray-gold horse with black mane, tail, and lower legs. Some of his long mane spilled forward over his left eye.

Considering Wickenburg, Choctaw rasped dust-filled fingernails over his scant trail beard. He guessed he looked like someone who'd spent a month in the mountains chipping at rocks for signs of gold and panning streams for color. His clothes — flannel shirt, denims, slouch hat — had most of the shape and color battered out of them, with patches at the knees and elbows. In some places they were little more than rags.

He was keen to rejoin the human race after enough lonesomeness to last him a considerable while. But he was also uneasy. A frontier town, spawned from a rough mining camp, was as full of dangers, in its own way, as any wilderness. Except these dangers were better hidden, and lurked in more unexpected places.

Choctaw shrugged at his own skittishness. How much trouble could he get into?

A rueful smile touched his lips at the thought. If there was trouble along the way, he usually managed to find it.

And he did.

■ ■ ■ ■

His first port of call on entering Wickenburg was the assay office. Choctaw haggled with the agent about how much the contents of his poke — the nuggets and dust he'd chipped and panned out of Vulture Mountain rock and stream — was worth in cash money. Which came out about midway between his highest hopes and worst anticipations.

Then he spent some of his earnings, first on a drink to cut the dust, then on a shave and haircut, and next on two sets of new clothes. He went to a hotel and booked a room for the next two nights, luxuriating in a bath the hotel provided.

Returning to his room, Choctaw dressed in one of his new outfits. He opened the window and gazed down.

Dusk and shadow were capturing Main Street. Judging from the noise below, the voices, laughter, and music spilling out, there was no shortage of saloons in Wickenburg, and the town was warming up for a lively evening.

This brash discordancy jarred in his ears, after the cathedral silence of the mountains. But it was the noise of people, and he

13

wanted to have people around him again.

He closed the window and stood in front of the room's only mirror.

He gazed at a young man six feet tall, medium build. Wearing a gray-blue shield front shirt, red bandanna, and black denims, his black Plainsman hat pushed back on his head.

Four weeks outdoors had burned his skin almost dark as an Indian's. He'd been dark complexioned to begin with, made more so by three years living in the Southwest. But, despite his nickname, his features had nothing Indian about them. He had dark hair but it was brown and tousled, not the straight blue-black of Indian hair. His eyes were as blue as a Swede's. As far as he knew he didn't have one drop of Indian blood in him. The nickname came from being born on the Choctaw Agency, at Fort Towson, Indian Territory. His father had been an army contractor and storekeeper there.

Choctaw studied the face, rubbing his smooth chin. He'd let the barber remove the mustache he'd been working on for a year or more and reckoned he'd stay clean-shaven for now.

Enough women had told him he was handsome for him to believe them. But there was a wariness in the eyes, and a tight-

14

ness in the mouth, which smiled slightly but seemed reluctant to do anything more, that told of the tension in him. He looked like someone who'd seen too much for his age, grown up too fast, and lived too much on his nerves.

Which was only the truth.

Now he owed himself some soft living, easy living, for a change. Starting tonight with a good meal, a few — most likely more than a few — drinks and a turn at the gambling tables.

Choctaw thought about strapping on his gun belt. He'd be heading out tonight with a fair amount of money on his person. But pistols and saloons were a bad mix. Trouble came when a fellow with a gun took on too much liquor, and a situation arose quickly out of one wrong word, or even one wrong look. So he decided to leave his revolver behind. He did slide a thin-bladed knife down the side of his boot . . .

Choctaw ate a fine meal in a good restaurant. He followed up by smoking a cigar, not his normal habit, but why not? Tonight he was out to treat himself. Then he made his way to a saloon.

It was called *The Golden Nugget.*

It was a fair-sized place, raucous with noise. Kerosene lamps hanging from the

15

ceiling gave dingy light, hazed over by tobacco smoke. Feet stirred sawdust. A long mahogany bar was jammed shoulder to shoulder with drinkers. Others stood around a roulette wheel, or sat at tables. A few poker games were going on. In one corner a couple of banjo and fiddle players strained to make themselves heard over the general din. It looked like an Anglo crowd, with only a handful of Mexicans present.

Choctaw managed to squeeze through to the bar. He bought a glass of mescal and stood with his back to the bar, nursing his drink and surveying all.

He was disappointed to see only one woman among the clientele. She dealt faro at a table. Maybe it was too early — his watch told him it was just 8 p.m. He expected *whirlago* girls would appear later and mix with the customers. But it had been a month since he'd seen any women and his eyes kept sneaking back to the faro dealer. She was pushing forty, he guessed, and running to fat. But he liked the way her hair was taken up, and how she filled out her frilly dress.

Then he noticed a large painting on the wall. It showed a young woman reclining on a couch. She wasn't wearing any kind of frilly dress, or any kind of frilly anything.

16

Choctaw forgot about the faro dealer and let his eyes rest on her a while.

An upraised voice lifted over the saloon noise.

"You four-flusher!"

Choctaw took his eyes off the nude in the painting and gazed at one of the poker tables, where two men appeared to be arguing. One sat with his back to the bar, so Choctaw couldn't make out much about him, save he was bareheaded and wearing a yellow vest. The young fellow facing him, sitting on the other side of the table with cards in his hand, was dressed in trail gear that was fairly nondescript, except he wore a large sombrero. But he didn't look Mexican. He confirmed that when he spoke, his accent as Texan as pecan pie. "What you saying, Harvey?"

Harvey replied, but his words were lost in a splurge of other voices. Maybe trouble was happening, but Choctaw had promised himself to keep out of that, and it wasn't any of his business anyway. So he went back to his pleasant contemplation of the nude, rolling a cigarette as he did so.

A chair scraped across the floor and an angry voice lifted. Reluctantly, Choctaw abandoned his study of the painting and gazed once more at the poker table.

Harvey was standing, addressing the man in the sombrero. The saloon had gone quiet around him, even the music-makers had paused, so Choctaw heard Harvey say, "You're a Goddamned bottom-dealer, Flynn!"

If Harvey was plenty mad, the Texan — Flynn — seemed unfazed. In fact, a grin split his long, narrow face as he leaned back in his chair, pushing his sombrero back on his head. "You calling me a cheat, *amigo*?"

"You been sharping us all night!"

On the frontier, men went to their guns over talk like that, but the Texan only laughed. "Nobody needs to sharp you, Harve. You play so bad you might as well give your money away!"

Harvey made a sound of anger. There was a bottle on the table. He grabbed it by the neck and swung it at the other man's head.

Flynn burst out of his chair. As he did so, he lifted the table, flinging it at Harvey. Cards, chips, money, glasses, bottles, and other poker players went flying.

Harvey dodged the table and struck again. But Flynn blocked the blow, catching Harvey's arm with his own upraised left arm. Then he swung a right-handed punch. It caught Harvey flush on the point of the chin.

18

The punch lifted Harvey off his feet. He hurled backwards, parting the crowd, crashed down on his back, and plowed across the floor. He came to rest at Choctaw's feet, the top of his head almost touching Choctaw's boot toe. He lay still while Choctaw gazed down at him, bemused.

Flynn hadn't lost his grin throughout this whole scrimmage. Now he bent and set the spilled-over table upright, while others scrabbled to pick up coins, dollar bills, chips, etc., strewn across the floor. The Texan addressed the room. "Now, that's what I call a sore loser!"

A couple of onlookers laughed.

At Choctaw's feet, Harvey stirred. He pushed himself up on one elbow. His right hand hunted around like it was looking for a gun. But he wasn't wearing a gun belt. His hand dived under his vest and came free and there was the gleam of metal in his fist.

Harvey raised his arm, aiming at Flynn's back, and Choctaw saw a small, snub-nosed object growing out of his hand.

A derringer!

Choctaw acted without thinking. He lifted his right foot and stepped on the back of Harvey's arm, pinning the limb to the floor. He drove the heel in hard, twisting it. Harvey cried out, his fingers splayed, and the hideout gun jerked from his grasp and skittered across the floor.

And then Flynn was there. He flashed Choctaw a look that was a mix of gratitude, surprise, and laughter. Meantime Harvey struggled to his feet. He clutched his stepped-on arm, breathing hard through his nose.

He glared at Choctaw in hatred, then turned the same glare on Flynn. He glanced back and forth between the two, as if deciding who to take on first.

He settled on Flynn. He swung a right cross that caught the Texan on the jaw and jolted him. But Flynn kept his feet and struck back. He showed his first punch had been no fluke, as his second one put Harvey back on the sawdust.

Harvey was game. He struggled up again, although this time he had to haul himself upright by clinging to the bar. He swayed, stared at Flynn bleary-eyed, and swung a wild uppercut that missed. Flynn launched his third good punch in a row. It impacted on Harvey's jaw with the noise of something breaking and the man was on his back once more. This time he stayed down. His mouth opened to groan. Blood flowed out of it over his chin and chest and pooled on the floor around him.

Choctaw sprang back to avoid any of this blood splashing the bottom of his new pants, but failed. He stared down at Harvey's broken face and felt revulsion, maybe even horror, even though the man had been a back-shooting son of a bitch.

Then he shifted his attention to Flynn.

The Texan rubbed his jaw, so maybe Harvey's punch had registered on him. At least it had displaced his grin. But a few seconds later the grin was back, and directed at Choctaw. The Texan extended his hand. *"Gracias, amigo."*

The other found he was smiling too. Something about the Texan's friendliness was hard to resist. Choctaw took the hand and shook it. *"De nada."*

And so Calvin Taylor met Declan Flynn.

CHAPTER TWO

Declan Flynn said, "We sure tied one on last night."

Choctaw nodded his head, which caused it to hurt even more. "We sure did."

They were sitting on a veranda on Wickenburg's main street. A ramada shaded them from the fierce 1 p.m. sun.

Stamp mills thumped away in nearby mines that gave this place its reason to exist. They also seemed to be thumping inside his skull. Music and harsh noise spilled from saloons. Clearly raucous life went on in Wickenburg twenty-four hours a day.

Choctaw gazed blearily down Main Street, which was fronted by a haphazard line of adobes, timber houses, tents, brush huts, false fronts, and bizarre hybrids of wood, mud, and rock. Maybe one in three dwellings looked to be a saloon. Traffic moved by: horsemen, carts, and a freight outfit, muleskinners sitting on their high wagons, cracking whips and turning the air blue with their language as they urged their mules on.

Two fellows were having a fight in the middle of the street, flailing away at each other while an encircling crowd yelled and egged them on.

All of which was plenty noisy and hurt Choctaw's head.

Declan rose unsteadily to his feet, swayed slightly, then made his way over to a horse trough. He dunked his head and splashed water over his face and shoulders.

Choctaw thought that might be a good idea. He did the same. The water was warm and maybe not too clean but he didn't care. He and Declan returned to the veranda. Declan had soaked his bandanna and got busy wringing it out over his head. Choctaw used his bandanna to towel his face dry.

He saw that his black denims, brand-new and spotlessly clean yesterday, were now scuffed and dusty. What had he been up to last night? He saw bloodstains on the bottom of his right leg and made a sound of disgust. He remembered how that blood got there, the breaking sound of Declan's fist on Harvey's jaw, and his stomach tightened.

Through his hangover fog, and the sun that hurt his eyes, Choctaw tried to piece together last night. Plenty of laughter, lots of booze coming. Him and Declan, going from one saloon to another, ending up where? There were flecks of straw on his sleeve so maybe they'd finished up bunking in a barn or a livery stable. He thought he could remember Dec saying that he was in the horse-trading business right now. Before that he'd been, variously, a cowboy, wrangler, and freighter. To which Choctaw had replied, "Me too."

Which was the truth, but a long way from the whole truth. He hadn't told the other man anything about his life with the Apaches.

He hadn't told Declan that plenty called him an Indian lover and some called him a squaw man. Or why.

Last night had been all about putting that behind him and just having some fun.

He was paying for it now though. He seemed to be sweating blood, out of his forehead and neck, so he used his soaked bandanna to damp that down. The aching in his head became a slow pounding, keeping time with one of the stamp mills.

Declan said, "Let's go eat something."

Choctaw groaned at the suggestion. "You want to eat, Dec, go ahead. I figure I'll just find a piece of shade to lie in for the next year or two."

Dec rose shakily to his feet, leaning against an upright.

He was a lanky fellow, maybe two inches taller than Choctaw. Twenty-two years old. He had a thatch of red hair and fair skin that freckled under the Arizona sun. He had managed to grow a decent mustache, which Choctaw envied. Maybe Dec's long face was more pleasant than handsome. But Choctaw guessed women would like him for his easy-laughing ways, his green eyes and reddish coloring. He wore nondescript trail gear, pants, shirt and vest. Like Choctaw, he wore no gun belt. The most distinctive item of his clothing, the wide-brimmed sombrero, hung down his back by a horsehair string.

Dec said, "My memory's kind of fuzzy . . ."

"So's mine! Wonder why?"

". . . But didn't you tell me you'd been raised up among a bunch of Indians?"

"My pa ran a store at Fort Towson in the Indian Territory."

"Raised among savages!"

Choctaw splashed water from the trough into his mouth, then spat it out, anything to get rid of the leathery taste. "Not hardly. That was in the Choctaw Nation. They're civilized Indians. That's what they're called. Live in towns . . . farmers . . . they're pretty much like white men."

Dec must have changed his mind about eating, as he sat back on the veranda. Choctaw told him, "You're the first Irishman I ever met with a Texas accent."

A small smile tugged at Dec's mouth. "I *was* born there — in the 'Emerald Isle.' But the first thing I can remember is being on a boat coming into Galveston Harbor. Being sick as a dog." He laughed. "Was raised in Nueces County." There was a pause, then he said, "Hey, didn't you tell me you'd been a wrangler on a horse ranch?"

"Yeah. Over in New Mexico."

"That's interesting."

Choctaw was about to ask the Irishman why it was interesting when he noticed two men approaching.

Dec gazed at these strangers and his smile became disdainful. "I was expecting this."

"What?"

The Irishman spat in the dust.

The newcomers strode up to them and halted half a dozen paces away. One said, "Looks like you boys sure tied one on."

Dec started to shape a cigarette. "That we did."

"My name's Finlay. I'm kind of the law 'round here."

Finlay was a tall man in his forties, without

much spare flesh on his frame. He wore a derby hat and a gray-blue frock coat, which must have been a burden in this heat. He eased back the wings of his coat, showing his vest underneath, and the pistol high on his right hip.

Dec said, "Don't see no badge. Just what kind of law are you?"

Choctaw was surprised at the hostility in Dec's voice, his easy friendliness gone. Finlay gave the Irishman a sharp look. It was a good face for frowning and giving accusing looks, being gaunt, with sunken cheeks and pale complexion. His wide handlebar mustache, dark turning gray, added to this stern picture. "Town council appointed me constable. I'm all the law there is here, until we get an officially appointed territorial marshal."

The second man spoke. "You fellers got any gainful employ in town?"

This man was short and shaped like a pear with the narrow part at the top. He was very fair in coloring, with a beard and mustache almost too pale to see. He also had a pistol on his right hip, his gun belt riding high on his expansive middle.

Choctaw asked, "What's that mean?"

"You working for anybody in Wickenburg?"

27

Dec said, "Just passing through."

Finlay frowned some more. "In which case, I'm advising you two to take your trade elsewhere."

"Our trade?"

"We're trying to build up a nice community here. We don't need no card sharps."

Choctaw's temper, which was always ready to come out fighting, stirred. "What?"

"If you're still around here tomorrow, say twenty-four hours from now, the town'll take a dim view of it."

Choctaw said, "I ain't no card sharp, mister!"

Temper pushed him to his feet, and made him glare at his accusers. Although it came to him as he did so that he could do little more than glare, as they had guns and he was unarmed — save for the knife hidden in his boot.

Dec addressed Finlay. "So you think we're a pair of card cheats?"

"That's right."

The Irishman made a small gesture towards Choctaw. "No need to accuse this feller. I never saw him before last night."

The pear-shaped man sneered. "Sure you didn't. You sharpers always work in pairs."

Choctaw's temper jumped in him again. "Don't call me a sharper you tub of guts!"

Pear-shape blinked, and his right hand moved towards his gun.

Finlay said, "Hold up, Slim."

Slim paused, and heat filled his face.

Dec said, "You got any proof I was sharping? Except what that feller Harvey said? He's the one you should be after. He come at me with a bottle. And then he tried to back-shoot me!"

Finlay nodded slightly. "We'd be dealing with him now if he wasn't laid up. You broke his jaw."

Dec looked shaken. "Jesus. I didn't mean to do that."

"You done it. We'll be moving him on too, once he's fit."

Nobody spoke for a minute, then Finlay said. "Like I said. Twenty-four hours."

Slim grinned, showing small yellow teeth. "Or else."

Choctaw said, "Or else what, big belly?"

Slim became red-faced again. Choctaw and the fat man got into a glaring contest. In part Choctaw was angry at himself for sounding like some kid. Finlay must have agreed as he said, "Things is getting a little childish around here. Now you two —" He gestured towards Declan and Choctaw "— just be sensible and heed what you've been told." Finlay coughed. It was a dry, racking

29

cough. He produced a handkerchief and pressed it to his lips. Now Choctaw understood his deathly pallor, his shriveled cheeks. Finlay took the cloth from his mouth and spat. "There's a tree down by the assay office. It's been decorated by eighteen fellers didn't heed what they were told. Don't you boys make it twenty."

Finlay walked away.

Slim did a little more glaring; then he turned and followed.

CHAPTER THREE

Choctaw watched the two so-called "law-men" walking down Main Street. He still felt hot with anger. He asked Declan, "We gonna sit here and take that?"

When the Irishman didn't reply, but merely shrugged, Choctaw said, "I ain't never been run out of no place."

"You get used to it."

"You mean it's happened to you before?"

"Once or twice. I just naturally end up butting heads with authority. I guess I just don't like nobody telling me what to do."

Choctaw sat back in the shade on the veranda. "Maybe I'm the same."

Declan got his grin back. "I reckon you and me are kindred spirits, young Choctaw!"

"My name's Calvin."

Declan rinsed his bandanna out over his head some more. With water streaming down his face he said, "We're misfits,

31

outsiders. We're bound to fall foul of the likes of them two. Especially when it calls itself the law." He made a contemptuous sound. "Law! Most lawmen I seen out here are crookeder than a dog's hind leg. They're either killers with a badge, on the take, or throwed in with the outlaws. Or all three."

Neither spoke for a while, then Choctaw asked, "So, what do we do now?"

"Something'll turn up."

"Maybe."

"You was lone prospecting, wasn't you? Up in the mountains. You could always go back to that."

Choctaw spoke with feeling. "No sir, I ain't going back."

"Why not?"

"It's not the prospecting so much. It's . . ." Choctaw felt a new wave of pain behind his eyes. He let it pass before he went on: "It's no good being alone in wild country. You've got to watch out all the time — for any hostiles still loose . . ."

"Indians?"

". . . For fellers riding the high lines — on the dodge from the law. Thieves and bandits and such. Some of them'll cut your throat just for your boots. That month up there by myself I was always looking over my shoulder, eating with one hand close to my gun.

Sleeping with one eye open, when I could sleep."

"Yeah?"

"On top of that I got so damn lonesome I ended up talking to my mule."

"It's when they start talking back to you that you should worry."

Both men laughed. Choctaw said, "No sir, the next time I go rock-scratching, it'll be in company." He glanced over at the Irishman. "You wanna go partners with me?"

"That's trusting of you, ain't it? How'd you know I wouldn't rob you, if we found any color? After all, the law says I'm a card sharp."

Choctaw shrugged.

Another freight outfit turned onto Main Street, hauled by oxen this time, bullwhackers walking alongside the teams, snapping whips over their heads, and urging the animals on. The air was filled with dust and salty language. The two young men watched this caravan pass, and park out front of some corrals.

Declan rubbed his soaked-through bandanna into the back of his neck. "I got a better idea than prospecting. Instead of scratching for gold that might not be there, I know where there's money just running 'round free."

33

"Where?"

"Coming down here from the north, I come through Mormons' Basin."

"So?"

"That basin is full of wild horses. I must have seen nearly a hundred of 'em. Catch 'em, break 'em, sell 'em for thirty to fifty dollars a head. More for stallions. Army wants remounts, ranchers need horses, everybody needs horses."

"Why you telling me this?"

"Can't break 'em on my own, boy. I need a partner. And you said you've been a wrangler. Will you throw in with me?"

"Let me think on it."

Dec slapped Choctaw across the knee with the back of his hand. "What is there to think about? We can get rich quick! A month, six weeks, we'd have enough money to last us all winter."

But, despite what he'd said, the Irishman then fell silent and let the other man think about it. Which Choctaw found to be hard work, given the load of pain in his head.

Declan asked, "How much money you got?"

"I dunno. I still got forty dollars left maybe."

"I got about the same."

34

"You must have done all right, horse trading."

"Yeah." Declan looked slightly uncomfortable for a second, then went on quickly, "How about we go in fifty-fifty, outfitting?"

"We got time to do that? We got to get out of town don't forget. So 'the law' says."

"Fuck 'the law!' And this place. We can go over to Vulture City and buy our supplies there. It's only ten miles."

Choctaw thought some more. As far as his hangover allowed. Declan let a minute pass, then asked, "Well? We partners?"

Choctaw thrust out his hand.

Declan grinned, took the other's hand, and shook it. "Partners!"

They both laughed.

Dec stood. "And to seal our partnership — let's go eat."

"Lead on, 'partner.' "

The Irishman set off down the street. Choctaw squinted a look at the high, fierce sun. Reluctantly, he stirred from the shade and followed.

They passed the assay office and came to a large tree. Both paused and studied it.

It looked like a live oak, or maybe an ironwood, a broad trunk from which a riot of thick, dark-gray branches sprouted. It was a peculiarly repulsive piece of nature,

Choctaw thought, entirely leafless, skin horny as a toad's back, smaller branches reaching out from the main boughs like wizened, clutching hands.

He said, "That is one ugly tree."

All the humor left Dec's face. He stared angrily, as if the tree had just spat in his eye. "Serves an ugly business."

"This the one Finlay talked about? The one they hung the eighteen fellers from?"

"Yeah. You ever seen a lynching?"

"No."

"Well, I have. Nothing I hate more! I'd like to chop it down myself."

He glanced around, as if looking for an axe to do just that. Choctaw shifted uncomfortably. He guessed these mood swings were part of Declan's character. Choctaw forced himself to grin. "Come on, partner. I'm hungry."

In an instant, the Irishman seemed to forget the hanging tree. He looked at the other man and smiled. "Partners — Taylor and Flynn."

"Flynn and Taylor!"

They laughed.

Dec slapped the other on the back. "After you, Choctaw."

Choctaw felt his grin slip. There it was again. He could travel this country end to end and still couldn't get loose of that damn nickname!

CHAPTER FOUR

Close to noon in Mormons' Basin.

Declan and Choctaw had been working the basin for eight days. They'd built three corrals for the mustangs they rounded up. But to date their tally was low — they'd only captured three horses, a stallion, and two of his stringers.

They had one of the stringers left to break, a blaze-faced claybank filly. Once she was done it would be the stallion's turn.

The claybank was penned alone in the largest corral. Declan had managed to get a saddle and bridle onto her and was about to get aboard while Choctaw leaned on the railings and watched.

Choctaw started shaping a cigarette. From time to time, he gave the surrounding land some study.

This was still Indian country — the range of those the locals called Tonto Apaches. He knew the Tontos weren't Apaches at all, mostly, but Yavapais. He knew this because, for the last two and a half years, on and off, he'd worked for the army, scouting against the hostiles. He'd been part of General Crook's campaign last winter when the army whipped the hostiles in several major fights. This seemed to have broken their resistance, and the past five months had been the most peaceful, Indian-wise, in the history of central Arizona. But there might still be a few renegades loose hereabouts, so you watched out for them.

And not just for them. Any Anglos or Mexicans in far lonesome places like this were likely to be running from the law, or bandits looking for what they could steal.

Choctaw was conscious of the "Yellow Boy" Winchester in the saddle scabbard of his buckskin horse, standing a few yards away. He also had a pistol, stowed with his gun belt in his saddlebags, too cumbersome to wear without need. There was a knife sheathed on his right hip.

His gaze roved over pink desert flats streaked with the green of mesquite. The walls of the basin rising blue in the distance. Beyond them purple mountains running against every horizon, an upside-down saw edge of bare rock under a vast blue sky. The Arizona landscape he'd grown used to, missing only the saguaro so prominent further south. He hadn't seen any north of the Hassayampa.

Some looked at this landscape and saw only useless desert. He saw a wild beauty that he loved.

It wasn't the scorching heat of summer but still plenty hot. Choctaw's once-new clothing had most of the color and shape battered out of it by dusty horse-breaking. Again he bristled a scant trail beard and mustache.

The claybank's whinny brought his attention back to the corral. Declan gathered the horse's reins, stabbed his left foot into the stirrup, and swung aboard.

The instant Dec's rump hit the saddle, the horse bunched her muscles and bucked. But the man clung on. Angrily, the mustang tried to get her head down so she could really go to bucking, but the rider kept her head up. The filly started pitching, grunting with her efforts. Yet the man stayed with her.

Choctaw yelled, "Hang on there, Dec! You got her!" He slapped his hat against his thigh.

Infuriated by the thing clinging to her back, the mustang took higher and wilder leaps, snorting and grunting, but couldn't shake her burden loose. Dec swayed and bobbed with the maddened plunging, twisting, and corkscrewing of the claybank. The rider stayed in the saddle . . . until he sat down a little too easy. The filly tossed him up with the highest buck so far, and swapped ends, and there was no horse under him.

Dec flailed into the air.

Falling, he struck against the top rail of the corral. And through it as it snapped under his weight. His descending body cleaved through the fence rails all the way to the earth.

There was a gap in the side of the corral.

Dec struck the earth and rolled away. The maddened filly went off around the corral like a firecracker, sunfishing and kicking backwards at the invisible enemies that had subjected her to this indignity. At the end of her crazed run, she made a tentative lunge at the break in the fence, then circled back.

Seeing what she was about, Choctaw yelled and set off at a sprint around the corral, to block the gap on the far side.

He got there just as the mustang vaulted through.

Choctaw grabbed at her trailing lines, got a hand to them, and was yanked off his feet. The claybank dragged him a few yards until he lost his grip. The horse took off to the west at a high lope.

There was a lot of dust.

Choctaw struggled up, coughing and blinking. He winced at the stinging of a scraped elbow and knee. At the same time Declan climbed shakily to his feet.

They gazed after the claybank, growing small in the distance.

Declan's face was hot with anger and he was cursing hard enough to make a mule-skinner blush. Choctaw walked over to him.

When the Irishman paused long enough in his cussing to catch his breath, Choctaw smiled and said, "Looks like you've got a busted fence to fix."

Dec glared. "You fix the fucking fence!"

Dec lifted his fist and punched the other quite hard in the chest. Choctaw felt his own temper flick and swung a punch in return, catching the Irishman on the shoulder. Dec slapped Choctaw's left cheek and then they were trading punches and half-wrestling with each other. Dec started laughing, typically switching from anger to laughter in a second. Choctaw glared his anger, and then he found he was also laughing.

After a minute of this sparring, the Irishman backed off a few paces, raising his hands to signal no more. They both laughed for a minute, then Dec said, "You fix the fence and I'll catch that gut-twister."

He used his sombrero to beat dust out of his clothes. If anything, his duds were even more battered and shapeless than his friend's.

Choctaw said, "Well, you know what they say, Dec. 'Ain't never been a horse that can't be rode — ' "

" ' — Ain't never been a rider can't be throwed.' " The Irishman scratched his trail beard. "Whose idea was it to go mustanging anyway?"

"Lemme see . . ." The other pretended to think, before grinning and saying, "I reckon it was yours!"

Declan grinned too. "Well, maybe it was." He glanced over at his paint horse, standing hipshot nearby. "You gonna be all right while I catch up that filly?"

"Sure."

Dec gestured towards the two horses in the other corrals. "Don't let nothing happen to them — especially that stallion." He walked over to the paint. He slid his Henry rifle from the saddle boot and inspected it. Then he ran the gun back into the scabbard. Declan gasped, placing his hand against his right side. "Maybe that damn claybank's busted *me* alongside that fence."

"Never mind, *amigo*. Just think about the dance in Lobo Wells this Saturday. All them *whirlago* girls."

"Dance?" The Irishman rubbed his fist into his back and made some more sounds of pain. "The way these mustangs is bouncing us about, we'll be lucky if we can still crawl!"

Declan rode off after the claybank and Choctaw set about plugging the gap in the corral fence. These fences had gotten broken before, so they kept a supply of poles and spars of mesquite at hand for any quick repairs. Choctaw ran a few poles across, lashing them together with strips of rawhide; he then strung a few lengths of rope across, and the break was temporarily fixed. Full, substantial repairs could wait for another day.

He broke his normal habit and worked through the afternoon. By 4 p.m. the job was done. Choctaw brewed himself a pot of coffee and ate some hardtack and jerky.

Next, he went over to the corral where they had the stallion penned.

The stallion stood at about sixteen hands. At a distance his coat looked black as oil, but up close you could see it was dark bay brown and almost purple, sheeny with sweat. Studying its lines, its fine points, its proud head, its dark, intelligent eyes, Choctaw felt a stirring of admiration for the animal's beauty.

He addressed the horse. "Tomorrow, you and me are going to play, huh?"

The stallion's ears pricked and slanted, pointing north.

Choctaw glanced that way and saw a small cloud of dust, growing bigger. It thinned and horsemen emerged.

He felt cold unease in his belly. He'd been careless, so busy admiring the stallion he'd forgotten to keep a lookout. He'd let two horsemen ride up to him unobserved.

They were now only a pistol shot away.

CHAPTER FIVE

Choctaw strode over to his horse and slid his Winchester from his saddle scabbard, watching the riders all the while.

They looked like Anglos.

He considered playing this hard from the start, pointing his rifle at the newcomers and calling out, "That's close enough." But before he could speak the riders reined in, maybe twenty yards off. Which was still closer than he should have let them get.

He took a quick glance at the country to the west, hoping Declan might show. But there was no sign of him.

Choctaw lowered his rifle, resting it against his right leg, his finger light on the trigger. He called, "Afternoon."

One of the newcomers touched his hat briefly. "You can call me Ike." He gestured towards the rider on his left. "This here's Kyle."

"Calvin Taylor."

"Mustanger huh?"

"That's right."

"All by yourself?"

At the question Choctaw felt the cold clay of fear in his belly. He told himself: *This is going to be bad.*

Ike was in his forties, lank, long-faced and rawboned. He wasn't carrying much fat on his six-foot frame. Under his wide-brimmed slouch hat, long brown hair showed, shot with gray. His handlebar mustache was also gray. The most striking feature about him was his paleness. He hadn't been out in the Arizona sun much of late. And his eyes were pale blue and cold, without one glimmer of friendliness.

Kyle was another tall, lean man, but much younger, maybe twenty-five. He had shoulder-length fair hair, mustache, and trail beard. There was a slight wildness to his eyes that was unsettling.

At first Choctaw hadn't taken these two for kin, but now he saw they both had the same long, sharp nose and long-jawed face. Kyle could be nephew or son to the older man.

They dressed like any nondescript cowboys or travelers. They wore pistols on their hips and also had rifles in saddle boots.

The horses they rode looked pretty

ganted. But the men looked hard-worn too. Scuffed leather and patches were in evidence. A layer of dust lay over them. They had a hungry look, maybe not just the product of hard traveling in desert country. If he was being uncharitable, Choctaw might have marked them as rawhiders.

He found he was being uncharitable anyway. He didn't take to these men. He didn't like the slow, deliberate way they inspected what was before them: the horses in the corrals, Choctaw's horse, the camp gear strewn about. Their eyes lingered on each item like they were doing a tally, then moved on. Most particularly he didn't like the way their scrutiny ended with the stallion. Both men gazed at the horse like a drunk looking at a bottle after a long dry, or a man long without a woman with his eyes on one.

He thought about Ike's paleness. He'd once seen another fellow like that. He'd been told this man had *prison pallor,* the hue of skin you got from years out of the sun, penned in a prison cell.

Choctaw chewed his lower lip. He wondered where Declan was. *How come there ain't never a crazy Irishman around when you need one?*

Until Dec showed, he decided to keep

playing this friendly. He asked Ike, "What can I do for you?"

But Ike ignored the question and spoke instead to Kyle. "What you think, boy?"

Kyle scratched his trail beard. "About a hundred and fifty for the stallion, maybe forty for the stringer."

Ike nodded. "Close to two hundred dollars."

Choctaw felt a smile working at his lips, although he couldn't imagine what he'd found to smile about. "Yeah, that's sort of what I figured to sell 'em for."

Now Ike smiled, genial as all hell. His teeth were bad though, yellow and brown with a few gaps showing. "Don't worry about that, boy. *We'll* sell 'em for you." He gave a short laugh. "Only question is . . ." He rested his right hand on his left hip, close to his pistol in its cross-draw holster. ". . . you gonna be nice about it, and let it happen, or are you gonna be stupid?"

Kyle's hands had been resting on his saddle horn. Now he moved them so they hovered at his side, the right one just a few inches away from the grip of his pistol.

Choctaw felt more fear, tight in his mouth and throat. He started to tremble slightly. He was still smiling like a damn fool, but the smile was fixed on his face as if it was nailed there.

Ike went on, "We ain't after trouble. We just wanna trade. Kyle's plug here for that buckskin of yourn. My old Spencer for your fancy Winchester." He nodded towards the corrals. "Your camp gear, them horses, for . . ."

"For what?"

Ike smiled, showing his bad teeth again. "Your life, boy."

Kyle laughed, making a noise halfway between a whinny and a bray. His laugh was as crazy as his eyes. "Or do you fancy two-on-one?"

That wild laugh jangled Choctaw's nerves, which were stretched taut as an Apache bowstring anyway. But he *had* been given an opportunity to back out of this. To let these rawhiders clean him out, and just hope Ike kept his word, about not killing him . . . Later, he and Dec could go after them, and get back what they'd lost. Sure it would be humbling, eating crow right now, but it was the sensible thing to do. The better part of valor and all that.

The stallion whickered.

Choctaw glanced at the horse, prowling restless in the corral. He thought of this animal in the hands of Kyle and Ike . . . Instantly, he forgot fear and knew only a

50

hot rush of temper.

"No trade!"

Kyle blinked, and his lips pursed in anger. His hands started to move.

Ike said, "No, boy."

Kyle froze his hands where they were. He glared some more, then darted a questioning look at the older man.

Ike gazed at Choctaw. His face showed disappointment, maybe even sadness. "Looky here, younker." He spoke slowly, like a man long practiced at keeping patient with foolish youth. "Like I said, we don't want trouble. This can all be settled peaceable."

Choctaw thought it over. Another chance to back away. But that would be backing away from keeping the stallion too.

He tried to put a curb on his temper. And failed. Before he knew it, the words were out of his mouth. "Get your thieving hides out of here!" He lifted his rifle, pointing it at the horsebackers.

Ike reared back slightly, like he'd just caught a bad, sharp stink in his nostrils. High color touched his weathered cheeks. Kyle flinched.

Choctaw seemed to be two people. The one talking and acting, and the other watching him do so. The second version of himself

51

felt some dismay. He'd had two chances to back out of this. Instead, he'd spat in the eyes of two armed men. Was he crazy? Did he think he could take both of them?

These last few years he'd developed a nasty habit of jumping into things without thinking them over first. A number of times it had landed him in spots like this. Eyeball to eyeball with dangerous men. Would he ever learn?

Would he live long enough to learn?

Kyle glanced across at Ike, as if he was waiting for orders.

Ike nodded slightly. Like maybe he was signaling something. Signaling what?

Choctaw tensed, bending his knees. He braced himself, ready to be ridden down by these men, to go down shooting.

But neither rider moved. The anger faded from Ike's face. He started to turn his horse away. Still keeping a hold on his temper, he said, "You got no respect for your elders, boy." Over his shoulder he added, "Somebody ought to teach you that."

Kyle wheeled his horse about too. Choctaw was surprised to find himself watching the riders' backs as they moved away from him.

He sighed with heavy relief, blowing out his cheeks. He felt almost dazed with it. He took his eyes off the horsemen and looked to the west, for any sign of Declan.

Which was a mistake.

Because the riders moved simultaneously, spurring their horses into sudden movement. Ike swung his horse to the left and Kyle to the right, cutting their horses around, circling back towards the man afoot. They came at him at the full gallop, pistols in their hands.

They yelled.

Choctaw jammed the butt of his rifle into his shoulder. He aimed at Ike as the man fired.

Ike missed.

Choctaw fired.

Ike came loose of his horse. He pitched sideways and hit the earth in a burst of dust.

Choctaw swung towards Kyle. The rider was almost upon him. Choctaw didn't have time to get his rifle back to his shoulder. He took the gun by the barrel, got a two-handed grip, and swung.

The butt hooked into Kyle's stomach. The blow scooped him out of the saddle. His horse plunged ahead, its shoulder catching Choctaw broadside, knocking him from his feet.

Choctaw struck the earth on his back. Hard.

All the wind seemed to be driven out of him.

He didn't know how long he lay there, dazed, trying to pull air into seared lungs.

But eventually he did move. Kneeling up and then climbing to his feet.

Ike and Kyle were both down. But as Choctaw reached full height, Kyle stirred too. He sat up.

Choctaw glimpsed the butt of his rifle at his feet. He ducked down, grabbed it, lifted it . . . and then he realized all he held was the stock, the barrel lay in the dust nearby. Striking Kyle, he'd broken the Winchester in half.

Kyle rose slowly and painfully to his feet, left hand pressed to his side. In his right hand he held a pistol, which he pointed at the other man's chest.

Choctaw stared stupidly. There was death, a dozen yards and a finger squeeze away. But he was too dazed to feel fear, or anything . . .

He could only watch.

Kyle squinted, taking better aim.

And then he seemed to fling himself backwards, as if yanked by an invisible rope from behind.

Kyle hit on his back. Dust rose.

There was the sound of a shot.

Choctaw stared at him a minute, not understanding.

In the tail of his eye, he saw movement. There was a boil of dust, off to the west, growing bigger as it came closer, and a rider inside it. It rolled nearer and thinned, revealing Declan on his paint, leading the claybank on a trailing line.

Choctaw walked over to Ike. He was dead, his face showing a faint surprise, his eyes wide open and a hole in his forehead. The back and top of his head were scattered all over the trail.

Moving to Kyle, Choctaw felt relief when he saw the man was still alive, eyes open and trying hard to breathe. There was blood all over his shirt and the top of his pants, pooling on the earth around him. There was a small hole in his shirtfront, almost dead center in his chest.

Kyle groaned and said, "Ma." It was a small, weak voice, almost that of a child.

Choctaw said, "You'll be all right." His words mocked him, like that was maybe the stupidest thing he'd ever said. He followed up with something nearly as lame. "We'll fix you up."

Kyle tried to speak again and blood came out of his mouth and nose, washing over his chin. Choctaw remembered there was a canteen hanging on one of the corral fences and moved towards it.

Kyle screamed. That stopped Choctaw in his tracks. The scream went right through him, even into his teeth.

He hurried over to the canteen, took it from its hanging place, and returned to Kyle. He unstoppered the canteen, kneeling over the fallen man. Then he saw Kyle was dead, eyes and mouth wide.

Choctaw glanced up at the sound of hooves. Declan reined in a dozen yards away. The Irishman had his Henry rifle in his hand; he rested the weapon across his horse's withers.

Choctaw expected him to ask questions. When he didn't, Choctaw said, "Rawhiders. They wanted to clean out the camp." His voice shook slightly. His arms shook too, which was how he always reacted to violence.

Declan remained silent.

Choctaw tried to give his friend a rueful smile, but doubted he made anything but a poor job of it. *"Gracias, amigo."*

The Irishman took a long, slow look around, turning in the saddle. When at last he did speak, it was to observe, "Looks like you busted your nice Winchester!"

CHAPTER SIX

Declan dismounted and studied the dead men. "Ike and Kyle Baker."

In surprise Choctaw asked, "You know them?" When Dec nodded, Choctaw said, "I figured they was related."

The Irishman started to shape a cigarette. "Nobody could work out how. I don't want to speak ill of the dead, but talk was . . . Ike was kind of fond of his own sister. You know . . . Inbreeding."

"Shit."

"I did some horse trading with them once. Up north. Word was bad on them, though. That most of the horses they sold was stolen." Dec lit his cigarette. "Well, I'll smoke this, then we'd better get to planting 'em."

"What? Ain't we gonna take 'em into the law?"

"What for?"

"You're supposed to tell the law, ain't you,

when you kill somebody?"

Dec made a dismissive sound. "Pack these dead bodies over to Lobo Wells? That's a long day's ride in the sun. They won't be any too fragrant when we get there. And I don't even know if there is any law in Lobo Wells to report to."

"Maybe there's a reward on 'em."

The Irishman looked disdainful. "No-accounts like them? Small change, if any. Meanwhile we'll be missing out on the real money we *could* be making breaking horses."

He took a long pull on his quirley and exhaled, watching smoke thin as it drifted towards the walls of the basin. "I tell you what we could do. We could cut their heads off and put them in gunnysacks, lug 'em into town, and hope they ain't too ripe when we arrive. You fancy that?"

"Not hardly."

"Then let's get to planting."

"One of us better read over them."

As soon as the words were out of his mouth, Choctaw was conscious how pious he sounded. Meanwhile Dec gave him a look of bewilderment and shook his head slightly. "I swear, how you carry on over a pair of rawhiders. Two polecats that was fixing to rob us blind and cut your throat."

"They said they wouldn't kill me."

"They give their real names?"

"Uh-huh."

"Then they'd kill you." Dec flipped his cigarette and emptied his lungs of the last smoke inside him. "But maybe you're right. Maybe we should say some good words over the dear departed." A smile twitched at his lips. "Maybe sing a few hymns and then maybe have a church supper."

He started to laugh and Choctaw felt a rush of temper. He cried, "You fucking bastard!" and launched himself at the other man.

They were back to wrestling and punching at each other. But somewhere in there they started laughing. And then they were too busy laughing to fight.

A couple of times a day they seemed to fall to sparring like this, rubbing away the itch of being crowded together in a harsh, desolate place, doing a back-breaking, dust-eating job. Most times it ended this way. This time they were laughing longer and harder than before; there was something almost crazy in how hard they went at it. They were laughing out tension, and the act of killing.

Later Dec and Choctaw found a place not too close to camp and scraped a grave out of the earth. They dug just as deep as might be considered decent, one grave for both men. Each body was covered with a blanket, then earth. Atop this they laid rocks, to discourage varmints. By the time they'd finished it was close to sundown.

Dec took his hat off and held it in his hands. He glanced over at his friend. "Do you know any words?" Choctaw was surprised at how somber Dec looked. And there was no sarcasm in his voice.

"Yeah."

"Say something."

"All right." Choctaw strained to remember. " *'O death, where is thy sting? O grave where is thy victory?'* " He paused because he'd forgotten the next words and then went on, " *'Jesus said . . . I am the resurrection, and the life: he that believeth in me, though he were dead, yet shall he live: And whosoever liveth and believeth in me shall never die.'* "

"Good words." Dec gestured towards the grave. "Better than they deserved."

"I think I got two different verses mixed up."

"Still, it's pretty. Where'd you learn that?"

"My pa fancied himself as a preacher. Especially when he was drunk. Which was plenty."

Dec asked, "Your pa was a preacher?"

"Just called himself one. He sure didn't act like a Christian, most of the time."

"My father swore off any religion. He hated it with a passion. He said it was the curse of Ireland."

"Yeah?" Choctaw realized how little he really knew about his friend. But that was how it was out here. An unwritten rule of the frontier was you didn't ask about somebody else's past.

Dec stared at the grave, frowning. He seemed to take burying harder than killing. "Let's eat."

It was an unusually silent meal. Silent afterwards too. Their campfire was an oasis of amber and rust in deep purple darkness. Both men stared into the flames. But if they weren't talking, other creatures filled the night with their howling and cries, spooking the horses.

Dec said, "The wolves and coyotes, trying to dig up them Bakers."

Choctaw nodded. "Yeah. Reminds me of —" Just in time, he caught his tongue.

"Of what?"

Choctaw had been about to say: *It reminds me of the Camp Walsh Massacre. When wolves and coyotes swarmed down out of the mountains to feast on more than one hundred*

61

murdered Aravaipa Apaches. But he hadn't shared that black reminiscence with Dec, or almost anybody. Instead, he said, "Nothing."

The humans fell back into silence, while the animal kingdom screeched and yowled about them.

Choctaw fashioned a cigarette. Tonight's food tasted like ashes in his mouth, although he couldn't remember what he'd eaten. He hadn't managed the appetite to stomach much, whatever it was. He saw Ike's blood and brains all over the trail. He heard Kyle scream.

Dec sighed heavily. "I wish we had some liquor left."

"Yeah."

"You'd think them Bakers would have at least one bottle in their saddlebags."

All at once Choctaw couldn't take any more of the gloom pressing down on him. He attempted to smile, and to his surprise, managed one. "Why don't you get out your Jew's harp? Let's have a wake."

"Not in the mood."

Choctaw pushed himself to his feet. "Goddamn it! I'm not going to sit here anymore, feeling bad 'cus I had to kill some horse thief who was trying to kill me."

"What you gonna do?"

"I'm gonna go over there and pay my respects."

"Huh?"

Choctaw touched his groin. "Piss on their graves!"

Dec grinned. He stood too. "I think I'll join you."

He laughed. Choctaw laughed. Both men grinned at the other.

After a minute, Choctaw lost his grin. "Maybe that's not such a good idea."

Dec also let his grin slip away. "Maybe it isn't."

They sat.

Around them predators howled and screamed.

CHAPTER SEVEN

Saturday morning and Dec and Choctaw were hazing their saddle band — the stallion and his two stringers — along the trail.

All the mustangs were broken now, including the stallion.

They crossed a tableland of rippling grama grass, waving knee-high. At the far side, the riders reined in and gazed westward.

There was a long, gradual slope before them. At the base a stretch of flat country and a freckling of buildings.

Dec said, "There's Lobo Wells."

Choctaw made a sound of disappointment. "Not much of a town."

"It'll have to do. Sixty miles of hard desert to the next place."

"Yeah?"

"It's just about all there is between Wickenburg and Hardyville."

Both men dismounted and spent some

time sitting, rubbing the cramps of long riding from their legs. Then they walked about, kneading the aches in their backs.

That done, they got out their bibles and started on the makings. The stringers whinnied and pushed against each other. Choctaw called to them, "Be gentle now!" Then he addressed Dec. "Not bad for two weeks bronc busting. A hundred and ten dollars apiece, maybe."

"Beats being a thirty-a-month cowboy."

Choctaw grinned. "Or pushing a plow."

Declan laughed. "Anything beats that!"

"So how do we go about this horse-trading business?"

"Go into town and throw these horses into a corral. Then we set out our stall. Spread the word about what we've got to offer. Sell to the highest bidder. Then we check into the hotel, have a bath, eat the biggest steak they got — and get drunk." Deep hunger came into his voice. "I got all the dust of Mormons' Basin to cut out of my throat. As for women . . . I tell you, boy, I am horny as a jackrabbit."

"Do we tell folks about the Bakers?"

"Fuck the Bakers!"

At Dec's upraised voice a few of the horses gave startled whinnies. Gentling his voice, he told them, "Hush up now."

"Maybe we should."

"Dunno, Calvin." Dec rarely used his given name, except when he was being serious, or, more frequently, mock serious. "Might not be wise."

"Why not?"

"You gotta realize in pissant places like this —" Dec gestured towards Lobo Wells "— mostly nothing happens. Folks get crazy mean with nothing happening. So they're always looking for a little excitement. Like maybe lynching a couple of strangers."

"Why should they lynch us? We killed them rawhiders in self-defense."

"That's just our say-so, boy. Our word against two dead men. All it takes is somebody in that town knows them Bakers, is a friend of theirs. He whips them up against us, they get liquored up . . . All I know is: I ain't gonna dance on a rope just to keep the locals entertained. You ever seen a lynching?"

"No. But you have. You already told me. What happened?"

It took the Irishman a while to reply. "Never mind. Best for all concerned if we don't say nothing."

An awkward silence came between them.

Choctaw thought about Declan's behavior, switching in an instant from happy-go-

66

lucky Irishman into darker moods and intense anger and back again. Hard about the law and lynching, but easy about killing. Filled with gloom at burying.

Choctaw came out of his reverie, conscious of the strained silence between them and wondering how to break it. But Dec did that for him, saying, "Let's not quarrel over the likes of the Bakers. Just respect me on these things, all right?"

"I always treat you with the respect you deserve."

"Good."

"Which is none!"

Dec rubbed his chin stubble. "Time you was reacquainted with some women. I been getting worried about you, boy. I mean, I seen you looking at that claybank filly real fond a time or two . . ."

Choctaw picked up a small stone and flung it. It missed Dec's right shoulder by an inch. The Irishman declared, "Tonight we'll probably be the richest fellers in Lobo Wells. Them women at the dance'll be all over us!"

Declan and Choctaw drove their saddle band into a corral on the edge of Lobo Wells and waited for potential buyers to show up. Which they did and soon.

The two mustangers ended up selling their horses to a local rancher named Nils Swenson.

Swenson leaned on the corral bars and gazed at the saddle band and — most particularly — the stallion in undisguised pleasure. Then he addressed the two mustangers. "You boys figure on going back to bronc busting?"

Declan looked up from the quirley he was fashioning. "Maybe."

Swenson took off his hat and scratched the back of his head. He was shortish but powerfully built, barrel-chested and square-faced, in his fifties. He had a shock of hair that might once have been as fair as his Scandinavian name suggested. Now it was silver with a grizzling of gray beard and mustache. His accent was singular, Texan but retaining a sibilance from the old country. He said, "I can always use good wranglers." The word came out as "wranklersss."

When neither of the others replied, he said, "Well, think about it."

Dec smiled. "Sure."

"Good money you've made. Now you're young men, so I ain't going to be so foolish as to tell you to spend your money wisely."

Declan glanced at Choctaw. They exchanged rueful smiles.

Swenson produced a pipe and pointed the stem at them. "You boys going to the dance tonight?"

Choctaw said, "Yes, sir."

"I'll be in town tomorrow. I expect to see you two walking around with sore heads."

The young men laughed. Dec said, "I reckon you will."

"And try and stay out of trouble, boys."

Choctaw said, "Sure will, Mr. Swenson."

Once again, he made a determination to himself to do just that.

And once again he failed.

CHAPTER EIGHT

The Saturday night dance was held in Lobo Wells's main saloon, which, alongside the one and only hotel, was the biggest building in town. Although Lobo Wells was more like a village, a shapeless sprawl of adobes, shacks, and tents with a population of maybe three hundred. Tonight that number was swelled by outsiders from nearby ranches, mines, and settlements coming to the dance. The saloon was a noisy place packed tight with drinkers, gamblers, and dancers. As usual a tobacco haze dimmed the kerosene light.

Dec took only a few turns on the dance floor. He said, "I am as clumsy as a three-legged buffalo on the dance floor. I guess my feet are too big!"

So Dec mostly sat and drank and Choctaw danced.

Word was there was a camp of Mexicans nearby, come in from Sonora to grow and harvest vegetables on an irrigated plain. It looked like plenty of them were in Lobo Wells tonight. A band that seemed to be wholly Mexican played *ranchera* music on brass instruments, fiddles, guitars, and *guitarróns*. Most of the girls dancing seemed to be Mexican.

Such as the woman Choctaw was partnered with. She looked to be in her thirties. Her name was Ina. Or was it Inez?

She laughed, her arms draped over his shoulders, leaning into him. "You like this music, huh?"

"Sure do."

She reached up and pinched his right cheek. "I like your pretty blue eyes, *querido*."

Choctaw smiled. "I think maybe you already told me that."

She laughed again. Choctaw was pleased he was making her so happy. But then someone cut in, and she was off dancing and laughing with him. Maybe laughing even harder. Choctaw leaned against the wall, feeling a slow pang of jealousy. Maybe he should shoot that cutting-in son of a bitch. Except Choctaw wasn't armed tonight — save for his old friend, the knife down the side of his boot. He turned his resentment against Inez, considering the

71

fickleness of women. Then he decided he was too happy to turn mean, and in a forgiving mood towards Inez, the cutter-in, and everybody. He felt a little tired from dancing anyway, and muzzy from booze. So Choctaw walked, slowly and carefully, over to Declan and sat at the same table.

Dec asked, "You all right?"

"I'm good, *amigo*. Pretty damn good."

"You sure been dancing up a storm with them hot *tamales*."

"How about you? You drunk yet?"

"Getting there. But —" the Irishman started speaking slowly and carefully, one word at a time, like he *was* drunk and trying to disguise it. "— I ain't. Figuring. On. Getting. Totally. Drunk. Otherwise my functions won't function. Later on, if you know what I mean."

He gazed around the room. Choctaw knew he was looking at the women in particular. Which was a pleasant thing to do, so Choctaw did the same. Most of the *whirlago* girls in view wore gaudy dresses, showing a lot of shoulder, cleavage, and ankle. Quite of few of them seemed a long, tired way past their best, but the clientele didn't seem to mind. Whatever these men were saying to them, it was sure amusing as there was a lot of female laughter.

72

Dec stared owlishly at a Mexican woman standing against the wall, smoking a short cigar, her face wreathed in smoke. She was old enough to be your mama and fat enough for almost two mamas, but Dec smiled at her and she smiled back. Then the Irishman glanced at Choctaw. "Oh, I forgot. You don't partake."

Choctaw shifted in discomfort. "You know . . . I tried it once with them gals. Wasn't to my taste."

Dec carefully poured himself another drink. "You waiting for some nice respectable girl to come along you can fall in *love* with? Well, you know, they're about as common as hen's teeth out here. 'Sides, they ain't gonna have nothing to do with a couple of sweaty mustangers."

"What do you mean, sweaty? I had a bath today. And a barbershop shave."

"So did I. Don't change the fact. Nice girls ain't gonna look at a pair of drifters. Until we get respectable —" Declan raised his glass in a toast to the woman standing by the wall, "— it's these females or no females."

Choctaw studied the back of his hands. "Yeah, well . . ."

"Sure, you might get an itch in your pants, but . . ." The Irishman drank. "That's the price you pay for not being lonesome."

An awkward silence descended, but maybe Dec didn't notice, a lot of his attention being directed to the whiskey he was drinking.

Choctaw said, "I think I'll go get a breath of air."

"Sure, *amigo.*" Dec smiled. "I'll be all right." His eyes moved to the woman once more.

His friend smiled too. "I figure you will be."

"Not just that, *compadre.* Something else before I get to the women." Declan rubbed his newly shaved chin. "Money business. Feller told me there's a poker game going on in the back room." With his thumb, he indicated behind him. "Big game. High stakes."

"You sure that's a good idea? Remember the last time you played poker?"

Dec laughed. "Won the pot, didn't I? You want to come along?"

The other shook his head. "I'm too drunk to play poker."

"I'm drunk too. I play *better* drunk." He reached out and slapped Choctaw across the knee with the back of his hand. "I swear. Agin' women. Agin' gambling. You're turning into a preacher!"

Choctaw didn't rise to that bait. Dec

stood, not quite steadily. The other said, "Watch yourself, *amigo.* Once you get behind closed doors . . ."

Unlike Choctaw, Declan *was* wearing a gun. Dec took his pistol — a Remington New Model .44 — out of the holster on his right hip. He laid the long-barreled weapon on the table. "Anybody tries to roll *me* . . . I tell you, Choc, the population of this shithole will go down considerable. They'll look around and remember the Alamo!"

"You've just made some good money, a hundred dollars, busting your back breaking them mustangs. Now you're gonna risk it all in a card game?"

Dec cocked his head as if thinking. "I'm so lucky. Most people only got one mother. I've got two." He took another drink. "Don't worry, *mi madre.* Just watch me turn that hundred dollars into a thousand."

"Well, good luck." Choctaw smiled. "By the way, Dec — fuck you!"

"And fuck you!"

"And fuck you too!"

The two young men smiled at each other. Declan holstered his pistol, turned, and made his way towards the back of the saloon.

After a minute or so, Choctaw stood. He headed for the door, easing through the crowd. As he threaded his way between two *whirlago* women, the one behind him grabbed his right buttock. He started to turn towards her in surprise and the other woman grabbed him somewhere else. And squeezed. He turned back towards her and she laughed and let go, fading into the crowd.

Choctaw thought maybe he'd forget his prejudices against *whirlago* girls. Maybe Declan had been right. He turned and looked for either woman but they were lost in the crowd.

He gazed into this faceless throng sadly. Then he returned to the business of clearing his head with some night air. He pointed once more towards the door. The noise in the saloon blared in his ears and he guessed he was drunker than he'd figured.

He was almost at the door, a few paces short of it, when a face swam out of the crowd before him.

This man placed himself directly in Choctaw's path. He asked, "You're Calvin Taylor, ain't you?"

Choctaw halted. The stranger's tone wasn't exactly unfriendly, but Choctaw still gazed at him warily. He told himself: *I'm going to keep out of trouble tonight.* He didn't want it with Dec, or Inez, or that son of a bitch who'd cut in. He didn't want it with this man now.

The stranger said, "You don't know me."

Choctaw smiled. "Right both times."

"I'm Billy Keogh. I'm a friend of Jack Adams."

At the mention of that name, Choctaw felt himself sobering up in a hurry. He gave up any pretense of smiling, or showing friendliness towards Keogh. Instead he glanced at the other man's waist, in case his hands were anywhere near a weapon.

But Keogh wasn't wearing a gun belt.

Choctaw looked Keogh over, for signs of a concealed pistol or knife. He couldn't see any bulge in the man's vest that might mean a hideout gun. He thought about his own knife, stowed in his boot . . .

Keogh asked, "You remember Jack Adams?"

Choctaw frowned at hard memories. He took his time answering. "Sure I do."

The other man nodded slightly. "You should . . . seeing as how you put three bullets in him."

CHAPTER NINE

Billy Keogh might be thirtyish, medium as to height and build. Nondescript as to clothes, hat, vest, pants. Fairish in coloring. Under his hat brim pale hair showed. And his face was clean-shaven and bland and should thus be hard to remember.

Except there was something unsettling about how this man looked.

Was it his weak, receding chin? The mouth and nose barely registered, pieces of flesh that seemed not quite finished off or fully formed. Or was it his eyes?

They were a cold blue. Protuberant, bulging under heavy lids, deep pouches under them. Very dead eyes, almost lizard-like and a small mouth that seemed fixed in a smirk. In a way this fellow was baby-faced, with any facial hair so fine as to be almost invisible. And yet the eyes were as empty as those of an old man weary of life.

Whatever, there was something peculiarly

78

ugly, almost repulsive, about his face.

Choctaw said, "Yeah, I shot Jack Adams."

"Shot him and left him a one-lung cripple."

"I've always been sorry about that."

Contempt touched Keogh's small mouth. "You're sorry?"

"Yeah . . . I'm sorry I didn't kill the son of a bitch!"

Keogh blinked his reptilian eyes. He stiffened and his hands twitched as if they wanted to reach guns that weren't there.

Choctaw went on, "Adams murdered a friend of mine. And he tried to back-shoot me. It's a wonder they didn't hang him, for all he's a cripple."

Keogh said, "That's 'cuz folks in Tucson ain't gonna hang a man . . ." He paused, lips puckered as if to spit, ". . . for killing an Indian lover!" For the first time he showed real emotion, beyond boredom and contempt, glaring his hatred. "A squaw-humping Apache lover just like you!"

Dimly Choctaw recalled he had a plan to be friendly to everybody, to stay out of trouble. That seemed a long time ago.

He swung a punch at Billy Keogh.

But maybe he hadn't fully sobered up because his aim was wild. He missed his target altogether and struck a man standing behind Keogh across the back of the shoulder.

This man turned slowly. Understandably as there was a lot of him to turn. He looked to be the biggest man in this room. Or maybe any room. Close to seven feet tall, a few axe-handles across with a chest and shoulders he might have borrowed from an ox. He had heavy mustaches and a beard covering much of his chest, a black thicket you could lose a small child in. A wide-brimmed hat was jammed down on his massive head.

Choctaw switched his attention from Keogh to this colossus. He didn't see the right hook Keogh flung at him, catching him on the chin and jolting him. But it wasn't much of a punch, not much strength behind it. Choctaw lifted his fist to strike back and the giant stepped between them.

He gazed down from his great height, breathing hard through bull-like nostrils. He told both parties, "You wanna fight — do it outside."

Choctaw tasted blood in his mouth. He touched his lower lip, which stung like fire, and his fingertips came away bloody. He glared at Keogh, who said, "I ain't heeled."

"Then get yourself a gun."

"I intend to. Say around noon tomorrow.

Out there." Keogh glanced towards the door.

"I'll be there."

"I'll see you then . . . Apache lover!"

Choctaw, answering to his temper, stepped towards Keogh, lifting his fist to land a punch on target this time. But a hand the size of a shovel descended from above and flattened its horny palm on his chest. The back of this hand was covered in wiry black hair and rested on his torso like some shaggy feral creature. Choctaw glanced from the hand up the length of the arm into the bulk looming over him, and past that into the giant's face.

This man said, "Outside."

Choctaw headed to the saloon door, stepping out into the night. He found an upright to lean on and gazed out into the street.

He thought about Billy Keogh, and his thoughts went past him to Jack Adams. And then they took him, as he knew they would, to Alope.

His arms started to tremble slightly. Not from fear, but from remembering.

Alope was an Aravaipa Apache girl. Just a squaw, plenty said. But she'd been the first girl he'd loved.

He lifted his eyes to the night sky. An inky vastness glimmering with stars. An icy void that held no answers. That couldn't shield him from his memories. Recalling what he'd been trying not to remember, these last two and a half years.

Alope the last time he'd seen her.

When he'd found her after the slaughter at Camp Walsh; after her murderer had used his rifle butt on her, striking down at her head again and again . . .

CHAPTER TEN

Choctaw returned to his hotel room. Declan was still out, presumably at his poker game, which could go on all night.

Choctaw went to bed but couldn't sleep.

He hummed with tension, trembling slightly. From fear of what might happen tomorrow? From jarring reminders of a cruel past he'd tried to escape but maybe never could?

What he needed now was the balm of unconsciousness but it wouldn't come. Minutes crawled endlessly, never reaching the hour. He was just about to abandon the whole process and get out of bed when sleep came after all.

He drifted through scudding dreams, of Alope alive and dead, and Billy Keogh standing on Main Street, and Choctaw saw himself staring into Keogh's sneering face, lifting the pistol in his hand, but he was too slow, because Keogh's revolver was pointing into his face, and the black mouth of the muzzle became an eye, a lizard's heartless unfeeling eye, and the lizard's eye swelled until it was the size of a boulder and then Choctaw heard the shot. Next, he was down at Keogh's feet, blood all over the front of him, pinned to the earth by the cannonball weight of the bullet in his chest, the ground becoming a dark copper lake he was sinking into, drowning in . . . the gunshot echoing, filling his head, becoming rumbling thunder . . .

Becoming snoring.

Choctaw blinked.

Daylight was filtering into the room through the shutters. He was lying tangled in bedsheets, wearing only his long johns, damp with sweat.

Across the room, in his bed against the far wall, Declan lay on his face with his mouth opening as he snored.

Declan tended to snore, most particularly when he was drunk. Which made sharing a bedroom with him a considerable trial. He sometimes approached the noise level of a herd of stampeding buffalo. Like right now, producing sounds that drilled into Choctaw's back teeth, and ought to have plaster falling from the ceiling.

Choctaw sat up. He wasn't just hungover

but disorientated from the flurry of dreams. His watch told him it was seven thirty. He climbed from bed and went barefoot out on to the balcony adjoining his room. He leaned on the balcony railings and gazed down at Lobo Wells.

A bird was trilling and he started to smile at the beauty of its morning song.

Then he remembered. Billy Keogh. Last night in the saloon. A lump of ice seemed to settle in Choctaw's belly, and tension began to sing through him again.

This might be the last birdsong he'd ever hear. On his last morning on earth.

Unless he turned coward today. He could hide in his hotel room, or get his horse out of the livery and flee town . . .

He remembered Keogh's gloating smile, his bulging reptilian eyes, the ugly man saying, "A squaw-humping Apache lover like you."

The chill of fear was replaced by hot anger. He decided he wasn't going to let the likes of Keogh run him out of any place. That would be betraying Alope, wouldn't it?

He washed in the basin, then dressed. He went to the wardrobe and got his gun belt, with the pistol — a Starr army .44 Converted in its cross-draw holster.

Not the prettiest gun: a chunky piece of black metal with a short grip. The only thing he liked about its appearance was the front sight, which was painted gold. It was heavy on the trigger. He'd chosen it because it was double action; you could cock and fire it with one movement, just a pull on the trigger. But Choctaw didn't care for it much, or for handguns in general. They were cumbersome, short range, and, compared to rifles, inaccurate. He couldn't remember the last time he'd fired this weapon.

Choctaw stepped out on to Main Street, expecting to come face to face with Billy Keogh, his nerves stretched taut in anticipation. He strode around Lobo Wells warily, his hand close to the grip of his revolver. Most particularly he was careful of anyone coming up behind him. Jack Adams had been a murdering back-shooter; why should his friend be any different?

He saw no sign of Keogh. But the man had said noon, not before.

So Choctaw went to a Mexican place doing breakfasts. In his three years in the Southwest, he'd not only learned to speak Spanish, he'd acquired an appreciation of Mexican food, music, and the culture generally. He ordered a bowl of *menudo* — beef soup — and then *huevos rancheros* but he was too tense to eat, barely finishing the soup and not touching the eggs. Mostly he breakfasted on black coffee.

The waitress asked, "Whassamatter? Food no good?"

Choctaw looked up from the cigarette he was shaping. "Sure it's good. Got no appetite, I guess."

The woman gave him a pitying, mother-to-child look. *"Pobrecito."* She pinched his cheek.

In the end they only charged him half. And the waitress rolled up a tortilla for him to take away.

Out on the streets he found a place in the shade of a ramada to sit, where his back was protected and he could look up and down the street. He smoked and watched life going on in Lobo Wells, which it seemed to do extremely slowly. Few people were about; maybe most of the settlement was sleeping off its Sunday morning hangover.

He felt a vague unreality. Pistol duels on Main Street happened all the time in dime novels. And they did happen in real life according to newspapers, but maybe only rarely, and only to hardened man-killers. He'd never seen one. When they did occur, they caused a sensation, making legends out of the likes of Wild Bill Hickok and John Wesley Hardin.

Choctaw decided he felt wretched. If this was the life of a shootist — the hot, dry throat, the gut-wrenching fear, the mouth tasting of ashes — you could keep it.

After a time, he felt a small gnaw of hunger. He ate the tortilla in stages, although he couldn't say what he was tasting.

He became aware that time had slipped by. He glanced at his watch and saw it was twenty after twelve. The killing hour had come and gone.

Could it be that Keogh was just a mouth fighter, all talk? That he wasn't going to show?

Choctaw decided to make one final attempt to flush out Keogh. So he prowled the streets once more. Again with no success.

He decided he'd done all honor demanded. Part of him felt an anticlimax, after what Keogh had put him through the last few hours. But mostly he felt relief. He'd celebrate not having to go to his guns with a good fierce whiskey someplace, and then retire indoors. Siesta while the afternoon sun blazed down.

He pushed to his feet, stepping out on to Main.

Someone called to him.

Choctaw's hand jumped to his pistol and he slewed around. He was a bare second away from having the revolver drawn when he saw who it was.

The rancher, Swenson, standing across the street.

Choctaw slid his hand away from the pistol. He let out a heavy sigh of relief.

The Scandinavian-Texan lifted his eyebrows in surprise. Choctaw smiled at the rancher, although he doubted he made anything but a poor, weak job of it. He opened his mouth to call a greeting.

"Hey, Apache lover!"

Choctaw froze.

He took a sidelong glance and there was Billy Keogh. Ahead and to the left across the street, standing a yard away from the sidewalk.

He held a pistol in his right hand.

CHAPTER ELEVEN

Keogh was dressed as yesterday, in nondescript hat and trail gear. His right arm hung at his side, the barrel of the pistol he gripped pointing at the earth.

So here we are, Choctaw thought. About to confront a past he couldn't escape. About to play Wild Bill Hickok.

But then it came to him he could do something else. Ignore this nonsense. Walk away as if this wasn't happening, as if Keogh wasn't calling to him.

Choctaw strode forward, down Main as before, but angling to the right, no longer pointing towards the saloon but at the next corner. He kept his eyes lowered, not looking at Keogh, pretending he hadn't seen him. He came level with Keogh and went past him and now his back was to his enemy. It felt a mile wide, muscles tensed and cringing, waiting for the smashing impact of a bullet against his spine . . .

Keogh called, "Don't walk away from me, you yellow bastard!"

Choctaw kept walking. Maybe nobody around would figure Keogh was shouting after him. The streets were almost empty; who else could he be calling to?

Choctaw rounded the corner and went right. He had no idea where he was going. He was striding up a long, wide street at the end of which stood a large, barn-like structure. The livery. Which was good. He could get his horse out of this stable and ride out of town . . .

The livery door opened and two men emerged. One he recognized as the old man who ran the place. The other was his friend the black-bearded giant from the saloon last night. These two started talking.

Keogh called, "I mean *you,* you red nigger lover! Turn and face me, or get it in the back!"

The two men by the livery must have heard. They turned and directed sharp looks at Choctaw and then past him.

Choctaw kept his ears closed to the pursuing cries. Only twenty more paces to the livery. All he had to do was cross that distance, and get his horse, and ride away from his memories, of Jack Adams and Alope . . .

An image flashed in front of Choctaw's eyes. Of Alope, as he found her.

He halted. He was a dozen paces from the livery.

He gazed down at Alope, at the ruin a rifle butt had made.

Anger coursed through him, at what was done to her. Someone should answer for that.

He turned slowly and faced Keogh.

This man was coming down the street at a quick walk. Now he slowed to a standstill. Heat flushed his cheeks.

Choctaw lifted his pistol from its holster and held it at his side.

There was a weight of coldness in his belly and his throat was tight but he wasn't sure if that was fear.

He took a quick glance behind him. The two men by the livery stared at him open-mouthed. He returned his gaze to Keogh and saw, standing some way behind him, Nils Swenson.

Choctaw judged Keogh was forty or fifty yards away. A fair shooting distance for a handgun. At least he had the sun to his back, while it was in Keogh's face.

"Choc!"

Declan appeared alongside Swenson.

Keogh shouted again. "I'm calling you,

you squaw-humping Apache lover!"

Choctaw forgot Dec, or Swenson, or any of the onlookers. He fixed his gaze on the slight figure forty yards away, with the pistol held at his side.

Keogh cried, "For Jack Adams!"

He jerked up his arm, pointing his pistol at the other man.

Choctaw started to move as quickly, lifting his own gun.

But a strange thing happened. A voice in his head told him: *Don't rush, do this slow, do it right. Let the other man hurry things, while you take your time.*

Calm spread over him, almost icy in its grip.

Keogh's pistol banged. Choctaw saw the dark gray gout of smoke, the burst hiding the man's face, then thinning and drifting across it. Choctaw's body flinched, waiting for the bullet. But he felt no impact. No whine of a near miss, yowling in his ear. Wherever Keogh's bullet had gone, it hadn't come close.

There was a stain on the pocket of the vest Keogh wore, a patch of dark brown just about where his heart would be. Choctaw held his arm straight out before him and put his front sight on that stain. But he decided that wasn't a steady enough aim, and gripped the underside of his right forearm with his left hand, bracing it.

A look of frustration, then anger, came to Keogh's face. He stepped forward, striding towards his enemy. Keogh fired again, the pistol jerking high in his hand. Another miss.

Choctaw stared along the top of his revolver, ugly black metal bulging out of his hand, down the length of the barrel to the gold of the front sight, and the brown stain beyond it, growing larger as Keogh strode nearer. Choctaw started to squeeze the trigger. Jesus, it was a hard, slow pull! He'd forgotten.

He saw smoke drift from the mouth of Keogh's pistol and heard the weapon bang a third time while he was still pulling, the working of the trigger so heavy it was like to sprain his finger. And Keogh was now only twenty yards away and still coming at him . . .

Choctaw squeezed and Keogh's gun banged again and Choctaw kept squeezing and then the gun bucked in his hand.

Keogh went down on his rump. He sat in fine dust that rose about him. The brown stain was lost as the whole of his torso was suddenly bloody. His face was plaster-gray with shock. He stared out of wide, dazed eyes. His mouth opened and words came out that Choctaw could only barely hear.

"I'm killed."

A gush of blood followed his words and Keogh sagged forward.

Choctaw strode over to the man sitting in the street. For some reason, his mind counted the paces he took and made it seventeen.

Keogh looked to be in serious thought, his eyes fixed on the earth between his splayed legs.

Choctaw realized the pistol in his hand was pointing at Keogh's face, and in a second, he would be pumping bullets into the head of a dead man.

He took his finger from the trigger.

Choctaw heard yells and swearing. He was aware others were coming towards him, some at the run. The world outside had become dim and far away, full of things that couldn't reach him, or matter to him.

But his numbness was easing for now he felt a sting of pain. It was high on the outside of his left arm. He touched it and felt ripped shirt fabric. A bullet had grazed him. There was a fair amount of blood but he judged it was only a nick.

His legs were rubbery beneath him and he swayed. He started shaking, harder than he could ever remember. Not even when he was a child, and had the chills and fever.

He sat, facing Keogh. So there were two men sitting in the street, one living and one dead, in the white blaze of noon.

CHAPTER TWELVE

Choctaw became aware of a hand resting on his shoulder. He glanced up at Declan standing over him. The Irishman asked, "You all right?"

In a weak, hoarse voice Choctaw said, "Sure."

Time passed. Maybe a fair piece of time. But then a hubbub of noise arose.

Dec said, "Reckon this is the law coming."

Choctaw glanced up. A group of six or seven men approached. Leading them was the black-bearded giant. He halted a few yards away with the others in back of him, most not even standing as high as his shoulders. One of them was the old fellow who ran the livery. Choctaw couldn't see Swenson anywhere.

The giant let a long-barreled pistol dawdle in his right hand, not pointing at anything in particular. He said, "Name's Parsons."

Dec said, "Don't tell me — you're the constable. What passes for law 'round here, till you get a territorial marshal."

"Ain't got a title. I head up what we got here — 'The Good Citizens' Committee.'" Parsons spoke to Choctaw. "Now, son — I'll take the gun."

Choctaw realized he still held his pistol. "Why?"

In answer Parsons held out his left hand, palm up.

Choctaw lifted his arm, holding out the Starr, and Parsons said, "Easy." He licked his lips. He gave the others a frightened look.

Another funny thing happened. The men back of Parsons seemed to react as one, flinching. A couple stepped back a pace or two. A strange look touched their faces. Choctaw slowly realized — everything seemed to be coming to him slowly — they were staring at him in fear. A bunch of grown men, and all of them afraid of him!

He decided he was enjoying this, all these fools scared of him, ready to jump like jackrabbits if he only said, "Boo!" He felt a smile of some kind, maybe tinged with contempt, he wasn't sure, touch his lips.

Hammers double-clicked.

He glanced over his left shoulder. While

he'd been showing his disdain for Parsons's bunch, another man had come up behind him. This fellow held a shotgun, both barrels levelled, aiming somewhere between Choctaw's head and the middle of his back.

Parsons made a small gesture with the barrel of his pistol.

Moving slowly, Choctaw passed the revolver to Parsons. The man with the shotgun lowered his fearsome weapon.

Choctaw let out a fairly substantial sigh. Tension drained from him. He saw others sag slightly, and make sounds of relief.

Parsons asked Choctaw, "You got any more weapons?"

"A rifle over at the hotel."

"On your feet, boy."

Choctaw stood.

Parsons said, "Doc."

A man stepped forward. He crouched down over Keogh. "Dead all right. Shot right through the ticker."

Someone said, "Jesus!" his voice full of awe. Others made similar admiring noises. Only then Choctaw noticed that some townsfolk had drifted over to join Parsons's original group, including women and even a few kids.

The doctor stood. "Better get this fellow to the undertakers, 'fore he gets ripe." He spoke to Choctaw. "Let's take a look at that arm."

"It ain't nothing. Just a burn."

Parsons addressed the gathering of townsfolk. "All right, we're done here. Everybody go on about your business."

Nobody moved. Parsons glared at them. Slowly, with obvious reluctance, they began to disperse, leaving only "The Good Citizens' Committee." And Declan. The dead man was carried from the street.

Parsons addressed Choctaw. "All right, son. Let's step on over to the jail."

"Why?"

"Because you're under arrest, that's why."

Choctaw gaped. "What? You saw what I done. It was self-defense."

"No doubt about it."

"Then why am I under arrest?"

"You can't just go gunning down men in the street, then wander off and have your lunch, you know. The Good Citizens' Committee agreed that when it come to a killing, the perpetrator would automatically be placed under arrest. Regardless of circumstances. Until the evidence can be reviewed in court."

Choctaw asked, "You mean this shithole's got a courthouse?"

"We use the saloon."

Dec asked, "And how long before court sits?"

"You're lucky. Next session is tomorrow morning." Parsons addressed Choctaw. "Now, let's get out of the sun, boy, and over to the jail."

"I ain't going to jail."

"Oh, yes, you are. Ain't safe having a fellow like you at large in our community."

"A fellow like me?"

"A gunman. A shootist."

"I ain't no gunman."

The livery owner piped up. "Sure acted like one." There it was again, in his voice: admiration.

Parsons said, "Now, boy, you can either walk to jail or be dragged there."

Dec said, "You can't arrest him. Especially when you said flat out it was self-defense. You got no right." The Irishman stood braced, as if he was the one facing Keogh half an hour ago. But he wasn't wearing a gun belt.

Parsons told him, "We can take you along too."

Dec said, "What I tell you about the 'law,' Choc? Four-flushers!"

Parsons scowled. "That does it!"

Choctaw said, "Dec, leave it. No point both of us ending up in jail."

Parsons asked, "That mean you're coming peaceful?"

Choctaw glared, breathing hard through his nostrils. His face warmed with embarrassment and anger. He said, "I'll come peaceful." His tone was even, but the words were bitter in his mouth.

When Choctaw emerged from "the courthouse" — the main saloon in Lobo Wells — at 11 a.m. the next morning, Declan was waiting for him. He lounged in a hickory chair on the sidewalk, in the shade of an awning out of the late morning sun. He looked up from the stick he was whittling as his friend approached. He asked, "How'd you get on?"

"Hundred-dollar fine."

"What?"

"Bastards!"

"What's the fine for? They admitted it was self-defense."

Choctaw sat on the edge of the veranda, still in the shade, his feet resting on Main Street. He told Dec the fine was for the "unlawful discharging of a weapon within town limits," plus court costs and the costs of burying Billy Keogh.

Dec said, "I wouldn't have paid it."

"It was either pay or thirty days' hard

labor with the road-building crew. And there's more."

"Don't tell me. Twenty-four hours to get out of town?"

"Yeah."

Declan lifted his whittled stick and flung it into the street in disgust.

Choctaw said, "Only applies to me. They don't regard you as an 'undesirable not conducive to the public good.' "

"You think I want to stay in this dung heap by myself? How was the jail?"

"I been in worse hotels. Which ain't saying much." Choctaw smiled ruefully. "My turn to get us run out of town. I'm starting to feel like you about the law. I can understand how fellows turn outlaw."

"Yeah." Dec took out his bible. "Like I said — you and me are kindred spirits, meant to run free. Can't be broke to anyone's damn plow. There's even a Mex word for our kind." He thought for a moment. "*Cimarrón.* Your Spanish is better than mine. It means —"

"It means wild. Untamed."

"Yeah, that's us. That fine . . . did it clean you out?"

"Still got nine dollars left. Hey, I forgot to ask. How'd you get on with your poker game the other night?"

Dec smiled. "Did real well."

"Good. Then we ain't flat —"

"Yeah, did real well . . . right until the last hand."

"What do you mean?"

Dec shrugged.

Choctaw asked, "How much you got left?"

"Oh, I figure . . . at least six dollars."

"Christ!"

"Easy come, easy go."

"It didn't come so easy as I recollect. Two weeks busting our backs mustanging, and we're broke again."

"No, we ain't. We got a whole fifteen dollars between us. More than two weeks' wages to a cowboy." Dec laughed.

"Trouble with you, Dec — you don't know when you're licked."

"That's 'cuz I ain't never been licked!"

Choctaw did something he hadn't done since before Billy Keogh: he laughed too. He laughed for a minute or so and felt the better for it.

Declan said, "Hey, didn't Swenson tell us he was looking for wranglers?"

"Yeah. I forgot that."

"That's it, then. Tomorrow morning we go over to his place. All of our problems solved."

"Maybe. When he said there was a job for

us . . . I wasn't a man-killer then."

"That feller was shooting at you. What else could you do?"

Choctaw remembered the gun bucking in his hand and Billy Keogh's shirtfront turning all bloody, blood coming from his mouth, and the words "I'm killed." A heavy silence weighed on them. Eventually Choctaw said, "You still haven't asked."

"Asked what?"

"About why me and Keogh came to guns. What he called me."

"I figure you'll tell me about it when you've a mind to."

Choctaw wondered if he was ready to do that yet. While he was thinking about it, he heard the scuffle of running feet.

Two young boys ran towards him. The kids slowed as they came nearer, halting altogether six or so yards from him. Brothers he judged, one gangling, about nine, one chubby, maybe seven. Across the street a woman called to them, although he didn't catch the words.

They stared at him and he gazed back. They were dressed the same, colorless shirts coming out of patch-kneed pants held up by braces, in material doubtless cut from the same cloth. The nine-year-old held a stick — actually two sticks, tied together to make a crude toy rifle.

Choctaw saw himself in these boys, playing in the canebrakes and sumac bushes back of Pa's store, climbing every tree in sight. He'd been crazy to play out all day, mostly as Kit Carson, picking off Indian after Indian with his own toy gun. Only he'd been dark and scrawny, where these kids had fair skin the sun brought out in freckles, round faces topped by shocks of light blond hair. The younger child was snub-nosed; the older had a gap in the middle of his upper front teeth.

The boys stopped staring at the man long enough to exchange glances, smile mischievously, and giggle; he guessed they were daring each other to be the first to speak. Choctaw started to smile too, and then the woman called again. "Thomas! George! Stay away from him!"

The younger child glanced at the older for instruction. The nine-year-old meantime looked at the woman, and then at Choctaw, torn between obedience and his fascination with the man sitting on the veranda. He said, "Ma —"

"You get over here!"

Choctaw saw even more of himself in this boy — he could never do as he was told the first time he was asked, either. He was about to say, "You mind your mother, son," when the kid turned and ran back to the woman's side. The seven-year-old pelted after him. The woman pulled both boys close to her. She spoke to them, but loud enough for him to hear. "Keep away from that terrible man." She gave him a stern, accusing look, then herded the children away.

Choctaw asked Dec, "What was that all about?"

Dec grinned. "You're their hero, boy. Now they want to grow up to be just like you."

When Choctaw snorted in disdain, the Irishman said, "It's true. And you can't blame 'em." He shook his head slightly. "I never seen nothing like that."

"Like what?"

"Like what you done. Standing there while that feller throwed all that lead in your face, like you hadn't a nerve in your body. Stood there cool as ice, and let him empty his gun at you. And then one dead shot back — right through the heart!"

"Dec —"

"Like you was Wild Bill Hickok or somebody! That's how legends get made."

Choctaw supposed he should be flattered. Maybe he *was* a hero to these kids. But at the same time, he heard the woman saying, "That terrible man."

"I ain't a legend. Don't want to be one."

"Yeah, well . . ." Declan picked a pebble from the dust at his feet and threw it down the street, where it kicked up more dust. ". . . Sometimes people get to be legends, whether they want to be or not."

CHAPTER THIRTEEN

Next morning Choctaw and Declan rode over to Nils Swenson's ranch, north of Lobo Wells.

The Scandinavian-Texan was out on the range where they had horse-breaking corrals. He sat in the "Opera House" — the top rail of a corral fence — watching one wrangler try and stay aboard a pitching mustang. The two young men approached on foot.

Choctaw managed to pin a small smile on his face, but he wasn't optimistic about what was coming. Swenson saw him and frowned. Which was only what the younger man was expecting.

Swenson climbed slowly down from the Opera House and stood waiting for them. He asked, "You've come about work?"

Dec said, "Yes, sir."

The rancher gestured towards a fire about a hundred yards away, where hands squatted. He said, "Go get yourself a cup of coffee, Declan."

Choctaw said, "You can say what you got to say in front of both of us, Mr. Swenson."

The rancher made a throat-clearing sound. He got busy filling his pipe, as if working himself up to what he was about to say. All the time he wouldn't meet Choctaw's eye.

Choctaw noticed the mustang had dumped its rider in the dust and was busy throwing itself around the corral. The wrangler rose slowly, groaning and rubbing his back.

Swenson said, "Calvin, you're obviously a good hand with horses. But —"

"But?"

"I can't use you, boy."

Choctaw had decided to try and keep his temper in check today. Making his voice low and even he asked, "Why?"

"Isn't it obvious?"

"Ain't you gonna tell me?"

Swenson chewed his lower lip. He seemed undecided about lighting his pipe. "I hire lots of young men. Most of 'em never get in any trouble. A few get in Saturday night fights —"

"Mr. Swenson —"

"Every once in a long time, they get in

110

something worse. If it comes to guns or knives, or killing, I let them go. I can't use them."

Choctaw's resolve to keep his temper in check was tested. But he managed to reply calmly, "What was I to do? That *hombre* started shooting at me. You saw it."

"Sure I did. I'm not saying it wasn't self-defense. But that's my rule."

"That ain't fair!"

"Nobody said life was fair, boy. Because of you, a man's dead. Maybe there's a woman ain't got a man now. Or a child ain't got a father."

Choctaw hadn't really thought about Keogh leaving anyone to mourn and know loss, how the killing might impact on others. He felt a cold unease in his belly, thinking of a child somewhere crying over Billy Keogh. *But Keogh had come looking for him, damn it.*

Swenson lit his pipe. "Some people just attract bad trouble. Maybe you're like that. You remind me of a young fellow I knew in Texas a few years back . . . name of John Wesley Hardin."

Choctaw's rein on his temper slipped. He raised his voice. "Hardin's a crazy killer."

Dec pitched in. "Killed a man for snoring too loud they say!"

111

Choctaw said, "I ain't like that."

Swenson nodded slightly. "No. Not yet. But trouble found him, like it seems to find you. And you're right handy with that smoke wagon, just like he was. On top of that, it didn't seem to bother you, pulling a trigger on another human being."

"He was fixing to kill me."

"I saw your face, boy. Bullets practically fanning your hair and you didn't bat an eyelid." Hadn't Dec said almost the same thing?

"It was happening too fast for me to be scared."

"I saw the same look on Hardin's face when he killed a man. And he was maybe younger than you."

"I ain't like Hardin!"

"Sorry, boy. Like I said . . . that's my rule." Swenson turned towards Dec, but before he could address him, Choctaw asked, "That the only reason you ain't hiring me?"

The rancher chewed over answering that one too.

The wrangler was poised to remount the lineback. He twisted the horse's ear and, while it stood immobilized by pain, swung up into the saddle.

Swenson took his pipe from his mouth. "No."

"I didn't think it was."

"There was some talk in town about why you and that Keogh fellow went to guns."

"You listen to street gossip, Mr. Swenson?"

"He called you an Apache lover. That you had an Apache squaw. Is it true?"

Choctaw glanced at Declan. The Irishman was staring at him. Choctaw asked, "And if it is?"

Swenson said, "I got nothing against an Indian that's peaceable. But *Apaches* . . . those devils . . . I've lost too many friends to them. The Tontos is quiet now, after the army moved against them last winter, but before then they was raising hell. All last year. I remember . . ." His face grew darker as he revisited bad memories. After a time he asked, "Well? Is it true?"

So here it was again, Choctaw thought. The past he couldn't outrun. Unless he lied about it. Denied it all. *I ain't no Indian lover.* That would be easy to do, and might save him a lot of grief.

He said, "It's true." Saying it, he felt a strange relief. "I lived with an Apache girl. In fact, I've been with two of them."

The rancher glared. "Then know this:

there's no place in my outfit for an Apache lover!"

Choctaw opened his mouth to reply but the words dried in his throat. He tasted something like a penny rusting on his tongue.

The rancher said, "Declan."

"Mr. Swenson?"

"There's still a job for you here if you want it."

Dec glanced over at Choctaw. The other looked away. He couldn't watch the Irishman betray him, end their friendship.

He saw the wrangler was back in the dust. Lying and groaning, bad hurt maybe. Two men lifted him and carried him to the side while the mustang buckjumped all over the corral, snorting in anger. A whole horse-breaking episode had played out before Choctaw's eyes, and he hadn't seen any of it.

He heard Declan say, "No thanks, Mr. Swenson. I'll stick with him."

Choctaw shot Dec a surprised look. "You needn't put yourself out of work on account of me."

The Irishman smiled wearily. "I'll stick with you, *amigo.*"

CHAPTER FOURTEEN

Declan and Choctaw rode north from Swenson's ranch.

Choctaw wondered why they were pointing this way. North of them was the whole northwestern quarter of Arizona Territory, which someone had described to him as "a blank on the map." Almost no settlements ahead, just a vast wilderness of deserts and canyons peopled by some Digger Indians. Part of it, around the Colorado River Canyon, wasn't even explored properly. Most settlements — Prescott, Camp Verde — were off to the east.

Choctaw guessed Dec was forging ahead blindly, in the direction he'd followed since leaving Lobo Wells. Choctaw was happy to tag along behind him for now.

The empty land climbed. They found themselves on high tablelands where knee-high grass rippled before a ceaseless wind. They nooned, sitting in a bare patch in the grass, drinking coffee from tin cups.

Dec said, "Lucky we outfitted in Lobo Wells. We're all right for coffee, tobacco. What we ain't all right for is grub."

"We was figuring Swenson would feed us. If we're lucky, we might find a mule deer. Or maybe a wild pig."

They drank coffee as the wind sang around them. Choctaw said, "Thanks, *amigo.*"

"What for?"

"Sticking with me back there. You shouldn't have put yourself out of a job because of me."

"I was getting tired of being bounced up and down by them crazy mustangs." Dec chewed at his mustache. "I'm starting to get hungry, boy."

"The way you go on about your belly."

"Probably got that from my pa. He used to talk about the Potato Famine all the time."

"Back in Ireland?"

"Uh-huh. I was too young to remember it. I do recollect him saying 'Now we're in America, we'll never go hungry again.' " Dec gave a disdainful laugh. "Thought of that last winter when I was close to chewing on my saddle leather."

"I recall an Apache once told me his band

got so hungry one winter, they ended up eating their moccasins."

The statement was out of Choctaw's mouth before he realized. He instantly regretted it.

Dec said, "I guess you've been around Apaches plenty."

Choctaw shifted uncomfortably. "Last few years I have. That's what I do mostly — scout for the army against the hostiles. South of here. At least in the warm months. Come winter I find what work I can." Seeing the skeptical look Dec gave him, Choctaw smiled. "Nobody ever believes me when I tell 'em I'm an Indian scout; they think I'm too young, but it's true."

The Irishman commenced walking about, stretching his arms. Choctaw asked, "Doesn't it bother you?"

"What?"

"That I lived with an Apache girl? That I've been with two of them?"

"Why should it?"

"Lots hate Indians. Especially Apaches. Hating Apaches is almost a religion out here."

Dec grunted. "Well, I ain't too partial to religion." He kneaded his back. "Where I was raised, folks was always talking about wild Indians. Comanches mostly. But the only Indians I ever saw were tame, begging or selling blankets. I can't hate something I've never seen." The Irishman walked over to his horse. "Let's find some mule deer."

Declan fed another mesquite stick into the fire. He said, "Hey Choc . . . you ain't hardly ate anything."

Choctaw glanced at the tin plate on his lap and it was true, half of his meat and most of his beans lay untouched. "Not as hungry as I figured, I guess."

Dec said, "I am." He leaned forward to the spit, where their meat roasted over the fire, gleaming with fat. Not wild pig or mule deer — the best they'd managed to scare up was a jackrabbit. The Irishman sawed off a portion with his knife, making small sounds of pain as the meat burned his fingers. Fat dripped into the flames, sending sparks upwards, cindery fireflies scattering across purple darkness. "So, what's putting you off your feed?"

Choctaw poured coffee into his tin cup. "I keep thinking about what Swenson said. Maybe he's right. Maybe I am like that . . . a natural born killer."

"You had to kill a feller throwed down on you. What the hell else could you do?"

"There was one point when I was going

to walk away from Keogh. Just ignore what he was saying."

"Wouldn't that have made you a coward?"

Choctaw shrugged. "It's only words."

Neither man spoke for a while. In the fire, fat hissed, logs popped. Comfortable sounds keeping the dark at bay.

Choctaw turned his cup in his hands. "I could have walked away from Keogh. Then I thought about —" He considered saying the name. Then he did. "Alope."

"Who?"

"The Apache girl I lived with. It was like Keogh was insulting her. That's why I turned and faced him."

"You don't have to tell me all this if you don't want to."

Choctaw thought hard about answering. A wolf howled in the distance. Right on time, as Choctaw's memories were back on the morning when wolves and coyotes descended from the high country to an unexpected banquet, the harvest of bloated corpses strewn around the Apache rancheria . . .

He said, "About two years ago I was working as a post hunter at Camp Walsh, over near Tucson. You hear about the massacre there?"

"Vaguely. I don't recollect the details."

"A band of Apaches — the Aravaipas — come in to Camp Walsh to make peace. The post commander let 'em stay there while the army was figuring what to do next. That's when I met Alope. We fell in love I guess."

"Yeah?"

"There was a lot of talk that the Aravaipas were still carrying on raiding, while they were being protected by the army."

"Were they?"

"No. It was a damn lie!" Choctaw was surprised at the anger in his voice. More than two years and it still got to him. He drank coffee, letting his temper ease down, then went on in a more even tone, "But a bunch of vigilantes believed it. Anglos, Mexicans, Papago Indians. They jumped the Aravaipas and killed a hundred of 'em. Mostly women and kids and old folk. Alope was —"

He had one more word to say and he couldn't. All this time and he still couldn't get that word past his lips the first time of trying.

"Killed."

His throat caught and his eyes stung as if they'd started watering. He decided that must be from staring into the fire. His eyes had been watering that day, too, from the smoke of wickiups set ablaze, and burning human flesh . . .

Choctaw sat back. "Talk got around that I was an Indian lover. A squaw man. That's how come I ended up shooting Jack Adams." He started on the makings. "I thought I'd put all that behind me by now. And then along come Billy Keogh. Which shows you can't never get away from your past."

A cold wind touched the back of his neck and he pulled up the collar of his canvas jacket. "In the meantime, there was another Apache girl. Nahlin. That went bad too."

Declan didn't speak, and Choctaw knew he wasn't going to ask about Nahlin. Choctaw said, "That was my fault. I was a mean son of a bitch to her. Treated her cruel."

Dec raised his eyebrows. "What? You beat your woman?"

"No, I don't mean I hurt her physically. Just words . . . I said cruel things to her. Treated her so mean she ran away. I was gonna go find her; it's always the next thing I'm gonna do, but —" He stared helplessly at the cigarette in his hands. "I ain't got 'round to it yet."

He felt drained from so much talk, unburdening his past. He sat, barely moving.

Maybe Dec felt the same, as he let out a long sigh. "There's a story. Sounds like you been through a whole lot for your age."

"I reckon."

Neither man spoke for a time, as the dark deepened around them. Choctaw said, "We still haven't talked about what we're gonna do next."

"Something'll turn up."

Choctaw smiled and shook his head slightly in a mix of affection and disbelief. "That's your entire philosophy, ain't it?"

The Irishman grinned. "It sure is!"

CHAPTER FIFTEEN

In the morning they rode on, no longer pointed north towards emptiness, but east towards settled country. Midmorning, they reined in and stared ahead.

Before them was forest. A dense green wall of it. All the trees Choctaw could see were ponderosa pines, slim sentinels climbing maybe sixty feet, endless thousands of them. It was close to the finest stand of timber he'd ever seen.

That would have been enough scenery in itself. But beyond the trees was a great escarpment, the sides of a vast plateau rising at least a thousand feet above the forest. It was an enormous rectangular block marching for miles against the sky, then tapering off east towards the White Mountains. Its flanks were sheer cliffs of hazy purple, patched with shadow.

He said, "I guess that's the Mogollon Rim." He pronounced it, Spanish-wise, as

"Mog-ay-on."

The Mogollon Rim was the southern rampart of the great plateau of the Colorado River. Choctaw had heard the river canyon splitting this plateau was bigger and deeper than anyone could believe, a gargantuan crack in the world. They said if you fell into it, you might spend three days falling.

Choctaw was used to magnificent scenery on a giant scale but this was something beyond his experience. Maybe Dec was equally awed, as they both sat a while not speaking.

Choctaw said, "Makes you feel about the size of a flea in a blanket, don't it?"

Dec grunted agreement. "Big country all right. But it's the forest that bothers me."

"Why?"

"That's bear country. If there's one critter scares me — it's a bear."

"Yeah?" Choctaw lifted his canteen and drank from it. "Well, we run into one, I'll say: 'Please, Mister Bear, chaw on my partner first, he's got more meat on him.' "

"Yeah, but it's all gristle!"

They entered the forest. They encountered no bears.

A few hours along, they broke from the trees into a meadow, startling a band of horses.

These animals flared into movement and fled before them. All save one. Each running horse cleaved its own path through waist-high grass rippling before the wind, manes bannering out, tails streaming behind. Horses running free was a sight Choctaw had always found pleasurable. For him that completed this picture of a mountain paradise.

The only horse not to flee was a sorrel, coppery hide flashing in the sun. It took a few steps away but its gait was awkward. It seemed reluctant to put its off-front hoof to earth, like that foot or leg was hurting.

Dec called, "Maybe we should get back to mustanging." He lifted his rope off his saddle and shook out a loop. "Nice little band of money running 'round here."

Choctaw said, "He's wearing a brand, *amigo.* Most likely the others are too."

"Huh?"

"So you don't want to be caught with your rope on another man's horse."

Dec rubbed his trail beard. "Fellow once showed me how you can change brands real easy. All you need is a jackknife and a running iron. Or maybe only a cinch ring. I hear that's how most of the big respectable ranchers out here got started."

"How?"

"By helping themselves to other folks' cattle and horses."

"You better put your rope away, Dec. Before somebody sees and gets the wrong idea." Choctaw shifted in the saddle. "Taking a cow when you're hungry is one thing. Most times the worst you'll catch for that is jail time. But stealing horses . . . you know what that gets you out here, *compadre*. A bullet or a rope."

"Sure. I understand that. If we was leaving a feller afoot in the desert say, or with wild Indians about, then we'd deserve it. But these horses ain't saddle-broke; we ain't setting nobody afoot. We'd only be doing what them ranchers did, starting up."

"Are you saying we should turn horse thief now?"

The Irishman glared. Choctaw gazed back calmly.

Dec gave something like a sigh. He hung his rope back on his saddle. "No, I *ain't* saying that."

"Good."

"All I'm saying is — being honest ain't filling our bellies, boy; the money's going fast and winter's coming on. I tell you, Choc, we gotta do something. It's getting to the point we either starve or . . ."

Dec let the words trail off. He stared at

126

something past his friend's left shoulder. Choctaw turned and saw a rider approaching from the far side of the meadow.

The newcomer was dressed like any Anglo cowboy. He looked to be only about seventeen or so. He smiled nervously, so Choctaw guessed he hadn't seen the rope in Dec's hand. "Howdy."

Dec gave the younker the friendliest version of his grin. "Howdy."

"You fellers looking for work?"

"Maybe. Your outfit hiring?"

"You'd have to ask the boss. He's just back there." He jabbed a thumb back over his shoulder. "Mister MacNee. Runs the Circle M."

John MacNee was a wiry fellow of medium height, in his fifties. He was something of a dresser, wearing a dark vest over a striped shirt, a necktie, and neat charcoal pants. His large gray Texas hat, almost swamping his head, contrasted with these town clothes, more suitable to a bank or store. He had silver-gray hair and mustache. His face was thin and had looked at a lot of weather, judging by the lines in it.

The rancher took a pair of eyeglasses from the top pocket of his vest and used a small cloth to rub dust off one lens. Then he perched the glasses on his nose and studied the two young men standing before him.

"I got work," he said.

If MacNee was native-born Scots, as his name suggested, he'd left the homeland a long time ago. His accent was Deep South, Alabama or thereabouts.

A coffeepot stood by the fire. MacNee hunkered down by it, lifted the pot, and poured into a tin cup.

"I got work," MacNee repeated. "For one feller." He gazed at Choctaw as he spoke, and the younger man guessed what was coming.

The rancher made a small gesture towards Dec. "For you." He drank, then told Choctaw, "Not for you, boy."

Not long ago that would have stung Choctaw into angry reaction. Today, he just felt a weariness, although not exactly disappointment. "Why not me?"

He got the answer he more or less expected. "I heard about you. You're the crazy kid Nils Swenson wouldn't hire, after you shot a man dead in a gun duel in Lobo Wells. The one they call 'the Choctaw Kid.'"

"Choctaw Kid!" Choctaw laughed in disdain.

"The half-breed pistoleer. I hear you killed

your man 'cuz he insulted your Choctaw mother."

"I'm not even part-blood Indian, mister. The feller I killed — I shot him in self-defense."

"I ain't gonna waste time augering. I know Swenson. He's a fair man. If he didn't take you on, there's a reason." MacNee stood. "I got plenty horses in my cavvy. But no kill-ers!"

Choctaw felt some temper after all. He glared. MacNee ignored him. He pointed at Dec with one earpiece of his glasses. "You still want the job?"

The Irishman shifted uncomfortably. He glanced at Choctaw, then at the rancher. "Sorry, Mr. MacNee. You take both of us . . . or none."

A little disappointment showed in MacNee's face. He shrugged. "Suit your-self."

Choctaw said, "Wait a minute, Dec."

Dec smiled faintly. "It's all right, Choc." He told the rancher, *"Adiós."*

He strode towards his horse. Choctaw hurried after him. "Wait a minute."

A dozen paces along, Dec halted, just a few yards from where their horses stood. Choctaw came alongside him.

He saw MacNee standing with arms

folded, watching them.

Choctaw said, "Listen, Dec . . . If you keep holding to that, neither of us is going to get a job. Work's so thin around here, might be better if we look separately anyway."

The Irishman blinked. He seemed puzzled, and then a slight look of pain touched his face. "Choc —"

"How much money you got left?"

"Just about enough for one day's bed and board I reckon."

"I'm the same. We're looking at a long, hungry winter, partner."

MacNee unfolded his arms. "You made up your minds yet? I can't stand around here, burning daylight."

Choctaw asked Dec, "How about we meet up in Prescott come Christmas? The Lucky Strike saloon."

"Choc —"

Choctaw forced a smile that he hoped was halfway convincing. "Don't worry about me. I'll be all right."

Dec rubbed his chin.

MacNee called, "Well?"

Dec nodded slightly. He tried to smile himself, without much success. "See you Christmas."

Choctaw reached out. He didn't quite

know what he was reaching for. A hand-shake? Instead, he touched his friend lightly on the left shoulder. Dec reached up awkwardly and patted Choctaw's arm.

He looked embarrassed and Choctaw felt the same way. He moved to his horse and climbed into the saddle. Only then did he look back at Dec.

The Irishman said, "The Choctaw Kid!"

Choctaw felt a genuine smile work its way on to his lips. Dec beat that; he grinned.

Choctaw said, "I think I will turn pistoleer. I'll start by shooting anybody calls me that!"

After a minute the grin faded, and the smile. The Irishman lifted a hand. *"Adiós, compadre."*

"Adiós."

Choctaw kicked his horse in the slats and rode off. A hundred yards along he reined in and looked back.

Dec had moved; now he stood alongside MacNee. Both of them were staring after him.

■ ■ ■ ■

PART TWO:
THE CRAZY R

■ ■ ■ ■

CHAPTER SIXTEEN

Choctaw came to the Crazy R.

This ranch was maybe a hundred miles from John MacNee's spread. Choctaw asked about who did the hiring and was directed to an area known as Baldy Flats.

A plain wearing a bristle of low grama grass, backed up against the enormous ramparts of the Mogollon Rim. Almost as bald as the name suggested, with only one visible tree, a gnarly, wind-stooped cottonwood. A few men in cowboy gear sat in its shadow.

A chuck wagon was parked nearby, its bentwood bows stripped of canvas leaving the interior exposed. A fellow was busy at the back of this vehicle; Choctaw took him for the cook from the apron he wore. A few yards away a large pot and a frying pan stood over a fire. From the smells coming from both, chow was nearly ready, and reminded Choctaw of his empty belly. He hadn't eaten since breakfast and it was close to 5 p.m.

The food smells, the murmur of human voices, reminded Choctaw of his recent back trail: crossing high, empty country, traveling in a line a little south of east, hugging the base of the rim that was always there, marching at his left hand. Feeling too much lonesomeness where there had been friendship, his rump and legs aching from too long in the saddle, eating too much of the dust a stern wind sifted into his face, at the same time knowing the gnaw of hunger.

He swung his horse clear of the chuck wagon. Range etiquette required you didn't risk getting dust into the food. He maneuvered his buckskin round a cowhand trudging up with an armful of firewood. Choctaw pointed towards a man sitting with his back to the cottonwood — a fellow in a blue-gray hat and dark jacket. He was studying the little book he held, most likely a tally book, a stub of pencil poised to write.

Reining in, Choctaw asked this man, "Captain Rawlins?"

"Cap for short."

"I hear you own this outfit. Who do I see about the hiring?"

Zachary Rawlins looked the newcomer up and down. He took his time about it.

136

"Mostly I leave that to my foreman, 'Dutch Henry' Kruger. That's Hank to you. But, as he's out on roundup and I'm here, I can do it. What's your name, son?"

"Calvin Taylor."

Rawlins thought about that a minute. Clearly he was someone who liked to chew things over. Literally. A plug worked rhythmically in his right cheek. He spat a thin stream of brown juice at the earth, then said, "Step down and help yourself to coffee."

Choctaw thanked him and dismounted. The coffeepot sat next to the frying pan. Choctaw hunkered down and poured himself a tin cup full.

Rawlins looked to be crowding sixty. He had a trimmed gray mustache and a fringe of beard that was gray turning silver. The hair that showed under his hat was mostly gray with a dash of its original dark color. Still a handsome man, for all his skin had seen a lot of weather. There was a spray of lines at the corner of his eyes that spoke of a lifetime of keeping them narrowed against the sun and focused on far distance. It was a hard face, darkened by the outdoors, but not without humor.

Rawlins said, "You'll notice I do a lot of sitting. But then I got to stretch some."

To match his words, he stood. He was maybe an inch or two over six feet, and hadn't put on much excess fat over the years.

The rancher patted his right leg. "This old pin ain't much good for standing and walking no more. Comanche war lance."

Choctaw said, "Jesus," and instantly regretted it. Some folks took against blaspheming. But Rawlins didn't seem to notice. "That was back when I was a Texas Ranger."

All of which might be an old man spinning a windy on a wide-eyed kid, but Choctaw was prepared to believe it. The old man's accent reminded Choctaw of home — it sounded pure, slow Arkansas. Rawlins's voice was low, had a lot of gravel and trail dust in it, but the result was more musical than harsh.

The rancher asked, "You work cattle before?"

"Over in New Mexico. Place called Rio Salado. Ben Tyler."

"No. Not familiar with that name. Who'd you work for last?"

"With a friend of mine. We was mustanging over near Lobo Wells."

"Horsebreaker huh? How come you still ain't at it?"

"My partner was called away someplace else."

Which was a small lie Choctaw had settled on telling, rather than the whole, complicated truth. Being as the truth was unlikely to get him work.

Rawlins said, "All right. Here's how I do things. There *is* work, seeing as it's fall roundup time. We got plenty cattle on the roundup ground need branding." The rancher spat juice. "We're always getting fellers after a job who swear they're cowboys. Turns out they don't know one end of a steer from another. They're just looking for a free meal. So, to weed them out . . . anybody new, we give a kind of a trial. First couple of days we put you through your paces. You don't get paid. Just grub and a place by the fire. If you shape up, you go on the payroll. That sound fair?"

"Uh-huh."

"One last thing. You on the dodge? Riding the high lines? Anybody after you?"

"No."

Rawlins gave the younger man some hard scrutiny, making him uneasy. The rancher said, "Well, as long as you ain't lying . . . you're hired."

Choctaw grinned.

A little smile worked around the older

man's lips. "You hungry? Young'uns usually is."

"Yes, sir."

"One thing this outfit don't never do is turn away a hungry man. Especially now, when it's getting close to feeding time."

"Much obliged."

"Been hungry too many damn times myself. Although I'm lucky. I get spoilt nowadays. Leastwise when my daughter's around to cook for me."

"Your daughter?"

"She'll be back here in a week or so. On her Christmas vacation." Rawlins's mouth relaxed into a full, unguarded smile. "She sure knows how to satisfy my innards."

"Kind of early for Christmas holidays, ain't it?"

"Not if you go to one of them fancy Eastern schools." Rawlins addressed the man standing back of the chuck wagon. "Hey, cooky!"

The cook turned towards them. He wore a derby hat, had a long, mournful face, mustache and full beard and a pipe hanging from his mouth.

Rawlins asked, "What you fixing to poison us with tonight, you old belly-cheater?"

The cook glared haughtily. Choctaw knew trail cooks were often men of temperament, who bowed to nobody, not even the big auger. Without taking the pipe from his mouth the cook replied, "You skunks are luckier than you deserve. Tonight it's my specialty — Sonofabitch Stew!"

CHAPTER SEVENTEEN

The air was harsh with smoke and the stink of branding.

It was the next morning and Choctaw stood by a branding fire. This was on the roundup ground, a wide plain below Baldy Flats, where Crazy R cattle were gathered.

It was the job of the Crazy R cowboys to spot any unbranded animals — what they called cleanskins or mavericks — among the herd and brand them. Mostly cleanskins were calves born since the spring roundup, with a scattering of full-grown animals who'd been missed last spring, or strays who'd joined the herd since then. Once the whole herd was branded, they'd be driven to late markets.

One of Rawlins's hands head-roped a dogie — a stray calf — and dragged it to the fire, backing up his horse. The foreman, Hank Kruger, approached on foot, taking hold of the taut rope snaring this animal. In a quick, practiced motion he flipped the rope over the calf's head. He reached down over the animal's back, grabbing some loose flesh on its far side, yanking the dogie towards him. Kruger kneed the near foreleg out from under the animal, and it went down on its side. The foreman sat on the calf's head, and another waddie splayed its hind legs.

Choctaw stepped forward, a stamp iron in his hand, brand dull red from the fire.

Kruger glanced up at him. Choctaw saw Cap Rawlins was watching him too, leaning forward in the saddle of his fine blood bay horse.

Choctaw rested the iron on the calf's hip but only briefly, as it wouldn't do to burn a brand too deep or set hair afire. There was the throat-catching stink of singed hide, an eruption of gray smoke, and the dogie bawled its pain — branding hurt like hell. Then it was turned loose and struggled to its feet. On its hip the Crazy R brand: a capital R upside down.

Rawlins wrinkled his nose. "Been smelling that for thirty years. Never have got used to it." Then he glanced across at Choctaw and gave a small nod of approval. He said, "That's branding. Let's see what you're like at 'cutting.' "

Cutting was about weeding unbranded cattle out of a herd with the aid of specially trained horses.

The afternoon of the next day Choctaw was riding a cutting horse called Blaze. Blaze was a handsome red dun with a coppery mane. His name came from the wide white stripe down the middle of his face. Choctaw had quickly made friends with him and judged he was plenty smart.

They rode close to the Crazy R herd. The longhorns milled around on long spindly legs, ugly, scrawny varicolored beasts, some of them wearing a spread of horns reaching six feet or wider. Hornless calves were scattered among them.

Choctaw scanned the herd for cleanskins. Thirty, forty yards off, Cap Rawlins reined in his bay and leaned forward in the saddle, once again watching him.

Choctaw spotted two mavericks: a runty calf bawling for its mother, and a big steer splotched rust and white, its horn spread reaching maybe seven feet. If he was going to shine in Rawlins's eyes, he needed to take on something harder rather than easier, so he pointed his horse at the steer.

The dun moved forward eagerly. They entered the herd and Blaze weaved his way expertly between tossing horns. Dust rose about them like a gauzy fog. Choctaw pulled his bandanna over his mouth and nose and squinted to keep stinging motes out of his eyes.

Horse and rider got behind the steer, nudging it out of the herd. The animal kept trying to duck back, to rejoin its fellows. The dun showed it knew its business, keeping itself between the maverick and others of its kind. Once or twice, it helped the steer along by giving it a quick nip on the rump. That way, horse and rider shepherded the cleanskin towards the branding fires.

Choctaw guided the cutting horse with his knees. As he did so, he lifted his grass rope off his saddle and shook it out, building a loop. He could snare the steer with a head catch, but a better way — though a trickier throw — was a heel catch. With Rawlins watching him, he decided to try the latter.

He was so busy planning that he took his eyes off the steer.

It whirled, trying to horn horse and rider.

Choctaw knew a quick fear: he'd once seen a rider horned in the groin. But Blaze reacted faster than he did. The red horse danced away. The steer made a few lunges after them, its corkscrewing horns jabbing like the tines of a pitchfork. Next it stood stamping up dust, bawling its anger, glaring out of red eyes. Then the steer forgot about fighting back, got its head down, and ran.

Horse and rider went in pursuit. They moved together with an easy rhythm. The horse was doing what it did best, and Choctaw felt excitement singing through him.

He readied his rope. The steer weaved ahead of him, looking for a chance to strike back at its pursuers. But Blaze kept on the brute's tail, driving it forward.

Choctaw threw. It was a low, sidearm cast. His skill — or luck — was perfect. The loop skimmed about a foot over ground level and went under the steer's back hooves, snaring both hind legs.

Then it was Blaze's turn. The horse skidded to a halt, braced with stiffened front legs, and the rope thrummed taut.

The steer's feet left the earth and it went down on its left cheek, leaving it lying side up. All Choctaw had to do was drag it the few yards to the branding fire. He and Blaze did so, raising a furrow of dust. A couple of men standing there took hold of the clean-skin. One loosed the rope and Choctaw spooled it in.

He found he was grinning. The cutting horse ought to be grinning too, after a job so well done.

Rawlins called, "Good throw, younker!"

Choctaw patted Blaze's shoulder. "This feller done most of the work."

"Shoot, I know *that*. If I was paying you both wages, horses'd get double the riders!"

Hard work in the fresh air and at these altitudes drove Crazy R riders to their saddle blankets soon after dark fell.

Bedding down, Choctaw felt the weight of his tiredness, the aching of his body, most particularly his rump, thighs, and legs, after how many hours in the saddle today?

A wind prowled, with the taste of winter in it. He pulled his blanket up under his chin and squirmed his toes deeper into his socks. He could hear distant singing, too far off to make out words. That would be the cowboy riding night herd around the Crazy R stock. He had a fine bass voice, and Choctaw was envious, as his singing voice was about as tuneful as an ungreased axle.

Out in the night a coyote yarred. In his mind Choctaw pictured this critter atop some high place, with his back arched like a bow and his cold nose raised to the sky. As

147

the coyote's voice lost itself in distance, behind the night herder's singing, Choctaw felt loneliness, to add to his weariness and aches and pains. As sleep came, he wondered how Dec was getting on, over at the Circle M . . .

CHAPTER EIGHTEEN

Next morning, Choctaw sat alongside Cap Rawlins at the fire, eating breakfast. The usual range diet of "Prairie Chicken" — bacon, beans, and sourdough biscuits.

Rawlins addressed the younger man. "Well, young feller . . . I reckon you'll do."

"That mean I'm on the payroll?"

The rancher gave a slight nod. "Uh-huh. As of right now."

Choctaw grinned.

Rawlins said, "I was gonna go over to Coronado Springs this morning anyway. You might as well tag along."

Choctaw swabbed up the last of his meal with a chunk of bread. "What for?"

"Got some horses over there I figured to bring in. You might as well look 'em over, start picking out your string."

Once they'd eaten the two men mounted up and rode.

Cap Rawlins, riding his bay, led the way,

pointing due west. The land climbed gradually, away from timber and grassy flatlands into terrain where the verdure thinned out, becoming sand and bare rock.

The beginnings of high desert.

Here Rawlins reined in his horse. He leaned forward in the saddle, staring off to the west.

The younger man looked that way also and saw a banner of dust trailing across the landscape, growing larger.

The rancher lifted his hat off his head and shaded his eyes with it, studying the oncoming rider. "Can't see right. Maybe that's Juan Ortega's horse."

Choctaw took his army field glasses from his saddlebags. Rawlins gave him a surprised look and forgot the frontier etiquette of never asking anything but the most basic questions. "Where'd you get those?"

The younger man didn't answer; he wasn't ready to tell the rancher anything about his life as an Apache scout just yet. Instead, he rode to the rancher's side and handed him the field glasses.

Rawlins lifted the binoculars to his eyes. "Juan sure enough." He frowned. "It ain't like him to scratch a horse. Not without a reason."

Juan galloped up. He reined in maybe a

dozen yards from them, so as not to kick dust into their faces or spook their horses. He let the dust settle, then walked his dun, which looked lathered and plenty hard ridden, over to the other riders.

He was taller than most of the Mexicans Choctaw had seen. He was about thirty-five. His most notable features were a large nose and his mustache, spreading wide below high cheekbones. He dressed like an Anglo cowhand, not a Mexican *charro,* save for the *chapajeros* he wore over his work pants.

He addressed Rawlins. *"Ladrones de caballos!"*

Choctaw translated Juan's words in his head. But Rawlins showed he could speak Spanish too. He said, "Horse thieves."

Juan nodded. "Drove off the herd at Coronado Springs." His voice rasped, maybe from the dust in his throat. "Six men. All Anglos, I think. I could've gone after 'em or come tell you." He looked sheepish, as if he figured Rawlins might think him a coward.

The rancher said, "No. You done right. Better than taking on six guns all by yourself. How many horses they get?"

"Eleven. All of 'em at the springs."

Something like pain touched Rawlins's face. "Some good cutting horses too." He looked over at Choctaw. "Including that one you was riding yesterday."

"Blaze?"

The rancher nodded.

Choctaw felt his own pain, mixed with anger, thinking of such a fine animal in the hands of thieves.

Rawlins said, "Come on, Juan."

He spurred the bay and rode off to the west. Juan followed. Choctaw galloped after them.

Rawlins pulled up his horse. As Choctaw came alongside him, he asked the younger man, "Who invited you along?"

"I'm on the payroll, ain't I?"

The rancher asked, "You got a gun belt?"

"In my saddle roll."

"Put it on."

"Awkward wearing that thing."

"Put it on now. Keep it on till I tell you otherwise."

The younger man thought about arguing, saying something like "You ain't my pa, don't talk to me like I'm some kid." Instead he did as he was told. Rawlins said, "All right. We can go now. But remember this, younker — if there's shooting, you skedaddle."

Choctaw stared in dismay. "You just told me to put on this damn pistol, now you tell

me to run if there's shooting! What do you
— ?"

Rawlins cut him off with "No more time
for talking!" He got the bay moving again,
and the others followed.

They came to Coronado Springs. It sat in
the middle of a desolate plain, marked by a
lone, twisted-about cottonwood. Two hundred yards short of it, Rawlins raised his
hand, signifying halt.

The rancher said, "If we pile in there, we
could wipe out any tracks those *ladrones*
left. So we go in afoots and poke around
careful."

He swung out of the saddle, and his men
did likewise.

They prowled around the springs, studying the earth.

Juan said, "Tracks are plain. No doubt
which way they've gone." He looked to the
west. Across a bald plateau towards a line of
hills, soft purple and shaped like knuckles,
their treeless outlines sharp-edged against a
sky so bright the eye flinched from it. "Into
the *malpais.*"

This time Choctaw translated out loud.

"Badlands."

Rawlins told Juan, "You get to the
roundup ground. Get help up here. I'll head
after these varmints."

Juan raised his voice in alarm. "You can't go after six men on your own, *patrón.*"

"I ain't crazy. I'm aim to trail 'em, not fight 'em. I'll leave a trail you can follow." Rawlins dismounted and started doing something with his horse's cinch strap. As he did so he told Juan, "Get all the men you can, and catch me up. Get Kruger if you can. Make sure word gets back to the ranch."

"Sí, señor."

The rancher glanced at Choctaw. "You go with Juan."

"No, sir. I figure I'll come with you."

Rawlins blinked. "You crazy?"

"I'm working for the Crazy R, ain't I?"

"Yeah. As a cowpoke, not to get yourself shot at. This is likely to come to guns."

"Don't matter."

"It *does* matter. I got enough to worry about, without thinking about you getting yourself killed."

"But —"

Rawlins made a sound of deep exasperation. "Will you quit augering? Your job is to go get help up here. So do as you're told."

Choctaw stared. His horse sensed his tension and shifted under him nervously.

Rawlins's face went from warm with anger to red with it. "Damn it, boy, times

154

a-wasting! Don't have me cussing you. I promised my daughter I'd quit cussing. Don't make me break my promise to her."

Juan said, "Come on, *amigo*."

The Mexican rode off.

After a moment, Choctaw rode after him.

They made the best speed they could, but you couldn't push a horse too hard over this kind of ground, with the full heat of day coming. They were maybe a mile along when Juan pulled up his horse.

Choctaw did the same.

They listened. There was a thin crackle of sound in the western distance.

Flat cracks that threw out long echoes.

Gunfire.

CHAPTER NINETEEN

After Juan and young Taylor rode off, Cap Rawlins mounted the bay.

As he did so he glimpsed a crawl of dust far to the west.

The rancher knew the country in that direction. It was barren and ugly, growing meaner every mile. He felt anguish for the stolen animals being hard driven over such terrain, as he was a man who loved horses.

Rawlins rode west. The sun climbed towards noon, and it grew hot. The wind was the breath of a furnace, rasping his flesh.

Impatience welled in him. Despite what he'd said to Juan, it was tempting to spur the bay into a hard run, to try and ride down these thieves. A crazy urge he resisted. There wasn't a whole lot of future in taking on six guns single-handedly. So he held to a steady pace and didn't push past it.

He also kept a wary eye out. There was a chance some of the men he pursued might double back and try to bushwhack him. They might do that to brush him off their trail. But they *were* thieves and they'd also be tempted to get hold of the bay, the rancher's rifle and gear, the money in his pockets. Maybe even his boots . . .

After a mile Rawlins came within rifle shot of Hopi Flats. He reined in and looked it over.

Nothing to please the eye: a hard pan of bare rock, rubbled earth, and sand under a metallic sky. You'd look in vain for trees or even anything green. Clumps of withered vegetation dotted about, none of them big enough to hide a jackrabbit. But what made the flats worth studying were the jutting rock outcrops and boulders scattered around its fringes. This was the first place he'd come to with good cover, where you might get yourself ambushed.

But there were a thousand such places ahead, and he couldn't avoid them all. So he booted the bay into motion and rode on to the flats.

As he passed beyond the first rocks, his back itched. His mouth was clenched tight, a chunk of fear in his throat, tasting sour in his mouth and lying cold in his belly. Easy to imagine eyes, or rifle sights, trained on you, from behind these blank stone faces.

But nothing happened.

Not until he was three quarters across the flats.

Ahead was one last piece of cover — a large, sun-blackened boulder — and then he'd be in open ground and heading into the foothills.

From the edge of this black boulder leaped a star blaze of light.

Rawlins knew what that was. He yanked on the reins, hauling the bay up, just as the shot came.

It missed.

By maybe two inches. It yowled so close to his ear he heard it say, "Cousin!"

The horse let out a shrill whinny. Rawlins spun the bay around, used spurs, and the animal took off back the way it had come.

Rawlins yelled, letting out his fear with that cry. His heart was hammering fast and hard enough to burst out of his chest. He crouched low against the horse's mane, reaching down, sliding his Winchester out of his saddle scabbard. Behind him a gun banged. His back was as wide as this landscape, expecting the bullet to drive him from the saddle.

He wasn't hit.

He drove towards a scatter of jagged rocks. From these rocks came another flash of silver brilliance.

Another burst of powder smoke.

Another bullet that missed.

Rawlins drove between these rocks and out into the open country beyond. He was out of the trap, maybe the bushwhackers would quit now he was on the run from them . . .

But a quick glance back showed him riders in pursuit, at the full gallop. Two of them. One of them yelled. A rifle barked.

The three riders hammered east, hooves clacking like castanets on hard rock.

Rawlins knew you could only run a horse this fast for a short distance — three miles maximum, even a fine animal like the blood bay. He reckoned he'd covered two miles before the bay started to wheeze.

But he still had a good lead over his pursuers.

And then the bay put its foot in a hole.

The horse went to its knees.

Rawlins pitched ahead. The sky tumbled crazily. He slammed into the earth facedown, plowing his own furrow. White dust erupted, swallowing him.

The bay struggled to its feet and fled.

Rawlins lay still. The fall had knocked all the wind, all the sense, out of him.

When he started to pull his scattered wits

together, he was grateful that at least he hadn't landed on his bad leg.

The mist of dust around him thinned. He squirmed over, glancing back, and glimpsed movement.

Two horsemen charging him. Riders with rifles in their hands. The nearest wore a green shirt, the farthest away a brown one. Hooves clattered on stony ground.

The rancher saw his Winchester lying on the earth before him. He grabbed it.

Rawlins was about to die alone on a vast plain, of less significance than a tick bite on this immensity, a victim of a couple of no-account horse thieves. His mouth twisted into a savage grin at this injustice. If he was about to cash in, he wouldn't go to Hell alone. At least one of these varmints would keep him company.

Green Shirt was thirty yards off. He guided his horse with his knees, his rifle raised to his shoulder. He came at Rawlins head on. He'd be on him in a shake.

Rawlins knelt up, pulling the rifle butt into his shoulder, aiming.

Green Shirt's rifle cracked; the rancher heard the whine of the bullet, viciously close.

Rawlins fired.

Green Shirt flipped back. His feet came

out of the stirrups. For an instant his body was balanced on the saddle, his legs straightening up into the air, like some circus trick rider performing. Then he cartwheeled backwards.

His horse kept coming. Rawlins flung himself aside as the animal hurled itself at him. A thousand pounds of horse passed overhead, blotting out the sky, as it vaulted over him.

Rawlins struck the hard ground on his bad leg. That brought such pain he screamed. It blinded him. He lay, lost in agony, knowing only his own suffering, trying not to scream again.

Then he was coming out of it, sprawled on his back, and Brown Shirt's horse was rearing over him, front hooves striking air.

Rawlins glimpsed the rider's bearded face, his wild eyes, the horse's flared red nostrils. There was a pistol in Brown Shirt's hand, pointed at the rancher's chest.

Rawlins realized he still held his Winchester. He started to bring it up, knowing he was too late, he'd be forever too late.

Brown Shirt plunged forward, pitching over his horse's head and striking the ground and rolling on, but rolling limply like he was a rag doll. And then the rolling stopped and the man was still while the dust he raised settled.

Rawlins fell on his back, as if his surprise had punched him in the face. Dimly he heard the echoes of a couple of rifle shots, chasing each other. He knew he was gaping like a damn fool. Stupidly he watched Brown Shirt's horse pelt off across the desert.

For a while pain returned to his leg and he lay, burning with it, sweat bursting from him. Slowly the hurt eased.

Rawlins heard hooves, coming nearer.

The rancher managed to raise up on one elbow. He gazed at the rider approaching from the east. This man reined in his buckskin a dozen yards away. He held a Winchester in his right hand.

Rawlins called out. His voice was thick with dust, cracked with thirst and pain. "Well, looky here! If it ain't Mister Calvin Taylor!"

CHAPTER TWENTY

Cap Rawlins sat, rubbing his bad leg.

Young Taylor asked, "You hit, Cap?"

The rancher shook his head. "I ain't been shot. Just fell on this damn leg."

But after a spell of kneading this limb, it felt healed enough to stand on. Rawlins got to his feet and limped over to the dead men. Two nondescript Anglos in battered trail gear.

Taylor sat out of the late morning sun, in the only shade hereabouts, under his horse's belly. He asked, "Do you know 'em?"

The rancher shook his head slightly. "No, but this backcountry's got more thieves in it than a dog has fleas. Needs a damn good scouring."

He ought to feel sorry two men had come to bad ends, one at his hands, even if they were horse thieves; but he couldn't. He was trembling slightly. Rawlins had been in enough violent confrontations to know that was normal reaction to the danger he'd just been in, and that he'd just killed a man. As was the anger building in him, driving him to lash out at something. He kept that reined in, making his tone even and neutral when he said, "That was good shooting, younker. *Gracias.*"

"*De nada.*"

"Nothing wrong with your eyesight, that's for sure." Then Rawlins's anger cut loose, putting an edge in his voice. "Can't say the same about your hearing. As I recollect, I told you and Juan to head for the roundup ground. Since when —"

But that was as far as the rancher got, because his eye caught a wisp of dust on the face of the desert to the east. He let his words trail off. He guessed it was Crazy R riders coming up. But you never knew who was haunting these wild places, so he rested his rifle across his arms.

Taylor must have seen too, because he stood and took the field glasses from his saddlebags. He passed them over to Rawlins. The rancher brought the binoculars to his eyes. "It's Hank and Juan."

Kruger and Juan rode up. The Mexican was leading Rawlins's blood bay.

Kruger asked, "What happened, boss?"

Rawlins told him.

The foreman said, "I got others coming up from the ranch. Should we wait for them?"

"No, they can catch us up."

Hank Kruger was maybe thirty-five, medium height, stocky and barrel-chested. He wore a dark blue shield front shirt, a big red bandanna, and a Texas hat. The most notable feature of his square, serious face was his dark handlebar mustache.

Rawlins felt anger warming in him once more. He addressed Taylor. "Now, as I was saying, I told you to head for the roundup ground."

Juan said, "I told him too. But when he heard guns, he took off after you."

The rancher went on, "Them was your orders, Mister Taylor. Not come back here and do something as fool crazy as a-rescuing me. Was you mine, I'd teach you better with the buckle end of my belt."

Taylor glared. "Well, I ain't yours. You're my boss. You ain't my pa, so don't be talking to me like you are!" He was clearly in the grip of some temper himself. "And if you want to teach me anything with your belt, old man, then let's have at it!"

He stood braced, as if he expected the rancher to come at him.

Kruger said, "Why, you little pissant . . ."

The younker switched his glare to the foreman; they got into a staring contest.

It could all come to fists in a moment, maybe even to guns. Rawlins looked at the back of his hands, flexed his fingers, and breathed out a long sigh. He gestured towards Taylor, putting mock wonder in his voice. "Well now — he even talks back to the big auger." He kept up the play-acting, shaking his head in disbelief. "I don't know what the youth of today's coming to!"

For a little more the tension held and then Juan laughed. The younker scowled, but then his lips twisted and he joined in. All Kruger managed was a grudging smile, but that was the best you could hope for. He laughed less often than it rained out here.

Rawlins let the laughter run on for a minute, then he said, "Well, this ain't getting our horses back."

He stepped towards his horse and Taylor said, "Cap?"

"Yep?"

Taylor looked at Rawlins, started to speak, glanced away, then back at the older man. "I'm sorry I spoke disrespectful."

The rancher said, "I forgive easy mostly." He gave his aching leg a further rub. " 'Course, if you do call me 'old man' again, I will tie you up in your own guts and hang you from a tree."

The younker smiled sheepishly.

They mounted up. Taylor asked, "Ain't we gonna bury these dead men?"

Kruger puckered his lips. It took him some seconds to find enough moisture to spit. "Buzzards and wolves got to eat, don't they?"

They rode west.

Rawlins's men were eager, but the rancher knew the country they were pointing into and kept an eye on his watch. After fifty minutes he ordered the riders to dismount and walk their horses for ten minutes.

As they got ready to mount up again, Rawlins took a small drink from his canteen — he'd rationed his men to one swallow — and rolled the leather-tasting water in his mouth. "I keep thinking about what this country'll do to them horses' feet."

Kruger said, "Remember boss: these bastards are after selling them animals, not ruining them."

"Yeah, but even so . . ."

Juan said, "They ain't lost yet, Cap."

Again, they rode for fifty minutes, then walked the horses for ten. They repeated this for the next two hours. They didn't pause to eat, but some of them chewed jerky as they rode or walked along.

The sun punished them, leaching sweat from men and mounts, and their halts between spells of riding and walking became more frequent.

They came upon one of the lost horses.

Rawlins recognized the cutting horse. "Whiskey!"

Whiskey was a handsome strawberry roan. Or had been. The gelding's coat was dark with lather and crusted with sweat. His head was bowed low, flies crawling at his nostrils and around his eyes. He stood with his near foreleg lifted off the ground. The leg was clearly broken at the cannon, as the bottom of the limb hung limply, twisted out of line with the rest.

It was a pitiful sight and Rawlins tasted anger like bile in his mouth and throat. He began to curse, remembering his promise to his daughter and biting his tongue just in time. But Kruger made up for it. Slowly, half under his breath, he worked his way through every oath Rawlins had ever heard.

The rancher said, "Looks like he fell and broke his leg. But they didn't have to leave him suffer."

Juan said, "They shoot him, gives away where they are."

"They could have cut his throat, God-damn it!"

The Mexican asked, "*Patrón,* you want me to —"

"No."

Rawlins drew his pistol and stepped alongside Whiskey. He stroked the horse's flaxen mane. The animal trembled, whinnying piteously, but not reacting at the touch of cold metal behind his left ear. The rancher spoke softly, his voice low and soothing. At the shot the animal dropped.

Rawlins stared down. He breathed hard through his nose. After a time, he glanced up and saw Taylor with his eyes fixed on Whiskey. There was an expression of undisguised anguish on his face that made him look very young. Rawlins guessed he was thinking about Blaze ending up the same way. Taylor had taken a real shine to that cutting horse.

Juan said, "Maybe we'll never catch 'em." There was a hint of despair in his voice.

Rawlins said, "We'll catch 'em." He gazed at Whiskey once more. It was a day of eyeball frying heat, but he felt a strange coldness. An icy hatred, the sort of feeling that would only be assuaged by killing. He walked over to the bay and mounted up. "We'll catch 'em today."

CHAPTER TWENTY-ONE

But they didn't.

They hadn't as much sighted the horse thieves' dust by sundown.

Rawlins said, "No point blundering around in the dark. We'll make camp and go after 'em at first light."

It was a cold camp, no fires. They ate hardtack and jerky, washed down with water. Today had squeezed most of the talk out of them; they ate and drank in dour silence except when Juan said, "These horses are getting pretty dried out, Cap."

"I know. But there's the springs the other side of Dead Mule Pass." He moved the chaw in his mouth with the tip of his tongue. "They're usually good."

Taylor asked, "How far's that?" All their voices rasped, cracked with thirst.

"Six, seven miles. We should make it maybe an hour after sunup. Then we can all have a good drink."

They bedded down. There was a chance the horse thieves might double back and attack them while they were sleeping. So each man took turns standing night guard, including Rawlins.

The night passed peacefully. They breakfasted at dawn, a brief revisiting of the same cold trail rations as supper. Within half an hour they were in the saddle.

The trail the pursuers followed switched from due west to northwest. This took them into rising ground, towards a run of bare hills.

Now Rawlins made them walk their horses twenty minutes every hour. The first time they did this Juan said, "They sure aren't hiding their tracks."

Rawlins answered him. "No. They're moving too fast." The rancher blinked his eyes, stinging with dust. The distant hills changed as haze shifted, from blurred and wavering outlines to jagged, sharp-edged ramparts brought into cruel focus. And back again.

Kruger said, "Hard enough to do this, without having to watch out for no greenhorn." He spoke to Rawlins, but looked sideways at Taylor.

The youth showed his temper again by rising to this bait. "I ain't exactly a greenhorn."

"No?"

Rawlins knew it was sometimes the fore-man's way to needle folks, especially those new to him, but right now the rancher had no patience for such nonsense. "Didn't act like no greenhorn at Hopi Flats."

Kruger started to grumble a reply, Taylor too, and Rawlins put an edge of temper into his voice. "You two want to fight, save it for those horse thieves. Then we'll see who's what."

They mounted up and rode on.

The horsemen reined in just less than a mile short of Dead Mule Pass. The mouth of the pass was in plain view, gaping before them, flanked by two great buttresses of black rock.

Taylor asked Rawlins, "We're going through that pass?"

"Sure. Springs on the other side. These animals are thirsty, and so am I."

The younger man pulled a face. "Looks like a good place to get ambushed."

The rancher grunted agreement. "True enough. But we go round these hills it'll take another half day. We'd be pretty low on water by then, and these horses near done. So I figure it's worth risking." He gazed towards the others. "What do you fellers think?"

172

Kruger and Juan studied the black jaws of the pass, their faces grim. Then both men nodded.

Rawlins scratched at the dust in his beard. "Let's hope we're lucky, and there ain't some bad *hombres* laying up there right now, with rifles pointing at us. But keep your eyes peeled. These varmints already bushwhacked me once. Any more and it'll be getting kind of tedious."

Kruger lifted his rifle from his saddle scabbard. The others did the same. The foreman was the first to ride towards the pass, then Juan.

Rawlins asked Taylor, "You coming?"

When the younger man didn't reply, the rancher turned his horse and rode after the others. He heard the clatter of hooves that meant the younker was following.

The horsemen rode up the slant, holding their horses down to little more than a walk. The ground started to be tricky, littered with rubble, loose stones, and shale. They came to where a long slope climbed before them, scattered with boulders, in places ramping up steeply, and then leveled off to flat ground that ran to the mouth of the pass.

Rawlins heard hooves crashing on stones and Taylor pushed his buckskin alongside

173

him. The younker held his field glasses in one hand. He called, "Hold up! Hold up, you fellows!"

They did so. The rancher asked, "What is it?"

Taylor said, "I thought I saw metal flash."

Kruger said, "I been watching the mouth of the pass. I ain't seen nothing. 'Sides we're still out of rifle range."

"I don't mean in the pass. I mean up there." The young man pointed at three or four boulders at the very top of the slope, at the beginning of level ground. Perhaps four hundred yards away.

Taylor passed the binoculars to Rawlins. The rancher trained them on the boulders. The younker said, "And I been watching the birds."

Juan gave him a half-incredulous look. "Huh?"

"A couple of times birds looked about to light there, then took off, 'stead of landing."

Kruger snorted in derision. "Birds!"

"Suppose these fellers are smarter than we think. We're watching to get jumped riding into the pass. That's the obvious place. So they hide where we ain't looking, 'hind those boulders. Old Apache trick. Get you watching for an ambush in one place, then spring one on you in another."

174

Rawlins asked, "How come you know so much about Apache tricks?"

"I worked a few army posts south of here. Picked up a few things from scouts there."

"Scouts? White or Apache?"

It took Taylor a little while to answer. "Both."

Kruger asked, "Cap, you gonna listen to this crazy kid?"

"Sure. I always listen to a feller who tells me I might be riding into an ambush." Rawlins did some more scanning with the field glasses. "I don't see nothing."

The foreman said, "Neither do I." He straightened in the saddle. "You ain't got the guts to go up there, kid, fine. You can stay back."

Taylor blinked and glared.

On the frontier, coward was an insult alongside liar, something you might be expected to go to your guns over. Rawlins said, "No need for that, Hank!"

But Kruger was already moving, pushing his horse up the slope.

Juan followed.

The rancher used the binoculars again, studying the ground ahead. He felt cold unease, his whole body clenched. He still couldn't see anything, but this terrain could hide a small army. And the slope directly below the boulders was more like a series of steps, with cutbanks and steep falloffs. In places the horses would struggle to find footing on loose soil; they'd be sliding around. It would be a very bad place to get yourself ambushed.

But he had to decide. He was thirsty, his horse was thirsty, and maybe there was nobody lying for them on the trail ahead. What the kid thought was the metal of a gun flashing could as easily be a shard of mica, or something equally innocent . . . He passed the field glasses back to Taylor, who asked, "You going up there, Cap?"

There seemed to be a wedge of granite in Rawlins's throat. He swallowed it, turned his horse, and rode up the slope after Kruger and Juan.

He didn't expect Taylor to follow; but hooves rattled on stony ground. The rancher glanced back and saw the younger man maybe ten yards behind him, riding forward warily. Rawlins felt a jab of guilt. Was this younker following his boss into danger, against his best instincts, out of loyalty?

They rode upslope, strung out in file: first Kruger, then Juan, Rawlins, and last Taylor.

But they didn't go far. Maybe two hundred yards.

And then they were ambushed.

CHAPTER TWENTY-TWO

Cap Rawlins had one warning.

The sun catching a gleam of metal from the boulders Taylor had indicated.

Rawlins started to yell but Kruger had seen; he was wheeling his horse about. Juan too. Both of them came plunging downslope at a full gallop.

A rifle banged.

Echoes of the shot knocked between walls of rock. Mixed in with that were at least two more shots.

Rawlins hauled in his bay. He jerked his Winchester to his shoulder and ripped off a string of shots towards the dark powder bursts among the boulders. Not in the hope of hitting anything, but to cover his fleeing men.

There was movement behind him. A quick glance showed him Taylor spurring his horse into a run. But the younker wasn't fleeing downslope; he was riding *towards* the gunfire, although at an angle to the left as he charged his enemies, which seemed a crazy thing to do.

Rawlins switched his attention back to Juan and Kruger.

They hammered down the slope towards him.

More shots.

Kruger's horse went down. The rider pitched over its head and rolled forward.

Dust boiled.

The foreman scrambled up, his feet churning rubble and shale. The horse stayed down.

Juan spun his horse on a dime and rode back towards Kruger.

Rawlins started to yell after the Mexican, telling him not to be a damn fool, but before he got the words out Juan's horse was rearing over Kruger, the rider reaching down.

The guns at the boulders went crazy.

Kruger grabbed Juan's arm and then the Mexican was leaning past him and falling headlong out of the saddle.

Rawlins called, "Juan!"

There was more gunfire and the Mexican's horse screamed, reared, and fell. Another burst of white dust erupted, hiding men and animal.

It took some seconds to thin, revealing a

horse and two bodies lying still. Then one of the men stirred, grabbed the other, and dragged him to where a cutbank jutted, giving them some protection from the bullets pouring down from above.

Rawlins had known fear plenty times, and was in the grip of it now. His instinct was to ride like hell away from those hidden rifles.

But he must be as crazy as Taylor because he was spurring the bay into a gallop. And galloping the same way. Upslope. Except he was pointing towards Juan and Kruger, where they sheltered against the cutbank.

So far he didn't think he'd drawn one bullet, but he drew plenty now. They yowled around his ears. He might have been on the flats yesterday, while death sang around him and fear breathed fiercely on the back of his neck.

The bay reared, balking at the gradient. Rawlins slipped from the saddle, making sure he came down on his good leg. The horse bolted. The rancher saw his ranch hands a dozen yards away, their backs to the cutbank. He ran towards them. A bullet spurted stones at his feet; he felt hot stinging pain on his right forehead and then he was slamming his back against the cutbank, sliding down and sitting at its base, his rifle laid across his knees, jammed between the two other men.

Kruger called, "Boss! You hit?"

"Don't think so."

"There's blood on your forehead."

Rawlins touched the blood by his right temple, which burned like hell. But it felt more like a scratch, maybe caused by a piece of flying stone, than a graze by a bullet. "It ain't nothing. What about you fellers?"

The foreman said, "Ain't even nicked. Juan . . ."

Rawlins looked. The Mexican's face was gray with shock, although he was still conscious. There was blood all over his shirtfront.

The rancher's stomach tightened with fear. He crossed to Juan's side and knelt by him, unbuttoning the wounded man's shirt. He used his bandanna to wipe away some of the blood that was all over the Mexican's torso. Meanwhile Kruger stood guard, his eyes narrowed as he gazed uphill, rifle raised.

As he swabbed away the rancher told Juan, "You stupid bastard! Who told you to play Goddamned fucking hero like that?" He recalled he'd promised something to his daughter a while back, but couldn't remember what it was.

Rawlins's tongue felt in vain for the chaw in his mouth; he must have spat it out. "We're pinned down here. They can just take their time playing with us. Let the sun work on us, and then, when it's dark, maybe sneak in."

"We're sure in a fix, boss."

Rawlins was the leader here; it was his job to keep his men's spirits up. But stating anything but the obvious in these circumstances seemed foolish. So his reply was: "We sure are."

The rancher had cleaned away enough blood to see there was a small hole in Juan's left side. He felt around and could find no exit wound. Blood had soaked the man's legs through and was still pouring, so he sat in a widening pool of it. The Mexican's eyes were closed. His breathing was low and ragged.

Rawlins felt an iciness spreading through him. Juan was gutshot and bleeding out, with the bullet still in him. Up here, so far from a doctor, that meant only one thing. Unless a miracle intervened.

Of course, Juan was a good Catholic and believed in miracles. Rawlins wished he did.

In a bitter voice Kruger said, "The younker was right."

"Taylor? Where is he?"

Kruger's face was bleak.

Rawlins felt alarm. "Well?"

"I think I saw him go down."

CHAPTER TWENTY-THREE

When the ambush was sprung, Choctaw
spurred his horse.

He drove the buckskin upslope.

He glimpsed dark gouts of powder smoke
from the boulders. Bullets keened, searching him out.

Choctaw pressed himself low against the
buckskin's neck. He veered his horse to the
left, riding at an angle to the hidden rifles.
He slipped down, hanging low to the animal's near side, so the horse's body shielded
him from the ambushers.

They splashed through loose stones and
rubble; then he glimpsed a brief stretch of
bare sand. Choctaw flung himself sideways.
He hit the sand on his back, grunting as air
left his lungs. But however winded he was,
he couldn't stay down. As the riderless
horse pelted upslope, he rolled to his feet
and headed for the cover of some large
rocks. He threw himself down behind the

nearest one, sat with his back to it, and laid his Winchester across his knees.

His nerves were jangling, he shook, his heart pounded, his throat was fiercely dry; all the reactions he'd become familiar — too familiar — with. He reckoned at age twenty he'd already been shot at more times than most people were in a lifetime. He'd even heard, although it was hard to believe, of folks who lived their entire lives and never got shot at once. However many times it happened to him, he couldn't seem to get used to it.

Choctaw took a peek around the edge of the rock.

His mad run had taken him almost to the top of the slope, nearly level with the boulders where the ambushers hid.

A rifle cracked as one of the bushwhackers fired downslope. And then another.

Both men were about a hundred yards away.

That these sons of bitches were still in cover, and firing, meant they hadn't slaughtered all of Rawlins's party in the ambush. There was at least one person left alive to shoot at.

Choctaw felt relief. He'd taken a real liking to Cap Rawlins. And he didn't want anything to happen to the other Crazy R men, not even a sour, scratchy fellow like Kruger.

A horse whickered. Choctaw saw his buckskin standing maybe five hundred yards away. He felt more relief, this time for the horse.

The angle of land made it impossible for him to see the Crazy R men. But if they were pinned down on the slopes below, their situation would be pretty desperate. And lying in the cruel eye of the sun could only get worse for them as the day wore on.

Choctaw used his bandanna to wipe away sweat. His right hand ached from gripping the Winchester so tightly, his finger on the trigger. He unhinged his fingers and flexed them, gasping with pain as he did so.

Despite riding through a hail of lead, he didn't seem to have been hit.

There was another shot from the boulders. This time a rifle far below answered.

Nobody was shooting at him. Maybe the bushwhackers assumed they'd nailed him when he fell from his horse, and hadn't spotted him moving after that.

Choctaw squinted upslope, regretting he didn't have his field glasses. If Juan had counted right, there were six horse thieves to begin with. Which left four. Given how much fast shooting the ambushers had done, maybe all four of them were here.

He noticed there was a low, pyramid-shaped hill above the bushwhackers' hiding place. Apaches had taught Choctaw the importance of commanding the high ground. If he could get up there, he'd be looking down on his enemies. He'd have these bastards, however many of them there were, cold in his sights . . .

To get there he needed to cross ground scattered with rocks and boulders, some of them big enough to conceal a man entirely.

He set about doing just that.

Choctaw made his way from one boulder towering a few feet above him to another. He stepped past it.

And almost walked into a man.

A stocky figure in a poncho, a jowly face, a black beard. He held a Springfield rifle, barrel pointing down, as he strode forward. He halted and gaped in surprise.

They were two yards apart.

Choctaw started to lift his Winchester but Blackbeard was quicker; he flung his rifle.

It struck Choctaw across his shoulder and the top of his chest. He staggered back. His feet slid on loose stones and he went down on his rump.

He pushed himself off the earth, got to a crouch, and Blackbeard sprang.

His shoulder caught Choctaw in the chest. Choctaw said, "Whoof" as air went out of him. He was driven onto his back, losing his grip on the Winchester.

Blackbeard half-sprawled over him, reaching down with his left hand, fingers clawing for Choctaw's eyes. Choctaw seized his enemy's wrist and yanked those fingertips away from his face. Blackbeard's right hand went to his boot. Choctaw guessed why even before he glimpsed the flash of metal. Blackbeard suddenly held a knife, the thin blade hooking up to take his opponent in the throat.

Choctaw kicked up. His foot took Blackbeard in the stomach. Choctaw straightened his leg, hoisting the other man into the air. Blackbeard pitched headlong, somersaulting, coming down on his back on a crash of stones, rolling, churning through them.

Slowly, both men rose.

Choctaw stared into Blackbeard's small eyes. For an instant the combatants seemed frozen in the same position, mirror images of the other, crouching ready to spring, mouths open and sucking for air. Except Blackbeard held a knife in his right hand.

He stabbed. Choctaw dodged, feeling the breath of the weapon on his left side and Blackbeard plunged past him, plowing to his knees. He squirmed around towards his enemy, starting to rise and Choctaw struck. He aimed for the jaw but his fist caught Blackbeard in the throat.

Blackbeard grabbed under his chin and fell sideways, making choking, strangling noises.

Choctaw glimpsed the Springfield at his feet. He lifted the weapon as Blackbeard rose, left hand to his throat, his knife in his right fist.

Blackbeard lunged at his enemy.

Choctaw jabbed with the Springfield barrel. Blackbeard impaled himself on the muzzle, grunting and doubling forward. Choctaw swung the rifle butt across, catching the other man's left temple. Blackbeard spun away. He pitched onto his face.

This time he stayed down.

Choctaw stared down at Blackbeard, thinking maybe he'd killed him. But the fallen man was still alive enough to groan.

Choctaw guessed they'd made plenty of noise fighting, but maybe the other bushwhackers were too busy shooting at the Crazy R to hear.

He picked up his Winchester, but kept hold of Blackbeard's rifle too. Thus awkwardly encumbered, he sneaked about until cover ended.

Before him was a long, gradual slope of bare rock. He went up it crouched over. The slope climbed to some jagged upthrusts of rock.

A dozen yards short of the rocks, Choctaw got down to his hands and knees. He laid aside the Springfield. Armed with just the Winchester, he crawled forward keeping the barrel of the rifle above the earth and free of any dust that might foul it.

He came to the edge, to a jut of rock just big enough to shield him as he knelt behind it. He pushed his hat back off his head, so it hung by its string between his shoulders, and risked a quick peek beyond.

Maybe twenty yards ahead and down were two men, their backs to him. They stood behind boulders that came up to their chests. Both had rifles in their hands and were firing over the rocks at their enemies downslope.

The man on the right was dressed in gray, in what looked like an old Confederate forage cap and shell jacket, even though the war had been over for years. Choctaw dubbed him Rebel. He called the left-hand man Yellow Shirt.

They were perhaps a dozen yards apart. Lined up before Choctaw like targets.

What he ought to do, he supposed, was

189

call out, "Throw down your guns" or something similar. Try and take them prisoner. Knowing it was likely, with men as desperate as these, that they'd show fight, rather than surrender.

Or he could simply squeeze the trigger twice. Then he'd be a hero, the man who wiped out the horse thieves gang almost single-handedly.

Why should he show them mercy? After all, stealing horses was a crime that merited only one punishment out here, whether from a bullet or a rope. Even if he took them alive, that's what they'd be facing. And trying to take them prisoner might put him in danger.

He rested his elbows on the rock before him, pulling the butt of the Winchester into his shoulder. He fixed his front sight on Yellow Shirt, aiming at a spot midway between this man's shoulders.

Choctaw's finger tightened on the trigger. All it needed was two squeezes; it was the easiest and safest thing to do.

But it was no use.

He couldn't do it.

A voice in his head said: *You ain't got the sense you were born with.*

Instead he called, "You're covered! Throw down!"

Both men jerked about, showing startled faces. They lifted their hands, although they still held their rifles.

Choctaw called, "Drop them guns!"

Rebel tossed his rifle onto the earth in front of him. Choctaw let his eyes follow it.

Yellow Shirt dropped sideways. As he hit the ground he jerked his rifle about, firing. Choctaw ducked back, firing instinctively.

Both shots missed.

Rebel changed his mind about surrendering. He dropped to his knees and grabbed his rifle. Scrambling up, he lifted the weapon to his shoulder, aiming.

Choctaw fired.

Rebel spun away. He slammed against the boulder behind him and went down.

In the tail of his eye, Choctaw glimpsed Yellow Shirt on his feet and running. Choctaw fired at him and missed. The horse thief sprang onto the slope below and ran down it. He ran like an Apache, zigzagging. Choctaw drove a shot at the weaving runner, missing again. He took a steadier aim, leading his target. But his finger was only starting to tighten on the trigger when Yellow Shirt doubled forward, pitching headlong.

There was the crack of a rifle.

Yellow Shirt rolled down the slope in a

long trail of dust.

Choctaw slumped forward against the rock, letting the Winchester slide out of his hands. He was suddenly very tired. The reaction he expected to happen did. He was surprised, however, at how violently he shook.

Once that passed, he scouted around for a way down from this high place, which meant picking his way carefully down a steep slope. He walked over to Rebel and turned him faceup.

Rebel was dead, shot through the throat. His blood had soaked his Confederate jacket and formed a great pool about him, still spreading.

Choctaw felt a sourness in his mouth. The black taste of killing.

Standing back of one of the boulders, he called downslope. "It's all right! They're cleaned out up here!"

A voice answered, muffled by distance. He hoped it was Cap; instead, when it came again, he identified Kruger asking, "Who's that?"

"Calvin Taylor."

"Show yourself."

"All right. Long as you don't shoot me."

Choctaw stood at the top of the slope and waved the rifle in his hand. After a time, he saw Kruger approaching, moving warily up the slope, his rifle at the ready.

When the foreman came to where Yellow Shirt lay, he paused and stared down. He said, "Well, I nailed *him*." Then he continued climbing, pausing maybe a dozen yards from the younger man.

Choctaw asked, "Where's Cap?" He felt dread, waiting for the answer.

"He's all right. How about you?"

"Nary a scratch. Where's Juan?"

Kruger's face darkened. It took him a little while to answer.

"Juan's dead, kid."

CHAPTER TWENTY-FOUR

Kruger went back downslope.

It was a long time before he reappeared. Choctaw supposed he'd been busy catching up the horses. He came upslope leading Choctaw's buckskin. Cap Rawlins rode after him, mounted on his bay.

Choctaw waited for them, pointing his Winchester at his prisoner.

The man in the poncho sat with his hand to his right forehead, where a vivid red and purple bruise was starting to show.

Choctaw called down to Kruger. "Where's your horse?"

"Dead. These bastards killed it. And Juan's horse. Which puts me afoots."

Choctaw gestured behind him. "No. There's three horses up here. Not ours. Theirs."

Kruger reached the boulders. He walked over to the dead man in the Confederate jacket and looked him over. He asked

194

Choctaw, "Your doin's?"

"Uh-huh."

Kruger gave him an uncomprehending look. "Just who the hell *are* you?"

Choctaw didn't reply. Rawlins rode to within a dozen paces of him and reined in.

Kruger asked Poncho, "Where's the horses you stole?"

The horse thief didn't answer. The foreman strode up to him. "On your feet."

The man stood. He made a fairly disagreeable-looking piece of humanity, with his face rounding into chins and his belly bulging out of his pants, his clothing ragged and dirty, all that overlaid with grime and sweat. His teeth were irregular and bad, his eyes small and sly.

Kruger asked him, "Where?"

The fat man made a gesture towards his throat. Kruger struck him backhanded across the mouth. Poncho staggered. The foreman's face warmed with anger. "Where?"

He punched the captive in the mouth. Poncho retreated a few rubber-legged paces, somehow keeping his feet. Again Kruger asked, "Where?"

The foreman breathed hard, his fists clenched. He said, "There's a good man, a brave man, dead on account of you sons of bitches. Got hisself killed saving me. Where's them horses, you tub of guts?"

He started slapping the prisoner about the face. Choctaw glanced at Rawlins, wondering how much of this he'd allow. But the rancher seemed more interested in kneading his bad leg.

Kruger went from slapping back to punching. The blow took Poncho on the chin and jolted him onto his rump. He sat, wiping blood off his lips, again gesturing at his mouth and neck, his eyes wide in pleading.

As Kruger lifted his fist once more, Choctaw said, "I think he's saying he can't talk. Maybe he's a mute."

The foreman sneered. "Sure he is!"

Rawlins asked the captive, "Can't you talk?"

Glancing at the rancher, Poncho shook his head violently, tapping his throat.

Kruger asked the others, "You mean he's a dummy?" The foreman inspected his bruised knuckles. "Maybe somebody cut out his tongue for lying."

Rawlins asked the prisoner, "You know where the horses are? Nod or shake your head, damn you!"

The captive nodded. Kruger jabbed the barrel of his rifle into Poncho's considerable belly. "Show us. Get on your horse and take us there."

The captive swung aboard a scrawny paint. Kruger tied the man's wrists to the saddle horn. Poncho rode off, his captors following, Kruger riding one of the horse thieves' animals.

They entered Dead Mule Pass. Poncho reined in and gestured to the left, at a cleft in the rock walls. Rawlins asked him, "Is that where the horses are?"

The captive nodded.

The rancher said, to no one in particular, "Don't that lead into a box canyon, as I recollect?"

There was the drum of hooves. A rider appeared in the mouth of the canyon, galloping towards them; then he veered off to the left, showing them his back, and rode north towards the far side of the pass. Kruger threw up his rifle and took a few shots at the fleeing man. Both missed. The rider's dust dwindled into the northern distance.

Kruger lowered his rifle. "What do you figure? That's all of 'em? Or are there some more hiding in the canyon?"

Rawlins said, "I guess we'll have to find out." He told Poncho, "You lead us in there, big belly. We run into another ambush, you'll be out in front. And you make a big target."

Poncho led them into the canyon. There was no ambush, no snarl of hidden rifles from cover. Of which there was plenty, rock-strewn slopes stippled with ponderosas.

At the far end of the canyon, where red-rock walls rose to make this canyon a box, they found their lost horses. They were caged inside a rope corral where they could graze on the grama grass waving to their knees.

The Crazy R men left their prisoner sitting on a rock, his wrists tied behind him and his ankles bound too, while they went over to the horses.

Choctaw rode straight up to Blaze, dismounted, and looked the cutting horse over. He made a sound of relief. "He's hard run but his feet ain't ruined. Ain't wind-broke yet. Rest and graze for a few days and he should be all right."

As it turned out, all the horses were in more or less the same condition and could be saved, except a blue roan left badly lamed. Kruger shot it.

As the echoes of the shot fled northward, losing themselves in the face of the Mogollon Rim, Choctaw stared grimly at the dead animal. Then he switched his gaze to the prisoner, sitting a couple hundred yards away. He asked Rawlins, "What we gonna do with him, Cap?"

Kruger answered. "What do you think we're gonna do?"

"Take him into the law."

Rawlins said, "Sheriffs and marshals you mean? Ain't none of them within a couple days' ride."

Kruger said, "To get to 'em, we'd have to drag that piece of scum over the roughest country on God's Earth, and all the time there's a chance he could get loose. And for why?" He found enough moisture to spit. "No, we got only one law for horse thieves."

"You mean we're gonna hang him?"

"Guilty ain't he? Was shooting at us, wasn't he? And don't forget Juan."

"I know, but . . ."

"But what? What's your objection to rope law?"

"I ain't got no objection. I got a friend who has."

Kruger looked puzzled. "What you talking about? What friend?"

Choctaw asked, "We gonna hang him, Cap?"

Rawlins appeared to be in the grip of some tension. He gave a long sigh, stretched out his fingers, and studied the back of his hands. "I sure don't like it, but I'm with you, Hank. Though I don't figure we should do it 'less we all agree."

The foreman gave his boss a surprised look. "Now Cap —"

"I figure that's how we're gonna do it."

Choctaw protested, "That puts it all on me!"

The rancher shrugged. "That's how it is, boy. It's your call. What should we do?"

Choctaw thought of Whiskey whinnying piteously, the broken fore hoof hanging. And the blue roan just now. He thought about Poncho. He felt distaste at the man's grossness, his eyes deep-set in flesh and the cunning in them.

He recalled bullets howling around his ears and cold fear in his stomach. The knife in Poncho's hands, thrusting at his guts. Staring down at the body of Rebel. And Juan lying dead.

There was an icy taste in Choctaw's mouth.

He said, "Hang him."

CHAPTER TWENTY-FIVE

The three men stood, hats in hands, staring down.

At their feet was a grave.

At least here, in a side draw off the box canyon, they'd been able to bury Juan decently in a few feet of earth, with grass to wave over him and trees to give shade. Not try and scrape a grave out of the rock and sand of the desert, a flimsy resting place varmints would soon root up. There was enough purchase in the earth to stand a cross — made of two branches tied together — shored up by a cairn of stones. A piece of tree bark was wedged into this cairn, white side up. On it was written in charcoal, from the end of a stick blackened in fire: JUAN ORTEGA NOVEMBER 1873. They'd lost track of what day it was.

Cap Rawlins had volunteered to speak the words, which would save Choctaw having to.

A wind played about them, the hot breath of the desert outside the canyon. It tugged at hair and bandannas, sandpapering flesh. Its low dirge was the only sound, save for the creaking of a rope.

The rancher cleared his throat, then said, "*'For we know that if our earthly house of this tabernacle were dissolved, we have a building of God, a house not made with hands.'*"

The rancher put his hat on. Kruger and Choctaw took that as a signal to do the same.

Rawlins said, "Let's eat something."

Choctaw had no appetite, didn't figure he'd want to eat anything ever again. Kruger strode off. Choctaw was about to follow when the rope creaked. He paused and turned towards it. He asked Rawlins, "What about him?"

The juniper dangled its obscene fruit, the man in the poncho.

Rawlins asked, "First time you seen a hanging?"

"Uh-huh. Ain't we gonna bury him, Cap?"

"No, boy. That'd defeat the object. Point is we're making an example of this feller. He's kind of a sign post, showing what'll happen to anybody else goes after my horses."

The younger man said nothing. He gazed

202

at Poncho.

The horse thief's head slumped onto his right shoulder, his eyes closed and his mouth open. He might have been dreaming in his sleep except his face, full of blood, was between black and purple. One pants leg was darker than the other, and on the earth below was a wide puddle, its darkness fading into the flinty earth.

They'd ripped off a rectangular piece of another dead man's yellow shirt. It was pinned to Poncho's chest. On the cloth was written, again in charcoal: HORSE THIEF.

Choctaw couldn't take his eyes off the hanging man. He saw Rawlins was also staring at Poncho, as if mesmerized.

The rancher came out of it first. He said, "Come on, son." He rested his hand gently on the younger man's shoulder, then walked off.

The wind lifted, the rope creaked like a rusted wheel, and the hanging man turned.

The Crazy R men made a cook fire in the box canyon near where the horses grazed. They brewed up coffee, chewing the same cold fare as before. Choctaw surprised himself and found some appetite after all.

After eating, Rawlins went off to relieve himself. The others hunkered by the fire, drank coffee, and smoked.

There was silence, save the eternal sear of the desert wind.

Choctaw glanced at Kruger. It came to him that the foreman had been giving him puzzled looks, sometimes sidelong, ever since the hanging. The younger man felt numbed, weary, resentful, other feelings he couldn't describe. Would having it out with Kruger ease some of whatever it was?

Choctaw said, "Less I'm wrong, I figure you're busting to ask me something."

Kruger took his time replying. "Maybe."

"So go ahead and ask."

The foreman took a slow drag on his cigarette, "All right. Who *are* you?"

"You know who."

"Do I? I know what you call yourself. But I don't know *what* you are."

"Huh?"

"You sure don't act like any thirty-and-found cowhand. You ain't much over twenty I'd guess, yet you know about Apaches. How they bushwhack folk. Pull Cap out of an ambush all by yourself like it's all in a day's work. Then you single-handedly take on a whole nest of these varmints and pretty much clean 'em out." He sipped coffee. "Only feller I ever met who was anything like you was this half-Mex. Apaches had took him as a child and raised him. Once he got loose of 'em he ended up scouting for the army. They called him 'Cimarrón' because he was a wild man, couldn't be tamed. Is that what you are, something like that?"

Choctaw didn't answer for a moment, held by his memories. "Maybe. What business is it of yours?"

Kruger blinked.

Choctaw thought what he might be feeling was dull anger. One way to ease that was by violence. He remembered there was a gun belt round his waist, a pistol in the cross-draw holster, almost forgotten because he rarely wore it. "I tell you what I am, Kruger, according to you. That's yellow. That's what you said."

He stood, letting his hands hang at his sides. "You still hold to that?"

The foreman glanced at the other man's hands, at the pistol he wore. There was, for an instant, a hint of fear in his eyes. But only for an instant. Kruger laid his cup aside. He stood and gazed at the younger man calmly. "No. I shouldn't have said that. I apologize. And before . . . you was right about that ambush. And I was wrong. So I guess I apologize for that too. But, if that don't make you happy . . ." He made a small gesture, as if to say: it's up to you what happens next. This took his right hand close to the grip of his own pistol, holstered on his right hip.

He waited and Choctaw waited and then Rawlins said, "What now?"

Choctaw had been so focused on Kruger he hadn't heard the rancher approach. The old man asked, "You two eyeballing each other again?"

Kruger said, "It was him pushing into it, Cap. Like he was a pistoleer, Wes Hardin or somebody."

In his head, Choctaw heard a man say: *"You remind me of a young fellow I knew in Texas a few years back . . . name of John Wesley Hardin."* Who was it said that?

He protested, "I ain't no pistoleer."

Kruger started to answer and Rawlins said, "Don't know who did what and I don't care. The last two days has been a bloody business. Six men dead. And I'm sick of it. You two want to go at it with your fists, fine. But there'll be . . ." He scowled, biting out the next words one at a time. "No. More. Killing."

The wind lifted, flapping around them like thick canvas, raising dust in a pale screen.

After a little while, Kruger extended his right hand. "I said I apologize."

Choctaw gazed at the foreman's outstretched hand. He didn't move.

Annoyance flickered over Kruger's face. Rawlins gave Choctaw a look of disappointment and shook his head slightly.

The foreman started to turn away.

Choctaw said, "Hey."

Kruger turned back as Choctaw thrust his hand before him. The two men shook.

Rawlins said, "What's this?"

Choctaw glanced at the rancher and saw he was staring off to the south. At the dust of approaching riders.

These turned out to be three more Crazy R hands. Choctaw only knew one of them by name, a fellow nicknamed Brazos. He was getting on in years for a cowhand, forty or so, with a drooping gray-tinged mustache and the melancholy eyes of a hound dog.

Rawlins gave the newcomers the hard news about Juan. He told them to guard the recaptured horses until they were fit to move, then herd them back to the ranch.

Brazos had news too. Rawlins's daughter was back from the East. She was waiting at Doan's Store for her father to collect her.

The rancher said, "In all these doings, I almost forgot about her."

Choctaw asked, "Where's Doan's Store?"

"That's the nearest bit of civilization.

Where we go for supplies. Twenty miles south of the ranch." Rawlins spat tobacco juice. "Well, it ain't gonna be me collects her. After the last few days these old bones need plenty rest. Somebody else gotta go."

Choctaw said, "I'll fetch her for you."

The rancher said, "No, boy. I figure you — and Hank too — earned yourself a few days off, after what you done. You need it too, even if you don't realize it."

Rawlins, Kruger, and Choctaw mounted up and rode south through the pass, then swung east towards home.

Barely a word was spoken. Silence pressed down. It was as if they'd been rendered as mute as the man they'd left dangling from the juniper.

Chapter Twenty-Six

Poncho swung on the rope. His bloated face was grape-dark above the noose biting into his flesh, and then his face softened into rotten purple-black fruit and his mouth opened and he spoke, as maybe he never had in life, his voice Billy Keogh's saying "I'm killed," and then Kyle Baker's calling for his mother, letting out a long scream, and Finlay's saying, "decorated by eighteen fellers . . . don't you boys make it twenty" and Dec laughing and saying, "That's one ugly tree . . . I ain't gonna dance on a rope just to keep the locals entertained. You ever see a lynching?" Yes, he had, he was seeing one now as the horse ran out from under Poncho, the man's stubby feet kicking wildly at the air and piss streaming down one leg and jetting out below his pants bottom, and as he turned on the rope Poncho's face became Billy Keogh's, lizard eyes bulging, and then Juan's and then, strangely enough, Dec's face, and then Choctaw saw himself turning in the air as the rope stretched and creaked and he heard his own voice saying, "Hang him!"

He woke with a jerk.

He was mostly out of his blankets as if he'd been writhing about in his sleep. It was full light, which meant he'd overslept. Unusual for him. He'd learned the importance of being awake at the crack of dawn, when Apaches liked to jump enemies. But he had been under the dead weight of tiredness when he bedded down last night.

There was the smell of bacon frying.

The young man sat up, blinking away the dream, still shaken by its vividness and cruelty. He kicked away his blankets and stood.

Slowly, it came to him where he was. They were camped a few miles west of Hopi Flats, almost back where the bloody journey of the last two days had commenced.

Choctaw picked up his boots. Carefully. Boots made a nice warm refuge at night; when he upended them, he displaced a fine rain of crawling critters, including a yellow-legged scorpion that fled with stinger aloft.

Rawlins was busy on breakfast — a cooked meal, not trail rations. He had a frying pan and a smaller pan resting on the fire he crouched over. A coffeepot stood nearby. Kruger wasn't in view, maybe off somewhere about his morning ablutions.

Choctaw approached Rawlins. "You let me lie in."

The rancher shrugged. "Sleep well?"

Choctaw poured himself some coffee. "I had a bad dream. About . . ."

The old man chewed at his lower lip. "About the hanging?"

"A lynching, wasn't it? Not a hanging. I can't seem to stop thinking about it."

He expected the rancher to chide him. Instead, Rawlins said, "I know how that is. I can still remember my first time like it was today. And that was what . . . thirty-five, six years ago?" He used a knife to flip bacon in the frying pan. "Bad business. I've seen good people go crazy with the hanging fever."

"Hanging fever?"

"When folks get it in their blood. Get to like it. That's the danger. Before you know it, you've hung the wrong man. God help me if I ever get like that." He probed the smaller pan with a spoon, turning beans. "What happened yesterday was pretty cut and dried. Wasn't no doubt about that feller being guilty. But the first lynching I saw . . ."

Rawlins poured himself coffee. It was a

little while before he continued. "I wasn't much older than you. Left my daddy's farm in Arkansas to go to Texas. To fight Santy Anny. Only by the time I got there the fighting was done. Santy Anny was whipped and Texas was its own republic. But that's another story."

"I'd like to hear it, if you ever want to tell it."

A smile worked briefly at the old man's lips. "Anyway, not long after I got there, to this little town, a girl was molested. A mob got liquored up. They dragged this feller out onto Main Street and hung him from a pecan tree. He was kind of the village idiot." Rawlins drank coffee. "Turned out he was innocent. His only crime was being simple-minded. But they was set on hanging somebody, so they picked on him. That's what happens. Folks use a lynch mob to settle old scores, or go for somebody who's different, like that poor old simple feller, or some Mex or Indian. After that, I swore I'd never lend myself to a lynching."

"So what changed your mind?"

"I ended up in a place where there's no alternative. No law for a hundred miles or more and thieves all over." He attended to the bacon and beans a minute, then said, "Nothing lower, in my book, than a body who'll steal a man's horse. But that don't stop 'em doing it. If I put the fear of the rope in 'em, maybe that'll stop 'em. Otherwise, I wouldn't have a horse left."

"But it's wrong to hang a man without a trial, ain't it?"

Rawlins gave a slight nod. "Sure it is. Ordinarily. Once the law gets here, we can quit. But until then . . . what else can we do?"

Choctaw thought over an answer. As he was doing so, Kruger's voice came from behind him. "You still carrying on about stringing up a horse thief?"

Choctaw turned as the foreman approached. Kruger said, "I don't understand you. You killed a couple of them fellers yourself. Shooting 'em didn't seem to fret you none."

"That's hot blood, ain't it? But doing it cold, being your own judge, jury, and executioner . . ."

"Like Cap said: What else can we do? 'Sides . . ." There was a pause, as if Kruger was deciding whether to go on or not. Then he said, "Don't forget something."

"What?"

"It was your decision . . . to hang him. *You* called it."

Choctaw felt an iciness roiling in his guts.

"I know . . . God help me."

Rawlins said, "That's a hard thing to say, Hank."

There was a pause. When Kruger spoke, his voice was low, his tone almost apologetic. "Maybe. Look kid, nobody — no right person — wants to do these things. I hate the rope business, but when there's no law, we ain't got no choice."

"No?"

"Out here a man has to kill his own snakes!"

CHAPTER TWENTY-SEVEN

Rawlins, Kruger, and Choctaw took their time returning to Baldy Flats. The Crazy R men there listened as Rawlins recounted the grim events of the last few days.

Choctaw asked him, "What do you want me to do now, Cap?"

"Nothing, boy. We rest up here a spell, ourselves and our horses, clear through to suppertime. Watch all these other fools do the work."

So they did. As they were finishing their evening meal, Rawlins told Kruger, "Hank, you and Taylor head back to the ranch house. I'll be along directly. I got to spruce up the place, make sure it's fit for a woman, now my daughter's about to arrive. Meanwhile —" he indicated Choctaw, "— find a place for this young feller in the bunkhouse. Make sure he's got all the comforts of home."

Choctaw smiled at the old man's sarcasm.

He'd been in a few bunkhouses and wouldn't have described them as overburdened with home comforts. But at least he'd be sleeping indoors, out of the cut of the wind and with something under him that should be kinder to his spine than hard Arizona dirt.

Kruger and Choctaw mounted up and rode south, with dusk coming down around them. They descended from Baldy Flats via some fairly steep trails, rode through belts of juniper and ponderosa pine, emerging into open country. After six or seven miles, the foreman said, "Here we are."

They gazed down into a valley that shadows were capturing. Buildings smudged the valley floor. They were brick shaped in the usual Arizona style of long, low-roofed adobes. Only one looked to be two story, which Choctaw took for the main ranch house, where Rawlins would normally live. Among the others there'd be a cook shack, bunkhouse, and various outbuildings like a blacksmith's shop and tack shed. Back of the houses there were corrals, a few fenced with poles. One was a big layout with adobe walls on three sides, built to be strong against thieves, as it needed to be.

The riders descended into the valley, and Kruger led the way to a building that he announced was the bunkhouse.

As he studied this dwelling, Choctaw's heart also did some descending. Mostly at the sight of the slightly peaked thatched roof. He didn't think thatched roofs were a good idea out here. They leaked when it rained — admittedly only a very occasional problem. More to the point, they were homes for tarantulas, scorpions, and other crawling varmints.

They dismounted and Kruger went into the bunkhouse, Choctaw following. The younger man wrinkled his nose. The stink wasn't unexpected, but it still caught at his throat. A compound of male sweat, old clothes and blankets, coal oil from hanging lamps giving dingy yellow light, and the licorice in tobacco plugs men had chewed and spat upon the floor. Overlying everything the reek of dried cow shit. It was disorderly too, with gear, boots, and items of clothing strewn about, in the slovenly way of most single men of Choctaw's experience. There was a bunkhouse joke: "Don't forget to hang your clothes on the floor, so they don't fall down and get lost."

Kruger pointed to a lower bunk. "You can bed down there. Just us two in here tonight."

Choctaw made his way to the bunk. Sure this place was a mess, and somewhat ripe, but at least he was indoors. There was even a floor of wooden boards under him, not the dirt floor you found in many bunkhouses. Maybe more importantly, there was a board ceiling, which would impede rain and stinging critters leaking down on them.

He glanced towards Kruger. The foreman sat on his bed, pulling off his spurs. He seemed to have the best spot in this room, a single bed, not a two-layer bunk that served everyone else. His sleeping place was tucked against the wall, draped in what looked like Navajo blankets.

Choctaw gave the blanket and bedsheets on his bunk a looking over. They had a faint, musty smell. It would be a small miracle if they weren't ticky, and he hated lice. But graybacks were a fact of frontier life.

Kruger must have guessed what he was about. "Any feller finds a crawler and throws it on the floor without killing it gets a ten-cent fine." He started pulling off one boot. "What you think about them rich college kids? Started on their vacation already. Unlike the poor damn cowboy, working his tail off up to Christmas Eve."

"Yeah."

"Still, nothing's too good for Miss Jade Rawlins."

"Jade? That's a real pretty name."

"She's the apple of his eye. Old Cap'd be a lot richer if he hadn't sent her off East, so she can get the best education. I guess that's a promise he made to his wife."

"Oh?"

"Missus Rawlins died a few years back. Mind you, if Jade was my daughter I'd spend on her too."

"A looker, huh?"

Kruger glared. "That ain't a topic that goes around this bunkhouse much — speculating on the boss's daughter. You can think about it all you want, these long lonely nights. But we don't talk about it."

Choctaw shrugged.

Kruger's lips formed into a thin, sarcastic smile. "Not that she's gonna be interested in you, sonny. Cap'll see her married off to some banker, or senator, or some rich feller's son. She ain't gonna be looking at no thirty-and-found cowhand."

Choctaw eased his spurs off his boots. "Still," he said, "it sure is a pretty name."

CHAPTER TWENTY-EIGHT

Just about noon, a few days later.

Choctaw had spent the time either resting up around the Crazy R ranch house or doing odd jobs: adding a lick of paint to the cookhouse, mending tack, etc., but mostly just gathering firewood. Which he didn't mind doing for a while, provided he ended up back on a horse soon.

The last couple hours he'd been mending fences in some outlying corrals. He'd built up a considerable lather and sweat, which he washed away with the tepid water in a horse trough. He was stripped to the waist, using his shirt to towel himself dry, when he heard a horse approaching.

Choctaw got the soap and water out of his eyes. He saw a rider coming nearer.

A young woman.

He pulled on his shirt and buttoned up, watching the newcomer all the while. What he saw was mostly brown: her chestnut horse, her jacket, her ankle-length skirt. She did wear a white blouse. Her hair was dark brown too. She was riding sidesaddle, which always looked a cumbersome business to him.

A couple of yards distant, she reined in and asked, "Are you Calvin Taylor?" Her voice was low, her accent cultivated.

"Yes, ma'am."

There was only one person she could be so Choctaw felt no surprise when she said, "I'm Jade Rawlins."

He already knew she was nineteen. Bunkhouse talk — which existed, despite Kruger's warning — was that she was a looker. Choctaw had been skeptical, knowing how the scarcity of women might exaggerate someone's charms in the eyes of lonely men. But bunkhouse talk had been right. Maybe her nose was a little short, and slightly upturned in a cute way. There was a French word for it he couldn't remember. She also appeared to have a small overbite. But these were tiny flaws; overall his first impression of her was that she was flat-out beautiful.

Her eyes were hazel, and touched with humor, reminding him of her father. Her hair was long and lustrous, falling straight below her shoulders. Jade's clothing didn't hide her shapeliness and full breasts.

He didn't realize he was staring until she said, "It's generally considered impolite to stare."

"Sorry, ma'am. It's just that . . . you remind me of somebody."

Which sounded the lamest excuse in the universe. Except it was true. It wasn't just that she was the first good-looking woman he'd been around in a considerable while. She *did* remind him of somebody.

"A good memory I hope."

"Yes, ma'am," he lied. He had no idea who she reminded him of.

"Will you help me down?"

"Yes, ma'am." He was itching to smile, but if he smiled too happy, she might think him forward. It wouldn't do to get fresh with the boss's daughter at the first time of meeting. So he kept his lips pinned tight.

Choctaw moved close to her as she slid down from the saddle. He took her gently under the armpits, then her body fell against him so he swayed back. For a second her breasts pressed his chest, and her lips were only a few inches from his; then she steadied herself, her hands resting on his shoulders, and he lowered her the last few inches to the earth. She was tall, maybe five feet seven.

She pushed back a strand of hair that had

come loose across her face. "Oh, I'm sorry. I slipped."

"Yes, ma'am."

She gave him an annoyed look. "Have you ever been known to say anything but 'yes, ma'am'?"

Choctaw thought for a moment, then said, "Yes, ma'am."

Her eyes narrowed in irritation; then she caught the humor in it and smiled faintly. "It's just that riding sidesaddle can be so awkward. I know some women out here wear divided skirts so they can ride astride a horse like a man. But that would be too shocking, wouldn't it?"

Jade spent a minute getting herself un-mussed, tossing her hair. Choctaw was reminded how nice that was to view, when someone with long, beautiful hair like Jade Rawlins did it. He was conscious of the places where her hands had rested on his shoulders, where her body had pressed against his. He decided he'd been out of the company of women for far too long.

She asked him, "If I was to ride around here like that, would you be shocked?"

Choctaw opened his mouth to say "yes, ma'am," changing it to: "I sure would."

"I don't believe you, Mr. Taylor. You must realize everyone's talking about you."

"Yeah?"

"The daring deeds you did. How you saved my father's life. For which I want to thank you."

Not knowing how to answer, he gave a small nod instead.

Jade went on, "They say you took on a whole band of murderous desperados virtually single-handedly. That you plunged into the middle of them with six-guns blazing, heedless of your own safety, not pausing until the last of the villains was slain. And yet you're so young. Didn't it bother you, killing so many men?"

"Not particularly."

"Then you must be a real ice-hearted, cold-blooded killer."

"Pretty much."

Jade's eyes widened slightly. She raised her eyebrows, as if finally catching on she was being mocked.

She gazed around. For a little time, it seemed she was more interested in her surroundings than him, then she said, "I like to go riding, but my father thinks it's dangerous, with so many bad men in this lawless country."

"It is."

"He provides me with an escort, an old Mexican, who's perfectly fine but . . ." She looked back at him. "If I had someone I *knew* could protect me . . . somebody who's already proved himself . . ."

Choctaw supposed this was when he should volunteer his services. But part of him was already a little wary of Jade Rawlins, so he said nothing.

Jade gave him a frosty look. In a voice just as cold, she asked, "Will you help me back up?"

Choctaw helped the girl get back in the saddle. This time she managed to keep a respectable distance between her body and his. She said, "I do so dislike riding sidesaddle. But that's how ladies are supposed to ride."

"So they tell me. Ain't had too much to do with ladies."

"Really?"

After another little pause, Jade said, "Maybe I will get myself a divided skirt, shocking or not. I've even heard that some women out here have started a fashion of riding around in pants."

"That they have."

"Oh, but that would be simply going too far, wouldn't it? I mean, if I rode round in front of everybody dressed like that, they might take me for a man."

Choctaw let the smile he'd been holding

back play around his lips. "That ain't likely."

Which he meant as a compliment, but it didn't work; the chilly look returned to her face. "You're forward, Mr. Taylor."

"Yes, ma'am."

Jade turned her horse and rode away.

Choctaw watched her go. He felt annoyed with himself. He told himself: Everything was going nice, then you had to ruin it — slap on that silly smirk, and make a sneery forward remark. He gazed at a small lump of sand in the earth before him. That lump hadn't done him harm in any way at all, but he still kicked it.

But he must not have ruined it after all. The next morning Cap Rawlins rode up to him. The rancher said, "We're starting a drive tomorrow. I'm taking a herd up to the Navajo Reservation."

Choctaw smiled. "Good. I'm itching to get back on a horse."

"You ain't going. You and Hank stay here. He'll be in charge while I'm gone. Meantime, my daughter needs an escort when she goes riding, and she's picked you."

Choctaw didn't know how he felt about that, but before he could speak, Rawlins turned his horse and rode off. The younger

man watched horse and rider dwindle into
the distance.

CHAPTER TWENTY-NINE

Jade Rawlins said, "I like your blue eyes, Calvin Taylor."

"I think you already told me that."

He closed his eyes, seeing red-tinged darkness where the sun played on his eyelids. Something tickled his nose. When it happened a second time, he opened his eyes reluctantly. Jade was stroking his face with a frond of grama grass. He smiled and brought his eyelids down again.

She rested her head on his bare chest. For a little while that was all she did and he started to feel drowsy. Then he felt her finger tracing the scar near the top of his left arm. She asked, "Is that a knife cut?"

Here an Apache called Packrat had marked him. "Yes."

Her fingertip pressed his right side, about halfway up. "Is that a bullet wound?"

He'd been shot there, at fairly close range, by a scoundrel called Lije Green. "Uh-huh."

Her finger left him, then he felt her touch again, on his temple above his right eye. "And that?"

He was surprised she'd spotted that scar, only a faint tracing now, after two and a half years. Where he'd been grazed by that backshooter Jack Adams. "Bullet wound."

"How did all this happen?"

He followed his usual course when she asked him questions. After a bit of silence, she made an exasperated sound. "You never tell me *anything.* You never ask about me. You won't tell me anything about yourself. I mean we never *talk* when we're . . . together."

He smiled at the slight coyness in her voice. "We're too busy doing something else." He let his hand slide down her bare back to her ass and rest on her right buttock.

"Everybody's fascinated about you, you know. There was even a newspaperman at Doan's Store asking about you. I'm surprised he hasn't come out here to interview you."

"Hope not."

"Why not? Are you a wanted man?"

"I dunno. Do you want me?"

Jade made a hard-breathing sound that indicated she was moving past exasperation into temper. Choctaw gave up trying to sleep — which would have been a bad idea anyway — opened his eyes, and sat up.

He and Jade were lying on a bed of grama grass in the shade of a juniper, atop a long slope. They were hidden in a bosky with a good view of the surrounding world. His Winchester leaned against the juniper within reach. The horses — his buckskin, Jade's chestnut — were tethered to a couple of mesquite trees at the edge of the bosky, grazing and chewing beans and bark off the mesquites.

Jade sprawled across his legs. Both of them were naked and he gazed at her in admiration. He bent forward, kissing the top of her head, resting his cheek in her hair a little while, then slowly began working his legs out from under her. She made small sounds of protest but eventually man and woman were untangled.

Choctaw stood, pulling on his pants, looking around carefully while he dressed.

When Jade sighed heavily, he glanced over at her. She was sitting up, cupping her breasts in both hands and studying them as if they'd changed in some way. Which, he was pleased to see, they hadn't.

She said, "I guess we've got to carry on with our morning . . . ride."

"Yeah. We're out too long, they'll come looking for us. And it wouldn't do for your daddy to find out what we're up to."

"I'd tell him you forced yourself upon me."

Choctaw laughed out loud. "You would too!"

Jade started to pull on her clothes. Choctaw fashioned a cigarette and viewed the scenery. Which was worth viewing.

Around them were meadows of lush grass that might climb to a horse's belly. Clumps of ponderosa dotted the slopes above, not massed into solid dark green ranks like elsewhere. But the earth was a burnt ocher color, so the slopes were a weird patchwork of green and orange. And above the timber reared massive red-rock cliffs, some ending in shapes and formations you couldn't believe. One like the back of a hand pointing upwards, with the fingers pressed together, another the biggest back tooth in the world. Each towered hundreds of feet into the sky.

But the strangeness didn't end there, because these huge blocks weren't uniform in color. Some were orange at the base, becoming soft purple higher up, then gray-white. Others were banded across the top in tidelines of yellow, green, and purple. All backed against the Mogollon Rim, its sheer face gray-blue and filled with shadow. It made a picture of wild and startling beauty.

Choctaw breathed deeply of the clean, fresh air. He felt the burn of high altitude in his chest. "This is sure pretty country."

Jade said, "You're always admiring this wilderness. You never tell *me* I'm pretty."

She paused, giving him the opportunity to rectify that omission. When he didn't, she asked, "Do you love me, Taylor?"

The question surprised him. He laughed out loud.

A quick glance showed her face growing thunderous. He laughed some more.

He picked up his shirt. Something struck him on the back of the shoulder. He guessed Jade had thrown a small clod of earth at him. He smiled and carried on dressing. A hard object struck his elbow. He said, "Ow!" That felt like a stone, not earth, and a damn sharp one. He saw Jade had her right hand upraised to throw some more. Rubbing his elbow he told her, "Quit that! Or I'll —"

"Or you'll what? My daddy'll hang you up by your toes if you lay a hand on me."

"Already laid a hand on you. I've laid *me* on you. Didn't notice you complaining when I did."

"Ha! Don't flatter yourself."

232

He buttoned up his shirt. No more flung objects came his way.

Jade said, "I was at a ball three months ago. I danced with a young army officer from West Point who told me I was the prettiest girl there."

When that brought no response, she said, "I've already had two proposals of marriage, you know. One was from a naval officer who is looking to be first mate of his own sailing ship."

"That's nice."

"The other was from a young man whose daddy owns a string of factories."

Again, she waited for him to respond, before saying, "He says I'm the most beautiful girl at Vassar."

After another pause, she demanded, "Why don't you ever say anything like that to me?"

There was another little silence. Jade asked, "Do you like me, Taylor? Because I'm not sure I like you. Well, do you like me or not?"

"Maybe not."

She glared again, but that quickly turned into a smirk. "Good. Because I think you're a bastard!"

He smiled.

Jade buttoned up her shirt. "I suppose you think I'm a bitch?"

Choctaw took a last drag of his quirley. "Pretty much."

"A spoiled-rotten bitch."

The young man resumed his study of the scenery. He felt her hand on the back of his shoulder and then her arms slipped around his waist. She started to nuzzle the back of his neck. "I try to be a good girl and not disappoint my daddy, be like he wants me to be, he's raised me to be, but . . ."

She turned his head towards her and they kissed. Which was plenty nice but he knew where it would lead. In another few seconds they'd be back down on the ground . . . With a considerable effort of will, he drew his head back. "We need to be moving."

"But —"

"No, Jade." He admired how mature he sounded, how sensible. Inside though, he was as lusty as hell.

They moved to their horses. As he prepared to mount up, Choctaw thought about how Jade was still pretty much a mystery to him. Including the mystery of who she reminded him of. She sure put him in mind of somebody. The feeling had only grown stronger these last few weeks he'd been her "escort." Just now it had almost come to him. Something about their situation, making love in a grove of trees, while two horses grazed nearby . . .

And then he remembered.

She reminded him of one of the two women he'd loved. Maybe the one he'd loved most.

It was glaringly obvious and yet he hadn't realized because Jade was a white girl. Take her skin and make it dark copper, her dark brown hair and make it so black it was almost blue, and the resemblance was startling.

She looked like Apache royalty — the niece by marriage of Cochise, no less.

The Chiricahua Apache girl, Nahlin.

CHAPTER THIRTY

They rode back towards the Crazy R ranch, Jade leading most of the time.

Which was fine by him, as, whatever else Jade Rawlins might be, she was plenty easy on the eye. For a riding hat she wore one of those black, flat-brimmed Spanish hats he'd seen high-born Mexican ladies wear. It made her look real pretty and he'd almost told her that, before deciding to keep to his rule of never complimenting her unless it was absolutely necessary. She was conceited enough!

Jade reined in. He came alongside her as she said, "Look." She pointed with the quirt in her hand.

They were entering another fine meadow of fall-cured yellow grass combed by the wind, at its deepest waving as high as a horse's belly. A meadow that sloped uphill towards a belt of timber under the rim.

Just short of the trees, maybe three hundred yards off, was a bare patch in the grass. Here a small fire lifted thin smoke. A man stood by it. Something blotted the earth at his feet.

Choctaw felt cold unease in his belly; it was fairly obvious what this fellow was about. The Crazy R hand took his field glasses from his saddlebags and had a better look, confirming his suspicions. The man by the fire seemed to be dressed like any common-or-garden cowhand. The object at his feet was a cow or calf down on its side, probably hog-tied.

Jade said, "Let me have a look." In her usual style — demanding not asking.

Reluctantly he passed the binoculars over. While Jade was looking, the distant stranger gestured. Even at this distance, and without the field glasses, Choctaw could tell what he was doing. Waving his hat left to right, a signal anyone in cow country would understand.

Jade lowered the binoculars. "You know what he's doing, don't you? He's changing the brand on that cow. And when he waved his hat — my daddy told me what that means."

"Signaling for us to stand off while he does it. Or swing a wide loop around him."

He could see temper start to show in

Jade's face. "We can't just stand by or ride on by while he steals one of my daddy's cows!"

"Oh, yes, we can."

Her nostrils flared in anger. "He's just one man."

Choctaw had been thinking about that. It bothered him that he couldn't see the man's horse. Presumably it was tethered back in the trees. What else might be hidden behind that wall of pines? More horses? More cow thieves? He said, "We can only see one man. Might be others about. And he'll have a rifle."

She glared at him, her anger turning to contempt. "So have you. I thought you were a big hero!"

"Sorry, Miss Jade. I can't risk —"

She spurred her horse hard and the chestnut lunged forward. Choctaw was expecting that. He reached out and grabbed the animal's reins.

Jade slashed across with her quirt. The braided leather lashes caught him across the back of his hand and wrist and stung like hell. He swore and let go of the reins. She kicked her horse in the ribs again and the chestnut jumped forward. He grabbed at the reins, missed, and she rode out into the meadow.

He called, "You're crazy!" but she wasn't listening. She rode at the half gallop towards the cow thief's fire.

Choctaw let loose another good oath and rode after her. He reached down and pulled his Winchester from the saddle scabbard.

Ahead he caught a gleam of metal: the man by the fire lifting his rifle. Choctaw's heart filled his throat as he saw, in his mind's eye, the woman jerking as a bullet struck her, toppling from the saddle . . . He called, "Jade! Hold up!"

He kicked the buckskin into a hard run and caught up with her, reaching across and grabbing the reins and hauling the chestnut up. She slashed at him with the quirt and one of the tails stung him, drawing blood from his chin; then he seized her wrist and stayed her arm.

She said, "You're hurting me!"

"I can't let yourself get killed over some feller stealing one cow."

"Your job's to stop cattle thieves."

"No, my job's to protect you."

It came to Choctaw that in having this argument they'd forgotten something fairly significant: the man in front of them with his rifle raised. This fellow reminded them of his presence when he called, "Well, well, Miss Jade Rawlins."

Choctaw glanced over at the fire. The man there held a rifle — maybe a Spencer — at the ready, but not aiming.

He was tall and slim, perhaps late twenties. His clothing was nondescript and battered, from his slouch hat with its front brim pinned back against the crown to his faded pants and shirt, which might have been blue once. His face hadn't been near a razor for a while. His right eye was covered with a large black patch. Take that away, and the dark fuzzing of trail beard and mustache, and you might describe him as handsome.

The calf on the earth bawled. Lying on the earth near it was a length of metal, shaped like a poker with a curved end. A running iron, principal tool of the brand-changers' trade. Just possessing such an instrument out on the cattle range had earned men jail time for cattle theft, if they were lucky. And it had got others hung.

Eye-Patch addressed Jade. "I worked for your daddy last fall roundup. But I don't expect you to remember me, Miss High-and-Mighty Rawlins. Even if I was right in front of you, you wouldn't have seen me. I was just a lowly cowhand."

"And now you're a brand-changer. A cow thief! My daddy'll hang you!"

Eye-Patch smiled.

Choctaw started to feel another layer of unease. This man was altogether too confident, given his apparent situation. Choctaw asked him, "How about if we just forget about this? Ride on like we didn't see you?"

Jade shot him a venomous look. "You'd let this thief get away with it? You're no hero — you're a coward!"

Choctaw ignored her. He told Eye-Patch, "We won't tell nobody we saw you."

A man called, "You're damn right you won't!"

The voice came out of the pines on the slope above.

The speaker stepped out of cover into view. A man with a Henry rifle pulled into his shoulder, aiming at Choctaw and then at Jade.

CHAPTER THIRTY-ONE

Eye-Patch grinned. "Figured you'd gone and left me, Asa."

The man on the slope grinned back. "Just watching, Ira."

He gestured with his rifle, telling Choctaw, "Lose the gun, boy."

Ira lifted his own rifle to his shoulder. "Do it careful."

Jade flung Choctaw an angry look, the fury in her eyes saying: *Are we going to stand for this?* He was afraid she might try and make a run for it. Fear for both of them made his throat as dry as a limeburners' hat. In a voice that croaked slightly, he said, "Just stand easy, Miss Jade. Do what they say."

He threw his Winchester into some deep grass a few yards away. He hadn't brought his gun belt with him. He was unarmed . . . save for the knife in his boot.

Asa descended the slope, his Henry held

at the ready. He didn't make much noise, treading a carpet of pine needles. On top of that he wore knee-high, snub-toed Apache moccasins, similar to the pair Choctaw owned.

Choctaw glanced at Asa and then at Ira, not quite understanding what he was seeing. Then he realized: these men were twins. They looked identical to him, except for Ira's eye patch. Even their clothing was similar. Studying their worn trail gear and stubbled, grimy faces, he was reminded of the Bakers. Rawhiders cut from the same ragged cloth.

Choctaw was told to dismount and obeyed.

Ira approached Jade. He took hold of her horse's bridle with his left hand. A puzzled look wrapped itself around his dirty, handsome face. "We got a peculiar situation here, brother."

Asa said, "Uh-huh. We was after cows and now look what we got." He strode towards Choctaw, halting six or so paces from him. He smiled, showing a gap in his front upper teeth. "Question is: now we got 'em, what do we do with 'em?"

Ira scratched his trail beard. "How much you reckon Old Man Rawlins would pay to get his daughter back safe?"

Jade said, "You wouldn't stoop to molesting a woman?"

Ira showed the gap in his teeth again. "Nobody gonna molest you, honey. You're valuable merchandise, we'd keep you safe."

He rested his hand on her leg. Jade cried, "My daddy'll have your ears!" She jerked the reins, trying to turn her horse away, but Ira held the bridle, keeping the animal still. He laughed.

Asa laughed too. "Spitfire, ain't she?"

He was watching his brother, Choctaw saw. The Crazy R hand was very conscious of the knife hidden in his boot, of how far it was from his hands, of how long it would take him to grab it and use it . . .

Ira moved his hand up to Jade's knee. She slashed across with her quirt. Choctaw glimpsed a line of blood on Ira's cheek. The twin jerked back, crying, "Fuck!"

Jade spurred her horse. It squealed and reared but Ira kept his grip on the bridle, even as his other hand went to his face.

Asa half-turned towards his brother and Choctaw sprang.

Choctaw's shoulder caught Asa mid-chest. Asa went down on his back. Choctaw spilled forward over him, sprawling facedown in the grass. He struggled to his knees.

Jade's horse danced around. Ira still had

one hand to the bridle and reached for the girl with the other. She cut at him, left and right, with the quirt.

Asa rose groggily to his feet. Choctaw made it to his full height and stepped towards the twin. He landed a fair right cross on Asa's jaw and the man staggered. He glared at his opponent out of eyes trying to focus.

Choctaw felt a little triumph warm in him and swung a roundhouse right at the other's chin. The kind of punch that ended a fight.

Only Asa shifted his head and the punch missed.

A fist floated up out of somewhere and impacted under the point of Choctaw's chin. Next thing he knew he was down in the long grass, blinking up at a dizzy, tumbling-over-itself sky shot through with leaping streaks of color.

He was down but not out. He forced himself upright, stood on rubbery legs, and swung another punch. Missing. This time the return punch caught him on the side of the jaw.

Then he was sprawling in the grass again, watching the world cartwheel. It was having a fine time throwing itself about overhead. After studying it for a spell, he managed to rise.

Once again, he drove a punch at Asa, but the man turned to smoke before him and his fist sailed through air. There was a crack like bone breaking, like Declan's fist on Harvey's chin, except this was on his chin. Next, he was lying in the grass a third time while everything spilled past him like some kind of rockslide.

Again Choctaw tried to stand. He made it all the way upright and dropped back on his rump. He sat and watched the shattered world slowly piece itself together.

His jaw was numb. Teeth were loose in his mouth. The iron taste of blood was on his tongue, and red liquid leaked onto his chin. His hearing was knocked about too, as sound was muffled. Asa stared at him and spoke; his lips moved, but Choctaw couldn't hear the words.

Asa stepped towards the other man. Choctaw watched him approach helplessly. He couldn't do anything about it; he doubted he had the strength to lift his arms in his own defense. He saw Jade and Ira watching him, the girl staring as if astonished.

Asa's lips twisted in a wolfish smile; his nostrils flared in triumph. He was clearly enjoying giving the other fellow a good licking.

There was a rifle shot.

Asa halted and glanced off to the west. Choctaw's hearing seemed to be fully restored; he heard distant yells and the drub of hooves.

Ira forgot Jade, letting go of her horse, running back towards the slope and the trees he'd emerged from before. Asa ran after him.

It took a very considerable effort but Choctaw managed to turn his head and look around. From the west two men rode towards him at the full gallop. The nearest was Hank Kruger.

Ira made it to the trees and vanished into cover. Choctaw tried to rise and failed. Kruger flashed past him, his horse grunting with effort, and pointed after Asa like a hound after a rabbit. The foreman held a rope in his right hand, shaking out a loop.

Asa bounded up the slope. He was almost at the trees when Kruger flung his rope. The lariat sang in the air. Asa was caught, the loop circling his body, yanking tight and pinning his arms to his sides. Kruger made his horse stand, legs braced, and Asa was jerked backwards, clean off his feet. He hit on his shoulders and rolled backwards, down the slope. Kruger started to drag him. He trailed the cow thief a few yards through a furrow of his own dust, then let the rope hang slack.

Choctaw saw the cowhand with Kruger was Brazos.

Ira emerged from the trees. He had his hands raised, palms forward. Two riders came out of cover behind him — men Choctaw recognized as Crazy R cowhands. Two boys still in their teens. They bunked with him but he couldn't remember their names. These waddies held pistols, pointed at Ira.

Ira paused, taking in the scene before him. One of the cowhands walked his horse into the cow thief, causing him to stumble forward and plow to his knees. Both riders laughed.

Ira sat and looked around, seeming more indignant than afraid.

Choctaw managed to stand. He swayed, as did the world around him, whilst the ground didn't seem firm underfoot. His jaw lost its numbness and started to ache.

Kruger addressed the cow thieves. "I remember you — the Gird brothers." He asked the girl, "Are you all right, Miss Jade?"

"Yes."

"Did they harm you?"

"No." Anger came into the girl's voice. "But they talked about kidnapping me and holding me ransom. That one —" she gestured towards Ira "— that filthy man put his hands on me."

Heat flushed Kruger's cheeks; he grunted and breathed hard through his nose. The other cowhands reacted too, stiffening and giving the twins hard looks.

Fear, panic, or a mixture of both, showed in Ira's face. "She's lying!"

The foreman said, "Shut up." He asked Choctaw, "What about you, boy? Looks like they beat on you some."

Choctaw wiped blood from his lower lip and chin. "It ain't nothing."

Jade said, "My gallant defender tried to protect me." Which ought to have been a compliment. Except she spoke with sarcasm bordering on contempt. Sneering to boot.

Choctaw felt something like hatred for Jade Rawlins. For an instant he let that show in his face as he glared at her. But she didn't catch his eye and Kruger didn't seem to notice. He was staring grimly at the two men sitting in the grass. Then he moved his horse close to Choctaw, making his voice low so maybe no one else would hear. "Take Miss Jade back to the ranch. She doesn't want to see this."

"See what?"

The foreman didn't answer. He went back to fixing the twins with a hard stare. His fingers tightened on the rope in his hands.

Choctaw glanced over at the other cowhands. Brazos regarded the prisoners and frowned. The teenagers glanced at each other as if sharing a guilty secret, nervous smiles playing around their lips. They looked to be anticipating some excitement, their eyes bright with eagerness and a young man's cruelty.

Choctaw asked Kruger, "You ain't gonna hang 'em, are you?"

"Get her out of here, kid."

Choctaw said, "Let's go, Miss Jade."

She looked for a moment as if she would argue. But when she spoke it was to Kruger and the others, not to him. "I hope you hang them!"

Jade turned her horse and rode off to the west. Choctaw rode after her.

They passed without talking through a belt of timber and into a further, smaller meadow. Halfway across this grassy swale, Jade said, "And you're supposed to be this great fighter? That cow thief certainly got the better of you. Easily." She showed him her sneer again. "My hero!"

Choctaw reined in. She hauled in her horse too, asking, "What is it?"

"Can you make your own way back to the ranch?"

250

"What? You're supposed to escort me all the way."

But Choctaw wasn't listening to her, or seeing her. He heard instead a rope creaking as a body turned in the air, the sound of urine spurting down a man's leg. He saw a bloated face, purple-black with trapped blood, above the noose biting deep into his neck . . .

He said, "You'll have to make your own way, Miss Jade."

She raised her voice in protest but he still didn't listen. He wheeled his horse about and rode back the way he'd come.

CHAPTER THIRTY-TWO

Choctaw returned to the big meadow.

Once his horse started plowing through deep grass, he reined in.

Hank Kruger's party and their prisoners had moved from where he'd left them. Now they clustered at the edge of the trees. Choctaw studied them through his field glasses.

He could make out general details, if not small particulars. All the Crazy R men were afoot. The Gird twins sat horses, both men stiff-backed; it looked as if their hands were tied behind them.

Choctaw rode out into the meadow.

Halfway to Kruger and his men, he paused and glanced back. He wasn't expecting Jade to follow him, but she did lots of crazy things he wasn't expecting. But there was no sign of her.

He rode on, reining in maybe ten paces from the nearest Crazy R hand. None of them held weapons, save Kruger, who let his Winchester dangle in his right hand, muzzle pointed at the earth. Choctaw laid his own Winchester across the saddle before him and studied the twins.

As he'd guessed, both men had their hands tied behind them. They sat their horses under a ponderosa.

These towering pines weren't as suited to lynching as junipers, their boughs being more slender, but this tree had a limb forking out of it that looked strong enough to hold two men. Ropes looped over this bough ended in nooses around the necks of the twins. Ira's right cheek was bloody, so maybe he'd been rough handled. Then Choctaw remembered Jade's quirt and felt an instant's sympathy with the cow thief, as he'd been on the receiving end of that himself.

The Crazy R hands studied him warily, although none made a move towards their guns. Kruger kept his rifle pointing at the earth.

The foreman asked, "What you want, kid? Where's Miss Jade?"

"Loose those neckties off those fellows."

Brazos gave him a startled look. "You're crazy!"

Kruger told Choctaw, "Never mind us.

You get out of here. Get Miss Jade safe back to the ranch, like I told you."

Choctaw said, "I can't let you hang them."

One of the teenagers sneered. "*You* can't let us? You gonna stop us, all by yourself? Figure four-to-one's good odds?"

Choctaw remembered somebody else saying something similar: Kyle Baker, on yet another occasion when he'd jumped feet first into trouble too big for him to handle. Only now he was against double those odds, and no Declan Flynn to bail him out.

Kruger spoke in a patient, reasonable voice. "You've changed your tune, Taylor. Last time you was real keen to see a horse thief swing."

"I know. I was wrong, God help me. But it ain't right to hang somebody over stealing just one cow."

"It's making an example, boy. 'Sides it ain't just cow thieving. They laid their stinking hands on Cap's daughter."

"I know, but . . ." Choctaw was stumped for a second, before working out an answer. "They still deserve a fair trial."

The second teenager snorted his contempt. "Fair trial!"

Kruger asked, in a voice more puzzled than angry, "You're ready to shoot all four of us to save these scum?"

"I'm looking at *you,* Kruger."

The foreman blinked.

Choctaw felt empowered with a strange sense of confidence he'd never known before. He seemed to speak in a voice not his own. As if he'd stepped out of himself and was watching another version of Calvin Taylor, bolder and more authoritative than his years merited, someone who made others listen and obey, who caused things to happen. He watched himself tell Kruger, "All that horseshit about how you hated — what did you call it — rope work? Rope business? Truth is, you like it, don't you? *You've* got the hanging fever, you can't wait to see these fellers swing."

The foreman stared back calmly. "So it's you and me, huh?"

Choctaw wasn't conscious of feeling any fear or need to hurry. He was icy calm. He remembered that was how it had been in Lobo Wells, facing Billy Keogh . . . "Uh-huh."

Kruger surprised him by smiling a strange half smile. He even looked relieved, of all things. "Well, boy, you've been pushing for this . . ."

The foreman moved his right hand slightly, holding his Winchester away from his side. In a second he'd flip the rifle up and they'd be firing at each other . . .

Kruger's eyes moved from Choctaw's face to something past him. The foreman's face changed, he lost that peculiar shadow of a smile, frowning instead. He turned and spoke to the men behind him. "Get the nooses off them two."

Brazos lifted his eyebrows. "What?"

Choctaw was also puzzled; then he heard the sound of hooves, a horse coming close. He guessed the cause for Kruger's sudden change even as he turned to look.

He'd been right: Jade Rawlins was riding up.

One of the teenagers still hadn't caught on. He asked the foreman, "You gonna let this son of a bitch buffalo us?"

"Do it."

As the twins were released from the nooses, Brazos asked, "What we gonna do, Hank?"

"We take these varmints back to the ranch. Cap should be back pretty soon. Maybe even tomorrow. We'll let him decide what to do with 'em."

Jade pushed her horse in among them. She demanded, "What's going on?"

Kruger said, "We're taking these men back to the ranch, Miss Jade."

Jade lifted her voice in anger. "You mean

you aren't going to hang them? After what these disgusting men did to me?"

"That's for your father to decide."

Kruger rode off. The twins followed, then the teenagers. Jade glared after them. Brazos told her, "Don't blame the foreman, ma'am. It was this young feller —" He gestured towards Choctaw, "— who was all for keeping them alive."

Brazos rode on. Jade asked Choctaw, "Is that true?"

"Yes."

She pursed her fine lips and seemed to draw in a particularly deep breath, as if biting down on considerable rage. He waited for her to do something: spit in his face maybe, or give him another taste of the quirt. Her horse must have sensed the tension in her; it half-reared and danced about. She was busy a minute controlling her mount, then she asked, "How could you? After you saw them lay their filthy hands on me?"

"I know. But you wouldn't think like that if you'd ever seen a lynching. Let me tell you —"

But he didn't tell her anything because she whirled the chestnut and galloped off.

They rode towards the ranch, Choctaw

bringing up the rear. Nobody spoke to him, or would hardly even look at him, most particularly Jade. Once or twice, he'd caught the teenage boys sneaking backward glances his way, their eyes bright with hatred.

Close to sundown they came to a rock formation called Red Mesa — although it was more salmon-colored — shaped like a lower back tooth, pushing up maybe a hundred feet. About five miles from the ranch.

Kruger dropped back and came alongside Choctaw. He said, "I guess you won't be the most popular fellow in the bunkhouse this evening."

"I reckon not."

"And as we don't want any more trouble . . . such as anybody else bracing you . . . best you bunk there tonight." He pointed to a small adobe hut at the base of the mesa, a line camp Choctaw had shacked in before — and once visited with Jade Rawlins. "I suggest you point there right now, unless there's something you got to get from the bunkhouse."

"There ain't."

"Stay here until you get told otherwise. The big auger should be back any time. I know you was in good with Cap . . ." Kruger rubbed his chin. "But standing up for them as laid their hands on his daughter . . . that ain't gonna set too well with him, I figure."

"Maybe not."

"As for this thing between you and me . . . well, I guess it can't be lived with. It'll have to get settled."

"I reckon."

Choctaw was expecting the older man to lay out a time and place for the settling. Instead, Kruger kicked his horse into movement and galloped ahead. Choctaw reined in and watched the riders dwindle into the distance. He sat watching even after they'd passed from sight and their dust had faded.

Choctaw decided being a hero, standing up for fine principles, was a good thing; at the same time loneliness was like an anvil, cold and heavy in his belly.

CHAPTER THIRTY-THREE

The adobe at Red Mesa was like most line shacks Choctaw had come across. A Spartan one-room affair running to the bare minimum of furnishing, including a narrow, iron-framed bed. It housed a frugal store of supplies and creature comforts, such as some well-thumbed newspapers and dime novels. The only unusual feature was a roof of logs, rather than thatch.

He hunted around for some liquor to take the darkness out of his mood. He found a whiskey bottle, but it was empty, doubtless used as a rolling pin to knead sourdough into biscuits.

Choctaw took to his bed soon after full dark but found it hard to sleep: too many thoughts in his head. About the ice-cold way he'd squared up to Hank Kruger and the other Crazy R hands. He vaguely remembered being told he'd been ice-cold before, when it came to guns . . . like Hardin or

Hickok. Was it Dec who'd said that, or Old Man Swenson? He thought about what might happen when he and Kruger came to their settling. And about Jade Rawlins. Just when he'd given up on sleeping, he drifted off.

An unfamiliar sound woke him. Rain drummed on the roof, then there was a good crash of thunder.

Choctaw went to the door and gazed out. The night was bruised with heavy, dark-gray clouds. Forked lightning cracked the sky, thunder clapped and rain sluiced down, so the earth swam under drifts of water. You could get some real thunderstorms out here, spectacular lightning displays and downpours that flash-flooded the countryside. But this was only a modest business. Already lightning was striding off to the east and the rain was slackening. Still, he was grateful for the wooden roof, as thatch would have leaked like a sieve.

He returned to his bed, listening to rain hissing outside, feeling warm and comfortable indoors. A feeling that always reminded him of childhood. He slept again.

When he woke, full day was coming. Rain eased to spitting, then died altogether. Sun steamed the earth dry. Meantime, Choctaw ate a frugal breakfast and set about his chores, as befitted a Crazy R ranch hand. He filled in a hole behind the shack that had been gouged out by the rain. He gathered and chopped firewood. Some of the fences around the corral, out front of the shack, needed repairing.

About 3 p.m. Choctaw took a break, sitting with his back to the adobe, smoking a cigarette. As he did so, he saw an approaching horseman.

He waited with his Winchester ready until he determined the newcomer was Cap Rawlins. Right then he dreaded this meeting; he could guess what was coming.

Choctaw leaned the rifle against the steerhide door of the shack and walked towards the older man. He called, "Cap."

Rawlins didn't return the greeting. Nor was he smiling. He reined in and leaned forward in the saddle, both hands on the apple. He gazed at Choctaw, grim-faced.

Choctaw asked, "How was the drive?"

"Fine. Didn't lose nary any cattle, did good business, and everybody got back safe."

"Good."

"But that ain't what I'm here to talk about."

Choctaw looked at the rancher's stern face, at his own boots, and then back at

Rawlins. "I reckon not."

"You seen them two fellers? Them two cow thieves?"

"No. Ain't you got 'em over at the ranch?"

"They broke out of where we had 'em."

While Choctaw was figuring out how to respond to that, Rawlins asked, "You got any coffee?"

"Yes, sir."

"Brew up a pot."

A while later, both Rawlins and Choctaw leaned on the corral fence.

The horses — Cap's bay, Choctaw's buckskin — stood by the trough on the far side of the corral, necks dipped to drink. Their tails whisked at flies.

The two men watched them. They gazed at the sky beyond, subtly changing into its dusk colors. Cap chewed tobacco.

Choctaw smoked. This was his favorite time of day, the land fire-colored, the sky mauve, air full of the strange scent of hot earth cooling.

"Some back at the ranch," Cap said, "think you helped them cow thieves escape. That you was tied in with 'em. Which is why you stopped 'em getting their necks stretched."

"I just hate lynchings."

"A few of the boys, they was all for coming over here and . . . seeing you about it."

Choctaw imagined the two teenage boys had been up for that. He felt the flick of temper. "You think I helped get 'em loose?"

"No." Rawlins took the chaw from his mouth and studied it. "We had 'em in an old wooden shack. But I hire cowpunchers, not prison guards. I reckon the feller standing guard must've took shelter when it turned into a gully washer last night. When that happened, them bad *hombres* pulled out a few boards and snuck off. I figure they got free without your help."

The rancher replaced the plug and chewed a moment. "I could be more concerned about how you let my daughter end up in danger."

Choctaw thought about how to answer that without speaking disrespectful of Jade. But Rawlins spared him the need. He said, "I do know Jade can be a might impetuous, inclined to rush into things, so maybe you ain't to blame for that either. No, that ain't the reason for what I got to do."

Choctaw almost smiled. "Let me go, you mean?"

The older man took a little while answering. "Got no choice, boy."

It was only what Choctaw was expecting.

After all, he'd been through something similar with Swenson and MacNee. Even so he felt some anger and resentment. But that only lasted seconds, before it was replaced by tired resignation.

Rawlins said, "Maybe what you done yesterday was right . . ."

"So I do what's right, and I'm the one gets fired. That ain't fair."

The rancher began to reply. Choctaw lifted a hand, palm forward. "Don't tell me. Nobody ever said life was fair."

There was a pause and then Choctaw said, "I saved your life, Cap."

"I ain't forgot that. And what you did, getting those cutting horses back. Risking your neck for the Crazy R. I'm beholden. On top of that you've been a good cowhand. But . . ."

"But?"

"If I don't let you go, there'll be killing. Sure as eggs are eggs. You and Hank have nearly come to guns twice. Or maybe one of the hands riled up about this business'll brace you. Then maybe you're dead, or I've lost a good top hand, or a good *vaquero*. I can't let that happen."

In the corral, the buckskin snorted hard down his long nose, three or four times.

The rancher rubbed at his bad leg, which

was presumably hurting after he'd stood so long. "Boy, I don't normally go in for advising, and could be I'm wasting my breath, 'cuz maybe you're a lost cause. But maybe you ain't, so I'll have at it."

Choctaw waited. He started shaping a cigarette.

Rawlins said, "You're hot tempered, boy. And prideful. Just like I was, when I was 'tween hay and grass. But the difference with me is you're damn handy with them guns. You don't scare. And it don't seem to bother you to pull a trigger on another man. That can be a pretty deadly combination. Adds up to somebody like John Wesley Hardin."

It might have been Swenson speaking, back at Lobo Wells. Choctaw glared at Rawlins. "I ain't like Hardin!"

"No. But I'd say you're looking to go down the same trail he's on now. Maybe he had his reasons too, when he started killing, but somewhere along the way he got to like it . . . got sick with gun fever like some get hanging fever. Stick on that trail and you'll end up the same way he will."

"How's that?"

"Dead before you're thirty."

Choctaw looked at the quirley he was

shaping. He'd made a considerable mess of it.

Rawlins leaned his back on the corral fence. "From a bullet. Or maybe you'll kill the wrong man and it'll be a rope." He inspected his chaw and started on it again. "Could be I'll hear about it, and you know what? I won't give a damn."

"Oh?"

"And you know why?" Rawlins gazed up at the sky, where the pale crescent of a new moon was beginning to show. "Because you'll have finished up like Hardin: a no-account killer, for all some folks think he's a hero, want to make a god out of him. Maybe that's true of all these dime novel pistoleers and shootists or whatever you call them. Maybe even Hickok hisself, for all he's a lawman. They're just no-account trash. When they die, they don't leave nothing ahind 'em save the hole they're buried in. That'll be you too, boy, less'n you get off that trail right smart. The ones I feel sorry for is the widders and orphans they make, and the folk they cause pain to that have to go on living."

Rawlins fell silent a spell, letting all that settle. Finally he said, "Well, that's my sermonizing over. After so much talk I could drink up the Hassayampa. Come over the ranch house and draw your pay."

He strode towards the shack, dragging his bad leg.

Choctaw leaned forward, both hands on the corral bars.

He decided he owed himself two things: a break from these far, wild places, and a good long drunk. What he needed was a town and people, in both cases the rougher and noisier the better. He recalled promising to meet up with Dec in Prescott come Christmas. He determined to do that and they'd get seriously drunk together.

Choctaw realized he'd lost count of time, because he didn't know how close it was to Christmas. He decided any fellow who lost track of Christmas must be pretty damn lonesome.

He turned, leaning his back against the corral fence, facing the sunset. In the dusk the mesa lived up to its name, standing the color of old blood against the sky.

■ ■ ■ ■

PART THREE:
RIDING THE
HIGH LINES

■ ■ ■ ■

CHAPTER THIRTY-FOUR

Next morning, after another night at the Red Mesa line camp, Choctaw took his leave of the Crazy R.

He idled along on the way south, only reaching Doan's Store close to sundown. But this place proved to be just a hole in the road, the store and little else, not even a decent saloon, let alone a hotel. He ended up sleeping in the livery.

Next day he rode on, swinging west towards Camp Verde and Prescott. The first settlement he came across, after maybe twenty miles, was Eichmann's Crossing.

The Crossing was an untidy collection of dwellings straddling a creek you could wade across in a dozen paces and not get your knees wet — and was only that deep because of recent rains. It lay on the edge of open country, with a green wall of pines to the west. As to size and population, the settlement was about the size of Lobo Wells. But

271

it did have a few saloons, and, late in the afternoon, Choctaw entered what looked to be the most substantial.

There were only a few drinkers, no women and one bartender present. The latter told him they had St. Louis Beer. It bore the curse of frontier beer — as there was no way of keeping it cold, it came warm. But Choctaw drained his glass anyway and then ordered mescal. He asked if there was a hotel in town.

The bar dog ran a well-used towel over a glass. "You're honored. We got two. Take your choice, mate."

Choctaw was having a little trouble with this fellow's accent. "You British? London maybe?"

"That's right, governor. Cockney. Born within the sound of Bow Bells."

A reference that left Choctaw mystified. He asked, "Which hotel is best, you reckon?"

There was noise from the street outside: horses riding in, and some voices yelling. A man entered the saloon. He announced to everybody present, "Sheriff's back!"

The barkeep asked, "They get 'em, Walt?"

"They caught one of 'em."

Walt exited. The other drinkers forgot their drinks and headed outside.

272

Choctaw asked the barkeep, "What's going on?"

"Horse thieves, mate."

"Huh?"

"Hit a ranch. Ran off all the horses in the rancher's corral. Why'd you think the town is so empty? Most of the men are out after 'em, riding in posses. But it sounds like the sheriff has got one of the bastards!"

There were cheers mixed in with the shouting. Choctaw took his mescal to the door of the saloon, then stepped out onto the sidewalk.

On both sides of the street onlookers gathered. Some waved and cheered. They watched half a dozen men riding along Main Street. Leading them was a man with a badge pinned to his vest.

Choctaw found he was standing next to Walt. He asked him, "That the sheriff?"

"Uh-huh. Sheriff Blackstone."

Blackstone reined in before an adobe, an ugly square box with a wooden board pinned over the doorway. This bore one word painted in white on a dark background: JAIL. The procession of riders behind him halted. The sheriff dismounted, then the others.

Blackstone was between medium height and tall. On the thin side. Nondescript clothing, save he wore a hat with a low crown and very wide brim such as teamsters wore. His mustache made a horseshoe, pointing downward over his mouth, and he wore a fringe of beard. But what distinguished him was the extravagant length of his hair, falling halfway down his chest. And the color of it, gray paling into white.

Choctaw asked, "Kind of old for a sheriff, ain't he?"

Walt said, "Don't let that gray hair fool you. Rufus ain't even forty."

"No?"

"Went gray premature. They say when he was still a younker — fifteen, sixteen — he saw outlaws murder his mother and father right in front of his eyes. Those bad men did terrible things to 'em. That turned his hair gray. Since then, he's been real vengeful on all lawbreakers."

For a moment Choctaw enjoyed this grim tale; then he wondered if he was listening to a windy. "You believe that?"

Walt shrugged. "Maybe not. Good story though, ain't it?"

Both men smiled ruefully. Walt said, "One part of it's true. That Blackstone's a mean bastard."

"Yeah?"

"His prisoner'll soon find out."

As if on cue, out of the throng of people out front of the jail, one man was pushed forward. He plunged off the sidewalk and plowed to his knees. This must be the prisoner, as his hands were doubled behind him, seemingly tied there.

Blackstone stepped off the sidewalk and stood behind the kneeling man. The sheriff held a short-barreled shotgun. He kicked the prisoner in the back, and the man almost toppled.

A couple of people laughed.

The sheriff told his captive, "Get up!"

Slowly the prisoner got to his feet. Blackstone told him, "In there." He indicated the jail with the barrel of the shotgun, then, for good measure, jabbed his captive in the side with it.

The prisoner stumbled but managed to stay on his feet. He turned and glared at the sheriff, who said, "Get in there!"

The captive entered the jail. Blackstone and several others followed.

The crowd began to disperse. Walt went back into the saloon, and Choctaw trailed along after him.

Up at the bar Choctaw bought drinks for himself, Walt, and the bar dog, who said, "Cheers, governor."

Walt produced a thin cigar. "We'll be having some entertainment soon I don't doubt."

The Englishman asked, "You reckon tonight?"

"Maybe. More likely when the other posse men get back. Say tomorrow night."

Innocently, Choctaw asked, "What kind of entertainment?"

Walt did a little pantomime, indicating a rope across a throat, the rope being jerked and someone strangling with his tongue thrusting out.

Choctaw asked, "But that feller's in custody."

Walt lit his stogie. "That jail's kind of leaky. Downright peculiar how many times somebody in there has got out somehow, and ended up decorating a tree."

The Englishman gave a knowing grin. "Yeah. Blackstone's good at catching 'em, but he's shocking careless about keeping 'em alive for trial. You know what I mean?"

Choctaw nodded slightly. "I know what you mean."

CHAPTER THIRTY-FIVE

Sheriff Blackstone had told his deputy to take over in the jail at 10 p.m. But this man was enjoying himself too much in the saloon. When he glanced at his fob watch and saw it was just gone ten, he said *"Fuck you, Blackstone,"* and ordered another whiskey.

He took his time drinking, letting the liquor warm his insides nicely before he stepped out into the cold night air. Which was getting plenty chilly, seeing as it was December in the Arizona high country. He regretted not having anything warmer to wear than his canvas jacket, which he pulled more tightly about him, jamming his shapeless hat down on his head.

He gazed ahead down the main street of Eichmann's Crossing. There was only a small slice of moon giving light and buildings were low and solid black under a sky of deep blue-black. Nobody seemed to be about. Nonetheless, the lawman slipped his hand into his right jacket pocket, feeling the comforting bulk of his Colt pistol. Reassured, he set off down the sidewalk towards the jail.

He resented catching this duty, babysitting some no-account horse thief who'd be decorating a tree in a day or two anyway, if he knew Blackstone. The deputy had planned a more pleasant evening with Diamond Tooth Annie, who operated out of a crib down on the line on the outskirts of town. And if she was otherwise engaged there was a Mex gal a few shacks along called Carmelita . . .

He reached the end of the street where nearly all the buildings were dark. The exception was the jail, a kerosene lamp burning behind the pulled-down blinds.

As he approached this building, he fished around for the key. Even with a few whiskeys inside him, he still remembered his professional duties enough to glance around while he did so. He didn't expect to see anything suspicious and didn't. He unlocked the jail door and pushed it open.

A board creaked faintly on the sidewalk behind him. The deputy felt himself sobering. He reached towards the bulge in his jacket pocket.

Something small and hard pressed into the middle of his back. A man — his voice slightly muffled — said, "Put both hands either side of the door in front of you."

"That a gun you got in my back?"

"Could be just my finger. You want to find out?"

The deputy decided this was a smart-mouthed son of a bitch. But he was also someone who moved real quiet, and it could well be the muzzle of a pistol he pressed against the other man's spine. So the lawman did as he was told. A hand patted around both sides of his body, found the revolver in his pocket, and removed it. The realization he was defenseless put an icy taste in the deputy's mouth.

The faceless voice commanded, "Inside."

Both men entered the jail. The door was eased shut behind them. The lawman was ordered to "Get the cell open."

The jail only ran to one cell. Inside there was a dark shape, sitting up on the bed against the wall. As the deputy began unlocking his cell door, the prisoner rose to his feet, asking, "What is this?"

The cell door swung open. The deputy felt a push in his back and staggered forward a few steps into the cell. He risked a glance back and saw his captor held a pistol all right. The lawman gazed into this man's face. Or rather his mask. Under the brim of his Plainsman hat, his face was shrouded in pale cloth, with eyeholes cut in it. The deputy felt an instant's fear at the stark inhumanity of this visage, before more rational thought told him it was just a man with a gunnysack over his head.

The lawman glared his hatred at the gunnysacker. "You son of a bitch!"

The masked man produced some rope and a bandanna. He told the prisoner, "Tie and gag this feller."

The prisoner didn't seem to know his rescuer, and he gazed at him warily. "We got a little *ley de fuga* going on here?"

The deputy knew what that meant. *Ley de fuga* was said to be a common practice of the *rurales,* the Mexican police. How prisoners they took managed to get free, mysteriously, and then were killed while attempting to escape.

The gunnysacker said, "You're being sprung, friend. 'Less you want to stay here."

The prisoner stood, unmoving.

The masked man made an impatient sound. "Decide!"

The prisoner did. He picked up the rope and tied the deputy's hands behind him, then used the bandanna to gag him and pushed him on to the bed. The lawman watched helplessly as he was locked in the cell, then prisoner and rescuer left, locking the jail door behind them.

The rescuer moved along Main Street and the prisoner followed. Both moved quickly but quietly, keeping to the shadows. The rescuer ducked into the mouth of an alley.

The prisoner turned the corner too, but then paused. He stared into the black maw before him. It gaped like the jaws of a trap, flanked by high walls, and he recoiled from entering. If he went down there would the night suddenly be ablaze with gunfire, would figures loom out of the shadows to shoot him down, Blackstone among them? *Ley de fuga*?

Again, he had to decide. And did.

He went down the alley.

At the other end, his rescuer stood. He held the reins of a saddled horse.

As he approached, the prisoner thought he recognized the animal.

The rescuer said, "Get on this horse."

As awareness dawned on him, the prisoner listened hard and was almost certain he recognized the other's voice, despite the muffling of the gunnysack. He asked, "You coming with me?"

The gunnysacker shook his head. "No. You better get moving, *hombre*."

Now the prisoner was sure. He smiled. He said, "Choctaw, ain't it?"

The gunnysacker made a sound of exasperation. "Goddamn you! How'd you get in such a fix?"

Declan Flynn laughed.

CHAPTER THIRTY-SIX

The deputy lay, bound and gagged, in the jail.

He felt a mix of emotions: humiliation at being taken so easily; anger at the injustice of the prisoner escaping. That fellow Flynn had sure grated on him, laughing and staying cheerful even in the shadow of death. The deputy had enjoyed thinking how a length of strangling hemp would cure his funning and japes. It would be others laughing as they watched the horse thief kick and dance . . . .

But now Flynn was free. And that other son of a bitch with him.

The deputy was also thinking of how long and uncomfortable this night was likely to be, him lying here trussed like a Thanksgiving turkey.

As it happened, his ordeal lasted less than ten minutes.

A voice called outside the jail. Lying back

in the cell the deputy couldn't hear too clearly, but guessed it might be Blackstone. Someone banged on the door, and then a key turned in the lock and the door opened.

Blackstone entered, his pistol in his hand.

The deputy was expecting to catch hell from old Rufus. Especially if he smelled whiskey on the other man's breath. The sheriff was very quick to anger, and hard — judging about everything. That he was visiting the jail was a form of rebuke in itself. He must have come to check up on the deputy, figuring he was maybe too unreliable to do his job.

Blackstone paused outside the cell. He sure looked in the grip of temper, glaring and breathing hard through his nose. As ever, the deputy was struck by how the sheriff's long hair and drooping mustache gave him a likeness to "Wild Bill" Hickok. An aged Hickok with his snowy hair and graveyard pallor. Thirty-six, thirty-seven years old, looking fifty-odd. The deputy had seen men with consumption who looked like that, but the sheriff didn't have any coughing sickness. Nobody seemed to know what ailed Rufe, but it sure wasn't getting any better. The way his eyes were starting to sink into his head and shine with fever brightness told its own story. In two years, he'd aged twenty, so how much future could he have left?

You could feel sorry for Rufe that fate had played such a dirty trick on him, that he was being pulled down by something too cowardly to show its face, some secret corruption in him nobody could find or name. Except the sheriff was so hard to be around these days. He was more or less permanently angry, sometimes in a cold rage, other times lashing out in temper at those around him. And when it came to wrongdoers . . . He'd once told the deputy, "I don't have any religious beliefs, you know that. But there's one instruction from the Good Book I do cleave to." His lips formed into a half sneer, which was the nearest he ever came to a smile. "That's to smite the wicked."

Blackstone entered the cell. The deputy expected the sheriff to bellow at him like a maddened bull. Instead, Blackstone kept his lips grimly pursed. As he set the other man free, he asked, "What happened?"

The deputy told him, finishing with, "They ain't been been gone ten minutes."

"Ten minutes!"

The deputy stood, kneading his wrists. The sheriff said, "Go over to the saloon and roust out the other deputies. But do it quietly. These two varmints can't have got far. Most likely they're still around, skulking in some back alley. Get the men searching — but, like I said, do it quietly."

"Sure, Rufe."

Blackstone lifted the pistol in his hand — a Smith and Wesson American .44 with engravings on the long barrel. "We'll get 'em." He used the front sight of the gun to rub a place on his furrowed cheeks, while he stared in cold anger. "We'll get 'em both."

Choctaw told Dec, "Get on this horse." He spoke in an urgent whisper. His nerves felt shredded, not just with the queasiness of fear, which he was too familiar with, but at what he was doing that was new, stepping so far outside the law.

His buckskin horse was nervous too, tugging on the reins he held.

Dec also whispering, "You better come with me. Else Blackstone'll be hanging you instead of me."

"Why?" Choctaw felt ridiculous, talking inside a gunnysack. He was tempted to pull it off, but resisted. "All I am is a fellow got his horse stole."

The Irishman grabbed him by both shoulders. "Which'll make you the main suspect. And him and his crowd, they're crazy to hang *somebody*. They'll settle on you, boy."

Choctaw shook his head. "I ain't coming."

"You're crazy, staying here."

"No, sir. I sprung you. That's it. I ain't getting in any more deep than —"

A voice called, "Hold it down there!"

Choctaw almost jumped out of his britches. He turned, glimpsing the dim shape of a man in the mouth of the alley. This newcomer ordered, "Don't move or I'll go to shooting!"

Choctaw and Dec swore, almost simultaneously. The Irishman grabbed at the horse, which squealed and tried to back away. But Dec held the reins, and hauled himself into the saddle. He reached down. "Come on!"

Choctaw stood helplessly. He'd been confused plenty in his life but rarely as confused about what to do as he was now.

A pistol banged. It was as loud as a thunderclap in this narrow place, and the bullet keened overhead.

The faceless voice called again. "Next shot goes low!"

The confusion in Choctaw's mind seemed to vanish instantly. To be replaced by his old friend: fear. Choctaw seized Dec's arm and swung up behind him. With both of them in the saddle, Dec whirled the buckskin and they charged out of the alley.

Behind them, the pistol cracked again.

Bursting onto the street, they almost ran head-on into a horse and rider coming along at a slow trot. Dec swung the buckskin aside, so it caught the other horse broadside on. This animal went down, screaming, and the buckskin also tumbled. There were two horses down in the dust, and three riders spilled onto the street.

Falling, Choctaw banged his shoulder, elbow, and knee. He floundered where he lay. He realized he was lying on the buckskin's reins. As this horse struggled up, he grabbed them and swung into the saddle. He glanced around for Dec.

The other horse was a gray. It rose slowly, shaking its head and whinnying. Two men were dark shapes lying at its feet. Almost simultaneously, both sat up. One rubbed his head. The other man rose and grabbed the gray's reins. Choctaw saw this was Dec.

The gray danced about but the Irishman managed to climb into the saddle.

There were voices, yelling. A body of men down the street moved towards them. Another man came out of the alley and halted. Moonlight touched his long pale hair.

Dec fought the gray's pitching, managing to get it settled. Some of the men moving

288

down the street broke into a run. The Irish-man put his back to them, spurred the gray, and hammered down the street, raising a small storm of dust.

Choctaw watched him flee. He spun his horse to gallop the other way. Only the onrush of yelling men blocked the street. He wheeled his horse around, so he was now pointing after Dec. He spurred the buckskin into a hard run after his friend.

In the tail of his eye, he saw the pale-haired man across the way raise his arm, pointing at him. Metal flashed on Black-stone's pistol.

Choctaw ducked low against the buck-skin's withers, gritting his teeth.

The pistol cracked.

Something tugged at the right-side brim of his hat. He felt the breath of the bullet on his right temple, the keen of its passing in his ear.

Galloping hard, Dec swung around a corner, out of sight. Choctaw stayed on his heels, putting an angle of buildings between him and his pursuers. They yelled and fired guns but he got clear.

Ahead of him Declan was a black seed, trailing dust, losing himself in distance. He cut west, pointing towards the darkness of

the forest.
And Choctaw followed.

CHAPTER THIRTY-SEVEN

When Choctaw awoke, he was sprawled at the base of a ponderosa. Maybe he'd fallen asleep sitting with his back to this tree.

Darkness surrounded him, but as he watched, it became less absolute, then hazy gray between the black sentinels of trees.

He sat up, groaning as sharp pains jabbed and ached in his back. It felt like he'd been lying on a bed of rocks.

It was dawn. Early light flooded the forest like a pearly mist, his surroundings showing the first hints of color, muted greens and browns. A blotch of shadow a few yards away became Dec, hunkered down with his rifle across his knees, his back to Choctaw. The Irishman squatted where the ground sloped sharply downwards.

Choctaw heard birds starting on their morning song, a squirrel chittering high above, and, distantly, running water. He pushed himself to his feet, gasping as this brought more pain to his back and legs. He was cold too, in the sharp December air. He shivered and rubbed his fingers together to warm them up, stamping numbed feet. Breath steamed before his face.

Choctaw saw their horses were upslope, their noses bound with bandannas so they wouldn't whinny to any strange horses in the neighborhood. He walked over to the buckskin and got his canteen. He also took a drawstring bag containing some jerky and hardtack from his saddlebags.

He trod a soft carpet of leaves and pine needles over to Dec, who didn't glance back at him. The Irishman was gazing down long slopes, stippled with rank upon rank of tall, slim pines, some of them scarfed in mist.

Keeping his voice almost to a whisper, Choctaw asked, "See anything?"

Dec kept his voice low too. "No." He glanced back.

Choctaw asked, "What happened to your face?" It was something he'd noticed before, but there'd been no time to comment on it.

Dec's left eye was closed, the eyelid swollen to twice its normal size, gray and purple. Bruises made purple blotches on his forehead and both cheeks; his lips were smeared with blood; and there was a deep gash on the side of his nose. He said, "Blackstone . . .

questioned me."

"Son of a bitch!"

"He wanted me to tell him where the other . . . horse thieves were."

"So you finally come to it. What you was talking about before."

"Huh?"

"You turned horse thief."

Dec flashed the other man an angry look. "Like hell I did. Is that what you think of me?"

Choctaw started to respond with his own anger; he felt a tinge of shame instead.

He chewed jerky, offering Dec some of the same. "So, what happened? You still with MacNee?"

"No. I got laid off after the fall roundup. There I was drifting towards Prescott, looking for work. I was camped out all by myself, and I wake up in the morning and there's half a dozen guns pointing at me. Blackstone and his posse, trailing horse thieves. I made the mistake of being on the same trail. *That's* my only crime, being an innocent bystander." The Irishman glared. "And if you call me a horse thief again, I'll knock you sideways."

Dec gave him another hard look, and then he was smiling like the friendliest man alive. "Which is no way for me to treat the man who saved my life."

Choctaw remembered how quickly this man's moods could change. And how hard his friendliness was to resist. "Is that what I did?"

"Sure. The posse was laughing about it. How I was gonna be the next one dying of 'altitude sickness.' You know —" He made a gesture indicating a rope around his neck, being pulled taut. "And now they're after you too."

"No, they ain't."

"What?"

"Look, Dec, I sprung you because I wasn't going to see you lynched. That don't make me a criminal."

Declan's bloody lips twisted into a sneer. "The hell it don't! You held up a deputy, helped a felon escape — what do you think that makes you? That's a couple of years' jail time, boy. At least. You think you'll be let off because it's a first offense? You crazy? I bet your face is on some wanted poster before today's out."

"How come? I had my face hid."

Dec grunted in exasperation. "Blackstone ain't stupid, you know. What do you think he'll be doing today? He'll be asking around. 'Seen any strangers in town recent, fellow about six foot, riding a buckskin horse?'

Didn't you speak to anybody at the Crossing?"

"Sure I did."

"Then he'll pretty soon have a description of you. And then when he finds out you've mysteriously left town, that your horse wasn't in the livery last night . . . that'll make you suspect number one."

"Christ."

"You give your name? Sign into the hotel?"

"No. I was just about to when I saw Blackstone bring you in. And I don't think I said my name to anybody."

"That's lucky. But you'll still be on some dodger. An 'artist's impression' of you, anyway."

"You seem to know a lot about this business."

"I'm just telling you how things are." Dec studied the slopes below a while before he spoke again. "Face it, *amigo*. We're both wanted men now."

Choctaw thought about it. Try as he might, he couldn't see a way out of this. If he turned himself in, threw himself on Blackstone's mercy, what would that get him? Most likely a case of "altitude sickness." In a defeated voice he said, "I reckon."

"With that crazy Blackstone on our heels."

"You figure he'll chase us much? Two no-account horse thieves?"

"It ain't *who* we are that matters, boy. It's that we got loose on him. We put a stain on his reputation. Mighty prideful fellow, Blackstone. And maybe he's more than prideful. Maybe he's crazy."

"You reckon?"

"He sure acted like it sometimes. Like when he was . . . 'questioning' me." Dec carefully touched a bruise on his cheek and hissed with pain.

Looking at the damage done to his friend's face, Choctaw felt a warm anger. "Yeah. The law!"

"No, I figure we'll only be safe when we're out of Blackstone's jurisdiction. Out of the territory if necessary."

"What? You mean out of Arizona?"

"Yep."

"If we're gonna travel all that distance we need supplies. Can we risk going into any of the towns 'round here?"

Dec chewed some jerky. "I've been thinking. There's some fellers I did some horse trading with. They have a little place a fair ways east of here. We could rest up there. If the worst comes to the worst, they'd loan us supplies."

"We looking for handouts now?"

"We ain't got much choice. Needs must, *compadre.*"

"I don't know."

"The other good thing about that idea is . . . where they are is only maybe thirty miles from the New Mexico line. Once we're across that . . . not even Blackstone would follow us into another territory."

Choctaw turned the hat in his hands. There was a tear along the right side of the brim. He remembered invisible fingers snatching at his hat, and Blackstone's bullet keening in his ear.

Dec gazed downslope, shifting the rifle in his hands. "What do you think?"

Choctaw's gut feeling told him staying with Dec might be a big mistake. Sure, the Irishman was a real friend and plenty fun. But he was plenty trouble too. Since they'd met it had been one scrape after another. Admittedly, Choctaw was prone to find trouble anyway, and would have found some of it without Dec, but this latest business had left him deep in a bad situation. And the unease in his guts told him sticking with the Irishman would only make things worse.

On the other hand, if they split up, Choctaw would be a wanted man, a hunted fugitive, all on his own. And the outlaw trail was a lonesome place to be without a friend. Dec asked, "Well?"

CHAPTER THIRTY-EIGHT

It was close to dusk.

They were resting their horses by walking them. Now Dec halted, hunkered down, and started on the makings.

Choctaw paused alongside him. He took his canteen off his saddle. Drinking, he took a careful look around. A habit that had become second nature since his Apache scout days, and one he'd sharpened up since his adventures in the Crossing. He found he spent a lot of time in particular looking back. Watching for any dust.

Dec lit his cigarette. "What you looking out for? Wild Indians after our scalps?"

"No. The Navajos north of us is pacified. Same for the Apaches south of here. And any locals — the Hopis and such — is friendly."

"I was forgetting you know all about this Indian stuff. What you keep looking back for, then?" When the other didn't reply, Dec answered his own question. "A posse?"

Both men spent a little time studying the land around them.

They'd left the green country around Eichmann's Crossing, far behind. Traveling east, they'd crossed high tablelands alternating between sere grass and bald desert, passing well south of the Crazy R, skirting the southern fringes of the strange region known as the Petrified Forest. Switching northeast, they found themselves once again facing the hazy purple wall of the Mogollon Rim.

Choctaw seemed to have fallen very easily into the ways of an outlaw. Then again, he'd been hunted before. All he'd done was swap one set of pursuers for another, Apaches for the law . . .

But they'd seen no signs of pursuit. Dec's theory was Blackstone would expect them to head west towards more settled country, not figuring on them doubling back, past the Crossing. And maybe the Irishman had been right.

Dec said, "Best to keep watching out, with the likes of Blackstone on our heels. Anybody else would quit, but a crazy like him . . . you never know."

Choctaw washed trail dust out of his throat with a mouthful of water, then spat it out on the earth. He asked, "Just where are your horse-trading friends?"

Dec scratched his trail beard, his rusty stubble most of the way to being a real beard. It helped mask the bruising to his face, which had faded during the last few days. Most particularly the ugly purple swelling of his eyelid had diminished so it just looked like a regular black eye now.

He pointed east, towards a low run of hills, salmon-colored, turning red in the sunset, halfway between themselves and the base of the rim. "There's a little pass, runs through those hills. Up there. Couple hours' ride."

Moving on once more, they came to the hills, which ranged west-east, and rode along the face of them. After a few miles, a narrow opening showed to their left, barely wide enough to allow two horsebackers to pass through riding side by side. Dec turned into this slit and Choctaw followed.

He did so reluctantly. He was naturally uneasy anywhere you could get trapped and this corridor made a dandy trap. Sheer walls rose sixty, a hundred, feet on either side. Riflemen atop them would have anyone trying to squeeze through below in a cross fire. Just a few men up there could slaughter an army. Fortunately, no enemies appeared, no overhead guns flashed or cracked.

Hooves rattled on rubbled earth and bare stone, saddles creaked. Echoes bounced eerily between rock walls. In places these ramparts leaned inwards, pinching close to each other, so the sky was a ribbon of fading light, and the pass filled with shadow. And then the way through widened again, spreading out until it was a couple hundred yards wide.

They startled some mule deer from cover. Watching the fleeing animals, Dec said, "Make good eating when we get to camp." Both men fired their rifles at the deer, bringing one down. Choctaw slung the carcass across his horse's rump.

They rode on. All at once, the sun was gone and gray darkness flooded the pass. Far ahead lights glimmered.

Dec said, "Well, here we are."

After some study, Choctaw identified blotches on this grayness he took for buildings. He asked, "This place is kind of well hidden, ain't it?" Sarcastically he added, "I guess your friends ain't too sociable."

The Irishman didn't reply. Maybe a hundred yards short of the buildings, Dec reined in and Choctaw followed suit. The Irishman said, "We better sing out. Otherwise, we just might get shot at, coming up in the dark, unannounced."

Choctaw saw a scatter of adobes and a well. One main building, a long, low-roofed structure with lights in the windows, a fair-sized barn, and a few smaller huts. In back there was a corral with high adobe walls on three sides. He asked, "What is this place?"

"I hear it's an abandoned ranch house. Feller started a spread but either Navajos scared him off, back when they was hostile, or drought finished him."

"It got a name?"

"Irishman's Wells."

Choctaw smiled. "Who called it that?"

Dec grinned. "I did — just now." He leaned forward in the saddle, calling, *"Mujeres!"*

Choctaw looked at his friend in surprise. "You got some women out here?"

"Didn't I mention that?" Dec lifted his voice again. "It's Flynn!"

A door-shaped patch of light showed in the main building and a shadowy figure emerged, woman-shaped, the slim bar of a rifle held across her body. She asked, "That you, Red?" A voice with an accent Choctaw couldn't pin down straightaway.

"Red yourself. We brung you some meat for the smokehouse."

"Come ahead."

The two men rode up to the main building and dismounted. Light from the doorway partly illuminated the woman. From her looks and dress, she appeared to be Mexican, a scarlet *rebozo* — a long shawl — draped over her shoulders, folds of it almost reaching her waist. A woman in her thirties, her hair hanging to her full breasts. A rifle sloped over the crook of one arm. She held a cigarillo. Smoke filtering down from her nostrils, she asked, "What you got there, Red?"

"Mule deer."

Dec strode up to the woman, hoisted her off the ground, and kissed her full on the lips. He kissed her quite a spell, while Choctaw tried to look someplace else. When Dec was done kissing, he lowered the woman to earth. "You pleased to see me, Luz honey?"

Luz touched his lips with her finger. "Always pleased to see you, *mi querido.*" Her gaze moved to Choctaw and she smiled. "Who's he?"

"That's my friend — Calvin Taylor."

Choctaw nodded, almost like he were bowing, and said, *"Mucho gusto."*

Luz gave a small laugh. "Your friend's got nice manners, Red."

Dec said, "Sure he has. Way he was raised.

He's the son of a king back in Europe."

Gently, Luz touched the corner of Red's damaged eye. She made a tutting noise like a disapproving mother. "You've been fighting again."

"You should have seen the other feller."

"Yes?"

Dec grinned. "There wasn't a mark on him!"

"You crazy Irish!"

"Now, *señora,* how about feeding two hungry men?"

He leant to kiss her again, but she held him at bay with a fingertip placed on the point of his chin. "You wash your face first. You could stand a shave too."

The Irishman laughed. He told Choctaw, "We're 'round women now, guess we got to make ourselves presentable. Best as we can, anyhow."

Choctaw said, "As I'm a king, you should call me 'Your Majesty.' "

Another voice spoke. "Hi, Red."

A woman stood in shadow in the doorway. Dec said, "Rosa, honey."

Rosa stepped forward out of the shadows. She was another Mexican woman, but this time maybe nineteen or twenty. She turned her eyes on Choctaw, asking Dec, "Who's your pretty friend?"

"Calvin Taylor."

She fluttered her eyelids. "*Hola,* Calvin Taylor."

"*Mucho gusto, señorita.*"

Rosa smiled. "He sure is pretty!"

CHAPTER THIRTY-NINE

They entered the main building.

A main room, a side room/washup. Two rooms in back, doors closed. The main room was laid out in a style common to the Southwest: an earth floor a foot or so lower than the ground outside, with a few clay jars of water dangling from the ceiling to help the room cool. Sparsely furnished with a long plank eating table, two benches flanking it, a smaller table, a few chairs. In one back corner a cookstove and shelves holding tins and cooking things. Kerosene lamps bathed the walls in sallow light.

The men washed their hands and faces, then sat at the long table, where there was a large bottle of tequila in a cane basket. The two men took a few snorts, while the women busied in and out.

Luz was red-haired. Choctaw had seen a few Mexican women like that, although he couldn't imagine how red hair got in there.

You could guess she'd been beautiful in her youth. But her looks were running down, time adding a hardness to her face and lines at the corners of her eyes. She still had a fine figure but was putting on a few pounds.

Rosa was tall, slim, and shapely, her dark hair falling to her shoulders, and strikingly beautiful. She wore a fairly clean white off-the-shoulder top and a wide ankle-length dark blue skirt, with bands of vivid color across the bottom. There was a scarlet sash around her waist. She complimented that with a large red flower above her left ear. A lot of Anglo women would consider such gaiety too daring; Choctaw thought it was real pretty.

When Dec inquired after the horse traders, he was told they'd gone to the nearest settlement for supplies. They were due back any time.

The women brought plates of food: tortillas and bowls of chili. Plain fare, but the men cleaned their plates. Serving it up, Rosa proved unexpectedly clumsy at times. She couldn't help brushing against Choctaw. Once or twice, standing next to him, she almost overbalanced, steadying herself by placing her hand on his chest or — once — on the top of his thigh. She apologized. When he accepted her apology she smiled and touched his cheek briefly.

The women went to the smokehouse, to start dressing the mule deer for the meal tomorrow.

The men passed the bottle between them. Choctaw thought about the feel of Rosa's hand on his chest and face, how long her hand seemed to rest on his thigh, and the look of invitation in her eyes. He smiled.

After a while he observed, "You and Luz seem real friendly."

"We are."

"But you called her *señora*."

Declan shrugged. "She's had a few husbands along the way." He drank, then passed the bottle. "Why? You interested?"

"Well, she is a fine-looking woman." Saying that, Choctaw realized his tongue was thick with drink. The tequila already weighed heavy on him, sinking him down in his chair. "But I reckon I might be fully occupied otherwise." He smirked. "Way Rosa's acting 'round me."

Dec snorted. "Sorry to disappoint you, Romeo, but Rosa acts that way 'round anything passes for a male. If you was ninety-three with only one tooth in your head . . . she's all over any man ain't positively repulsive."

"You'd be safe then."

It was Dec's turn to smirk. "I figure I just about broke the record with Rosa. I'd hardly said hello before she had my pants off!"

The Irishman took a turn with the bottle before saying, "Anyway, I thought you was agin' loose women."

"I'm kind of weakening in that regard." That was another sentence that took a little journey before it came untangled out of his mouth.

Dec studied his friend owlishly. "I swear, you are a contradictory fellow. You won't lay with whores but you're happy to go with . . ."

The Irishman let the words die out. Choctaw listened to the sudden silence. He seemed to have sobered up considerably. He glanced over at Dec. The Irishman was pushing his tongue around in his mouth like he was hunting something to spit out.

Choctaw asked, "Go with who?"

"Nothing."

Choctaw felt a cold anger, something he'd never felt towards Dec before. He said, "What was you gonna say — go with squaws?"

"Forget what I said."

Choctaw pushed himself up in his chair. His cold anger was warming. "Is that what you was gonna say?"

Something thumped into his chest and slipped onto his lap. It was the bottle of tequila.

Dec said, "Drink!"

Choctaw stared at the other man, who wouldn't look at him, but was busy instead on the makings. "But —"

"Get outside of that bottle."

Choctaw stared some more. He glared through a minute or so of silence. Then, grudgingly, he lifted the bottle to his lips.

Dec studied the quirley in his hands. "You drunk yet?"

"Getting there."

"We shouldn't fall out. Not now we're partners in crime."

That was another sobering thought. But Choctaw decided he'd done enough sobering for now and took another drink. He said, "It's a hard thing — to be innocent, like you — to do what's right, like me — and still end up with the law after us."

Dec said, "My pa once told me something like . . . the law ain't made by God, it's made by man, and man's imperfect. And the people who administer the law, 'specially out here, are for sure imperfect."

"You can say that again."

"So we're the victims of blind justice, boy. Our kind are bound to bump heads with the sorry specimens that pass for lawmen out here."

"No, sir. This is as far as I'm going down that trail."

"Yeah?"

"Soon as I get over the New Mexico line, my criminal day's'll be over." That sentence proved to be another tongue twister.

The Irishman said, "We sure got the sorrows of the world hanging over our young and innocent heads."

"I reckon."

"Only one solution to that, I figure."

"There is?"

Dec lifted the bottle. "Get drunk!"

CHAPTER FORTY

Rosa said, "I like your blue eyes, *querido.*"

"I think you already told me that."

Choctaw gazed into the darkness behind his eyelids. Something tickled his cheek. When it happened a second time, he opened his eyes. The interior of the barn was black, becoming dark gray. Rosa's nose almost touched his. She stroked his face with a piece of straw. He smiled and brought his eyelids down.

She rested her head on his bare chest. For a little while that was all she did and he started to feel drowsy. Then she rolled away; he heard straw rustling.

He got more comfortable in the hay, which he and Rosa had stirred up considerably. He felt rested from sleep and sated from lovemaking. But now that he was awake, he acted out of the caution born out of his life on the frontier. He listened.

Outside, birds were tuning up their morning songs. Horses snuffled in the corral. First light, break-of-day noises. He tried to identify anything untoward, noises that might indicate, for example, Rufus Blackstone's posse lurking . . .

But he heard nothing more ominous than the trilling of a canyon wren.

A match struck, and then a little later another one. Reluctantly, he forced his eyes open. Rosa had lit a kerosene lamp, which stood on an upended bucket. She sat a few yards from him, her back to an empty stall. She'd pulled on a shirt but hadn't buttoned it up, so her breasts showed. She was lighting a cigarette.

He caught the smell of marijuana. She didn't smoke normally, just hemp on certain occasions, such as after sex.

He said, "Try not to burn down the damn barn."

He had a dim memory of entering this barn for the first time: he'd been fairly drunk and Rosa led him by the wrist, steering him inside. He seemed to have spent half his time the last few days in here with Rosa. The other half he'd passed in the main house getting drunk with Dec, with Luz joining in sometimes. Rosa didn't drink much, pouring her wild young energies into her other vices.

Rosa took a deep inhale, holding in for a long while. Exhaling, she asked, "What you thinking about, huh?" When he didn't reply, she said, "You thinking about Rosa and how good she fucks?"

"Could be."

"You think she's maybe the most beautiful whore in Arizona?"

"Is that how you think of yourself — as a whore?"

She shrugged. "Why not? That's what I am."

She passed him the cigarette. The last time he'd smoked this stuff had been the previous winter, holed up with some Apaches — friendlies scouting for the army. They'd been pursuing Yavapai or White Mountain Apache renegades through the Mazatzal Mountains, but torrential rain had forced them to shelter in a cave. Maybe he'd taken peyote about the same time — his memory was a little fuzzy.

Rosa asked, "You think I should be ashamed of what I am? A woman has to do what she has to do to survive."

"I ain't saying you have to be ashamed."

He passed the cigarette back.

Rosa asked, "Why is a woman always judged for fucking and not a man?"

"I ain't judging you. If there's anything I

315

hate, it's folks that are real quick to judge others, quick to condemn. Especially the ones call themselves Christians. Like my pa. They seem to forget that bit about 'Judge not and thou shalt not be judged.' Sanctimonious sons of bitches. I know people have to do what they have to do."

But his little speech was wasted on Rosa. She glared at him. "Bastard!"

"I just said I ain't judging you."

"Son of a bitch!"

He sighed in defeat, sat up, and reached for his pants. He seemed to annoy the women he came across real easy these days. Admittedly sometimes that was deliberate, but it was when he was trying to be nice to them, they seemed to get most riled. Maybe his taste just ran to scratchy females. On the other hand, the last two women he'd known — Rosa and Jade Rawlins — were probably two of the three most beautiful girls he'd ever been involved with. And the third was Jade's Apache twin, Nahlin.

He felt what he always did when he thought about Nahlin — unease, and a tinge of shame at how he'd driven her away. Why didn't he go look for her? It was more than two years.

His information was that Nahlin was living — if she *was* still living, which was always an uncertainty, given the precarious lives Apaches led — with the Nednis. Wildest of all the Apache bands, the Nednis camped far down in Mexico, in the high mountains of southern Sonora. Penetrating that almost unexplored wilderness would be plenty difficult, not to say dangerous. But it wasn't fear for his life that prevented him going after her. It was another kind of cowardice.

Rosa was still railing against him, although she'd used up her English cuss words and was now cursing him in Spanish. She paused in this tirade to ask, "Who are you to judge me?"

Buttoning his shirt, he said, "I ain't judging you."

"Given what *you* are."

"And what am I?"

She gave him a surprised, isn't it obvious look. *"Un ladrón."*

"No, I ain't!"

Rosa laughed derisively. "Sure!"

"Why'd you call me that?"

Instead of answering, she sneered her contempt, then returned to her cigarette.

Choctaw stood and pulled on his boots. Picking up his rifle, he crossed to the barn door. Rosa's words had puzzled him. More than that, they'd annoyed him, but not so much he forgot caution. Particularly now he was a wanted man. He stood back of the door as he eased it open and peeked between door and jamb.

He heard the canyon wren some more, then the thrumming of quail fluttering from the mesquite. And then a rumbling.

It sounded like a bunch of horses running towards him.

Maybe enough horses to mount Rufus Blackstone's posse.

His stomach tightened. Tension hummed through him. He eased the door open until he was peering through a slit three inches wide.

But he couldn't see much. The gut of the pass was black as coal, then, as he watched, its darkness became hazier and grayer. It changed again, becoming green, fading to pink as the new sun poked up over the mountains. Out of this pink light came movement. Six or seven horses galloping towards him, trailing roiling dust, then two more. These last two bore riders, dark man-shapes with what might be ropes in their hands. They herded the riderless horses up to the corral. A man dismounted, presumably to open the corral gate, their saddle band poured inside, and the man remounted. He and his companion rode over to the main house. Choctaw heard them call out as they approached the building. All the time darkness hid them, their faces and their clothing.

The barn was about the same distance from the main house and the corral. Choctaw walked over to the latter. By the time he got there, the new sun was shining gold, flushing the eastern sky, and light flooded the pass. He counted eleven horses in the corral, meaning seven newly arrived. As they milled about, he studied the brands they wore and frowned.

The front door opened in the main house and a man stood against the light. He called, and it was Dec. "Hey, Choc, come meet my friends."

Choctaw strode over. Dec entered the main building and Choctaw followed him indoors.

Two men in battered trail gear stood with their backs to him, talking to Luz. Something about them looked familiar. Cold unease touched his belly as he started to remember, and then both men turned towards him.

Choctaw halted and stared. The newcomers stared too. One smiled, showing a gap in his front upper teeth. He said, "Looky here. Ain't this a surprise?"

His companion nodded. "It sure is."
Choctaw was surprised too.
He was looking at Asa and Ira Gird.

CHAPTER FORTY-ONE

The twins seemed to be dressed the same as when he'd last seen them. Only everything was dustier and dirtier. Their faces were dark with trail beards and drawn with tiredness.

But as they stared at him their eyes became alert, their hands edging close to their guns. Ira had a long-barreled pistol hooked through his belt, while Asa carried his in a cross-draw holster on his left hip.

Choctaw's hand tightened on the rifle he held in his right hand, muzzle pointing at the earth.

Luz must have noticed all this. Her eyes widened in alarm and she took a step back.

Dec asked, "You know each other?"

Ira rested a finger on his eye patch, adjusting it slightly. "We met up at the Crazy R."

Asa joined in. "This feller was nursemaiding Jade Rawlins."

"Huh?"

"Zack Rawlins's daughter."

Ira moved his finger across his face, from the right eye patch to a red wheal lying over his left cheekbone. He spoke with hatred. "That bitch almost took my good eye."

Asa showed his gap-toothed grin again. He told Choctaw, "As I recollect, you're the *hombre* I was giving a good licking to when we was interrupted."

"I'm also the feller saved you two from getting lynched."

The Girds thought about that. Asa said, "I guess we should be grateful, brother."

Ira smiled. "Yeah. We surely are." The twins managed to sneer simultaneously.

With his eyes still on Choctaw, on the rifle in his hand, Asa asked Dec, "How'd you know him, Red?"

"We're friends."

"Huh?"

"That's right, boys. Just like you and me are friends. We got a house full of friends. So I expect everybody to get along real nice." There was a little pause, then the Irishman went on, "I'd ask you to remember that." He gazed at each man, saving his hardest look for Choctaw. "All of you."

Ira replied first. "Sure, Dec. Any friend of yours . . ."

Then Asa. "Sure. This man saved our

lives. So we can put away any differences."

Choctaw remembered before, one or both of the twins showing they could speak good English if needed. Maybe they'd started educated, raised properly, before falling low.

Asa glanced at Choctaw. "That all right with you, boy?"

Choctaw considered his response. He'd just settled on "Go fuck yourself" when Dec spoke for him. "It's all right with him."

Choctaw started to protest, then thought about it.

Ira scratched his trail beard. " 'Sides we ain't gonna be here long. We'll rest up today and head out tomorrow. So we got no time for quarrelling."

Dec asked, "How come? You only just got here."

"I know, but we got word there's stage going through Zuni Pass day after tomorrow. Carrying a real sweet strongbox. A nice little Christmas present. We figured to help ourselves to that, then hole up for the winter."

"Yeah?"

Ira gazed at Choctaw and smiled. "So no need for anybody to butt heads."

Choctaw decided the twins pretend friendliness was worse than their undiluted hatred. But before he could make anything of it,

Luz asked the Girds, "You *hombres* want to eat?"

Ira said, "All right. I vote we have breakfast and then get some sleep." He seemed to be the leader, the main decision maker of the brothers.

Asa said, "Suits me."

Dec said, "I'll leave you to it." He picked up a bottle and two tooth glasses from the table and stepped towards the door. At the threshold he paused. "You coming, Choctaw?"

Ira lifted his eyebrows slightly. "Choctaw? You ain't the feller involved in that shooting at Lobo Wells?"

Asa joined in. "Killed three men I hear. 'The Choctaw Kid.' The half-breed pistoleer."

There was that look again on the Girds' faces, this time — admiration.

Choctaw scowled. "I only killed one man. And I ain't no half-breed."

Dec asked, "You coming, *amigo*?"

Choctaw stepped towards the Irishman. He walked towards the door, trying not to show the twins his back as he did so, keeping his eye on their guns and how near their hands were to them. The Girds saw that and smiled.

He followed Dec outside. There was a

long plank table set up out front of the building, with a bench on either side. The Irishman sat on the farthest-away bench. He poured into the two glasses. He drank slowly, not looking at the other man.

There was still a chill in the air, easing as early sunlight strengthened. The horses stamped their feet and made restive noises in the corral, while birds cleared their throats with their first songs of the new day.

Dec indicated the glass on the table, smiling a little. "Drink, *compadre.*"

Choctaw leaned his rifle up against the wall. "The horses your . . . 'friends' brought in are wearing at least three different brands."

"So?"

"Those fellers ain't horse traders. They're horse thieves." Choctaw moved over to the table, but didn't sit. He stood, glaring at the other man. "Is that what you are?"

Dec looked at the glass in his hand, the table, the corral, the walls of the pass, and back at the table. At last, he spoke. "Yes."

"Huh?"

"That's what I am, Goddamn it!"

CHAPTER FORTY-TWO

Choctaw sat on the bench. He picked up the glass on the table, studied the liquor in it, and set it down. "When Blackstone caught you, you wasn't no innocent by-stander, was you? They caught the right *hombre*. Or one of 'em."

He glanced at Dec but the other man wouldn't meet his eye. Choctaw went on, "And the trading you was doing with the Bakers — I guess you knew it was stolen horseflesh. Didn't you?"

After a moment, Dec looked up. He managed a tired smile. "Sure." He turned the glass in his hand. "And I didn't get laid off by MacNee. He caught me and the Girds cold-branding. You know what that is?"

"Uh-huh. Just another way of stealing cattle. And that poker game in Wickenburg, when that fellow called you out for cheating . . ."

The Irishman shrugged. "You sided with

the wrong feller there. Truth is, I'm a real bad man, boy. I'm a horse thief, cow thief, smuggler, card sharp. I've robbed stages, banks, stores. I got my face on wanted posters in Texas, New Mexico, Utah, and Nevada. And Arizona too, since the Crossing."

"You wanted for a killing?"

"No. But I'll say this. It ain't 'cuz I wasn't prepared to. I shot at plenty, just never killed nobody."

"So you were lying all the time . . . You must have thought I was the greenest rube alive."

Dec sneered. "I sure did. I couldn't believe how slow you were catching on. It was right before your eyes and you couldn't see it."

Choctaw stood. He walked off a few paces, then paused. He gazed into the distance, at mountains growing red as the sun climbed, not really seeing them. In his mouth he tasted betrayal, a friendship that was maybe never real, with one half of the friendship secretly laughing at the other all the while. He reckoned cold snake must taste like that.

He said, "I ain't completely stupid. I got suspicious at times . . . like when you was talking about how easy it was to change the brands on those MacNee horses. And just now Rosa laughed at me and called me a *ladrón.* A thief. But I still wouldn't listen. It was like I didn't *want* to see it."

"Why not?"

Choctaw glanced at the other man. "Because you're my friend."

For an instant pain showed in Dec's face. His mouth tightened, and then the sneer returned. "There are no friends, boy. Surviving in this world — that's all that counts."

"Is it?"

"So many questions!"

Choctaw stood over the table and lifted his glass. He drank. The fire of the liquor mixed with the bitterness in his mouth. "Just one more."

"Yeah?"

"Why?"

Dec laid both hands on the table before him and studied them.

Choctaw felt a sneer of his own form on his lips. "You learn all that from your pa?"

He reached for the bottle and something struck him hard across the mouth. He staggered, lost balance, and fell. The earth slammed into the middle of his back and air grunted out of him.

The Irishman stood over him. Dec's right arm was raised, and there was blood on his knuckles and the back of his wrist. His face filled with color, was almost as red as his hair. He pointed at the man on the ground. "You can call me anything you like. You can call me a thief, a liar —" He paused, breathing hard through his nostrils. "But don't never bad-mouth my father!"

Choctaw pushed himself up on one elbow. His lips were torn, stinging, and he tasted blood, while a trickle of it ran down his chin.

Dec was poised, ready to pitch himself down on the other man. Right then, Choctaw decided he hated Dec. He hated the man for playing him for a fool, for using their friendship to his own advantage, sneering at his gullibility and trust. He found himself thinking, for the first time when it came to Dec, about guns. About the pistol holstered on the Irishman's right hip. About his own rifle, leaned up against the wall.

Dec breathed hard some more. But then he settled back on his heels, and Choctaw felt his own tension ease.

Dec said, "My pa was the straightest man I ever knew. If he found a dime on the street, he'd hand it in to the church poor box. He was as honest as the day is long." He laughed harshly. "A lot of good it did him."

The Irishman sat. He took his time filling his glass. Slowly his angry color faded. "He tried farming, horse ranching . . . never got one dollar ahead. He was poor in Nueces County and poor when we moved up to Milam."

Slowly, Choctaw got to his feet. He dabbed at his bloody lips with the ends of his bandanna.

Dec inspected the skinned knuckles of his right hand. "We had a little horse ranch. Pa, me, my brother, a year older than me. And yes, it was an honest business!

"One day, when I was away, three fellers rode by our place. Rough-looking customers on hard-run horses. My daddy figured they was on the dodge.

"They traded their horses for the three we had in the corral. By 'traded' I mean they did it with their hands on their guns. In other words, trade or get a bullet.

"What could my pa do? He hardly ever even carried a gun."

Dec glanced up at the other man. "You don't believe me, do you?"

"Why should I believe one word you say? Everything else was lies."

"Not everything."

"No?"

The Irishman glared. "Believe what you like!"

Choctaw sat and poured himself a drink. Neither man spoke for a minute, then Dec said, "Anyway, them bad *hombres* was barely out of sight when a posse showed up. Turned out those three horses was stole. My daddy hardly had a chance to speak before him and my brother was carted off to jail."

"They get a trial?"

"Trial?" Dec snorted in derision. "That country was as sick with 'hanging fever' as they are around here. 'Sides, nobody would have believed us. We was strangers, newcomers. Poor, shantytown Irish. I got word about it and got to town, but I was too late." He paused, then said, "A mob had already busted my pa and brother out of the jail. Dragged them off into the woods. By the time I reached them, they was . . ."

Dec lifted his glass to his lips. But, instead of drinking, he placed the glass back on the table. He said, "My daddy and brother was both swinging from an alamo tree."

Choctaw couldn't seem to get a glass to his lips either. Both men sat in silence, staring ahead, until Dec said, "The fellers done it was having a party, laughing and passing a jug around in the moonlight. They were still wearing their masks and gunnysacks over their heads like the cowards they were. I watched from cover. I was gonna start firing on them bastards, cut down as many as

I could before they got to me, but . . ."

His voice caught and became small as he said, "I didn't."

Dec rose and walked off a few paces. He stood with his back to the other man. "Then the main feller there, maybe even the one whipped my daddy's horse out from under him, pulled off his mask and guess what? It was the sheriff, the local law.

"I was seventeen and that's the day I turned outlaw. When I saw what the law really was. That's my 'why'!"

Choctaw lifted his glass, and this time he managed to drink. "So what happened to your pa and your brother nearly happened to you at the Crossing."

"Yeah."

" 'Cept they were innocent and you were guilty." Choctaw rubbed his thumb along the side of the tooth glass. "When you hang, you'll deserve it."

"That's for the Almighty to decide, ain't it? Besides, I ain't gonna hang. Watching my daddy kick, strangle slow . . . and nothing I could do about it . . . I made a promise to myself then and there that nobody'd string me up. If it come to it, I'd shoot myself first. Better a bullet than a rope!"

The Irishman returned to the table. "You've never seen a lynching . . ."

"I have now."

"Then you know."

Choctaw recalled the fat man turning on the rope, the purple-black face, the stream of piss. "Yeah."

"Still want to judge me?"

Neither spoke for a while, until Choctaw said, "Well, I reckon this is where we part company."

Dec gave him a look with some pain in it. "Where you gonna head? New Mexico?"

"Probably."

Choctaw touched his bloody lips and hissed. With one finger he probed inside his mouth.

A slight smile quirked at Dec's lips. "Still got all your teeth?"

"A few are kind of wobbly." Choctaw half-smiled too.

The Irishman poured himself another shot. "What you say, *compadre*? Shall we get drunk one last time?"

They were in the same place at sundown, at the outside table. They were still drinking. Drinking and talking about old times. Laughing plenty. Dec paused in laughing to pour for both of them.

The Irishman said, "There is something else you could do, you know, Choc. Rather than taking off for parts unknown."

Thick-tongued, Choctaw asked, "What's that?"

"You could throw in with me. I got a real easy little job lined up."

Choctaw glared at the other man.

Dec raised his hands in a gesture of surrender. "I know. That'd make you a real criminal, not an accidental one. But I'm talking about you joining up with me, not the Girds. I wouldn't expect you to hook up with the likes of them."

Choctaw drank.

Dec said, "It ain't a bad life. I ain't talking about murdering anybody. Nobody needs to get hurt." He started to shape a cigarette. "Sure, there's right and wrong. I was brought up like you to do what's right. And I'd've stuck to that if the world was a fair place. But it ain't. It's unfair and corrupt. Ain't it? My pa and brother was innocent, and look what happened to them. You rescued me from getting lynched and now you're wanted. You loved a girl and because she was an Indian you had to kill a man. You ended up in jail, run out of town. Swenson wouldn't hire you because you're — what did he call you? An Indian lover?"

Choctaw tried to remember. That took effort, considering how hard he found it to even sit upright on this bench. He scowled and said, " 'There's no place in my outfit for an Apache lover.' "

"That's what you're going to get all the time. Think they'll ever accept you? You fight wild Indians to make the country safe for those bastards, you risk your scalp, and what's your reward? To be an outsider."

Later — maybe a good while later, maybe while they sat at the table or were someplace else — Choctaw heard the Irishman say, "Face it, *amigo*. They'll never let you fit in. I told you, you're like me. A misfit."

"Uh?"

"Cimarrón."

"You're the *cimarrón*. Me . . ." Choctaw stared owlishly at the glass in his hand. "I'm a terrible man. That's what I am."

"You play by their rules, you'll always be left outside. Well, I say — fuck their rules! Rules they make to suit themselves and keep the rest of us down. Fuck any law when it comes out like those fellows in Lobo Wells, or Wickenburg."

"Or Blackstone."

"Yeah. Like that son of a bitch." Dec poured for both of them. "So . . . this job I got lined up . . . you in?"

Neither spoke for a while, then Choctaw asked, "Easy, you say?"

335

"Easy, safe, nobody gets hurt."

Choctaw didn't answer. Speaking was becoming hard work. Even getting his drink to his lips without spilling it.

Dec said, "Think on it."

Their "last" drinking session went on into the night. And into the next one. Maybe into the one after that, Choctaw wasn't sure. All he remembered were long stretches of partying and drinking with Dec and the women, interrupted with bouts of lovemaking with Rosa. And maybe not just her. At one point he awoke to find himself lying on the floor, or maybe in bed, tangled up in Luz, although he had no clear memory of the experience. Whatever, Dec didn't say anything, so maybe he didn't mind sharing his woman.

Somewhere in there, Dec asked him once again to throw in with him. On the easy little job.

And, this time, Choctaw said yes.

CHAPTER FORTY-THREE

Choctaw woke in the bed he normally shared with Rosa. But he was alone.

It was 4 p.m.

For the first time in he didn't know how long, Choctaw awoke without a hangover. The ills of drunkenness — sore head, muzziness, bloated tongue, a mouth tasting of sawdust — were gone, slept out.

He dressed and went into the living room. He had to step over the many dead soldiers littering the floor. The ranch had obviously been well stocked with booze, but surely they'd drunk most or all of it by now.

Choctaw saw the door of Dec's bedroom was slightly ajar. Through the crack between door and jamb, he glimpsed Dec in bed with Luz, both of them asleep and mostly covered by blankets. Luz rested her head on Dec's bare chest; his mouth was open and he snored. Choctaw was impressed she could sleep so close to such a terrible, teeth-rattling racket. Then again, she was used to it.

Choctaw closed Dec's bedroom door, went to the door of the main room, and gazed out. He looked for any dust, which might indicate the Gird brothers returning. They were due back any time. It might also indicate a posse.

For wanted desperados, he and Dec had been damn careless in their time here, mostly too busy with drink and women to keep any kind of watch. A passel of school-kids could have sneaked up and captured them, let alone a fierce enemy like Rufus Blackstone.

In losing his hangover, Choctaw had regained some appetite. He scraped together a tortilla of various ingredients, washing it down with black coffee. Neither Dec nor Luz stirred out of their back room. Rosa didn't appear either and Choctaw went looking for her.

Her horse was gone from the corral. Choctaw wondered about that while he saw to his own mount. The animals had been neglected while their owners were busy getting drunk and fucking the Mexican women. Choctaw gave his horse a generous portion of hay and plenty of water. He also talked to it gently and petted it.

He thought about Dec. Friendship, he thought, was a damn strange thing. Sometimes it seemed to bring as much pain as pleasure, as much confusion as certainty. And how much of it had been real, as far as Dec was concerned? And how much was lies, like those the Irish-Texan told so easily?

There'd been too much laughter in there. Too much fun. It couldn't all have been lies, could it?

Abruptly Choctaw remembered his promise to Dec. To throw in with him on the easy job he had lined up. To willingly become what accident and circumstances had forced him to be: an outlaw.

Here his road forked. He could keep his word to Dec and go one way, or back out and go another. Turn off this trail before it was too late. Before it led to . . . Choctaw tried to remember what Rawlins had warned him of, at Red Mesa.

At least riding the high lines promised some excitement. Even if it was on the wrong side of the tracks.

But what was right and wrong? The Aravaipas at Camp Walsh had been innocent, trying only to live in peace, and were murdered, more than a hundred old men, women, and children. When the Anglos and

Mexicans who slaughtered them were brought to trial they'd been acquitted, by a jury that deliberated less than twenty minutes. The men who'd killed Alope and others had been celebrated in Tucson as heroes. How was that right?

He heard voices: Swenson, *There's no place in my outfit for an Apache lover,* and then Billy Keogh, *Folks in Tucson ain't gonna hang a man for killing an Indian-lover . . . a squaw-humping Apache lover like you.*

Aloud, Choctaw said, "Sons of bitches."

Anger warmed in him. If that was right, to hell with it, he'd rather be wrong. He'd rather be on Dec's side than theirs. Standing next to the Irishman, a gun in his hand, a gunnysack over his head, on Dec's easy little job . . . To himself he said, "I'm in."

Choctaw noticed the buckskins ears were pricked, slanting forward, towards the east. Choctaw looked that way also.

There was a riffle of dust on the desert floor.

It could be the Girds. If it was a posse, it was a damn small one, three or four riders.

Nonetheless, Choctaw felt unease. He slid his Winchester out of the saddle scabbard and led his horse around behind the barn. He used his bandanna to bind the buckskin's nose and mouth. His rifle hanging in one hand, he peeked around the corner of the barn at these newcomers.

Three horsebackers. Shadows were lengthening towards the walls of the pass, and the light weakened as the sun fell westward, so Choctaw couldn't make out much about them. But one of them appeared to be leading a mule on a trailing line. Then they reached the most distant of the outbuildings — a shack used as a store or tack shed — maybe a hundred yards off, and reined in, and Choctaw could see them clearly.

The Girds. One of them led the mule, which carried packsaddles. The other twin also held a trailing line, which ran back to the third horse and rider.

Seeing this rider, Choctaw felt his jaw drop. He was surprised it didn't thump to the earth, so great was his astonishment. His belly felt like it had fallen out too. He knew he was gaping like a damn fool. Just like he had the other day, at first sight of the Girds. But this surprise even beat that one.

Because the third rider was the last person he expected to see. She was hunched forward in the saddle, and it looked like her hands were bound to the apple. She was gagged and she stared out of wild eyes while the wind whipped her long, dark brown hair across her face.

"God almighty," he said. "Jade Rawlins."

CHAPTER FORTY-FOUR

Choctaw watched the twins and Jade Rawlins enter the shack. The brothers emerged, mounted their horses, and rode over to the main house.

He stood, wondering what to do. But his thinking, angrily demanding answers, took him nowhere. He strode over to the main house.

Entering, he saw the men sitting at the long table, Dec facing the Girds. Luz was at the stove, busy with pots and pans. He smelled bacon frying.

As was now his habit when it came to the twins, he looked for their guns. But their gun belts and holstered pistols were piled up on the small table a dozen yards from where they sat, their rifles leaning against the wall.

He asked the Girds, "What's this? How come you got that woman with you?"

Ira gave him a look of distaste. "You seen

343

her, huh? You got sharp eyes, boy."

"Well?"

"When we stopped that stage for that strongbox, guess who else was aboard? Off to spend Christmas with her aunt in Santa Fe."

"Kind of a coincidence, ain't it? Sure you didn't know she was traveling on that stage?"

Asa smirked. "Maybe we did."

Ira had an airtight of tomatoes open before him. He fished one out with his knife, eating it cold off the blade. "So we got the strongbox *and* her."

"Didn't she have no escort?"

"Sure. Two Crazy R hands and an old Mex woman."

"And them fellers just let you take her?"

The twins looked uncomfortable and avoided anybody else's eye. Neither answered; Ira sucked on the tomato while Asa chewed on a thumbnail.

Dec made an impatient sound. "Well, did they or didn't they?"

At last Asa spoke. "One of 'em made a fight of it and got left."

Choctaw felt alarm. "You mean you killed him?"

When there was no reply, his alarm became dread. He'd liked a fair few of the men who worked for the Crazy R. He asked, "Who was it?"

"I think they called him Brazos."

"Jesus Christ!"

Dec glowered. "I said no killing, boys."

Asa lifted his voice in protest. "What else could we do? We had him covered but the crazy son of a bitch still come at us. He gave us no choice."

Choctaw said, "So we're in it for murder now! And kidnapping a woman, by God!" For a moment he was too full of anger, or something like it, to speak. When that eased, he said, "You know how folks are about anything done to women. *White* women anyway. Right now, there'll be posses all over Arizona getting up to come after you."

The one-eyed man sneered. "Don't you mean 'after *us*'?"

From where she stood by the stove, Luz said, "He's right — bad, stealing a woman."

Ira scowled. "Who asked your opinion?"

Man and woman glared at each other in hatred. Luz muttered one word under her breath. Choctaw still heard, it was a Spanish word, and a pretty dirty one.

Asa asked, "What you say, bitch?"

Dec raised his voice slightly. "Hey!"

The twins switched their hard, angry looks from the woman to the Irishman. He

345

seemed about to smile slightly, then didn't.

Luz appeared behind the twins and gave both the same venomous look. She banged plates of food down on the table before them. She glared down, as if she was about to spit into each of the meals she'd served up. Then she went into her bedroom.

Choctaw addressed the twins. "Taking Zack Rawlins's daughter? You crazy?"

Asa gave his smirk another airing. "Yeah, like a fox."

"You sure you want Rawlins on your trail? I seen him hunt men before. He won't quit till he has your ears!"

"You make him sound right fearsome."

"That's because he is, you damn fool!"

Asa's smirk vanished; he got back to glaring. "Don't talk to me like that, kid." He glanced over at the table, at his gun belt, and Choctaw, already plenty tense, got more so.

He said, "You ought to know how fierce he is. You nearly got your necks stretched last time you was on the Crazy R."

Ira said, "We ain't forgot what we owe that old bastard. And his high-and-mighty daughter." He scowled and touched the quirt mark on his cheek.

"Then you know what to expect."

"Let me tell you what I know about Rawlins. For one thing, he's plenty rich. For another, he sure dotes on Miss Jade."

Asa said, "Yeah, that's kind of his blind spot. He won't see her for what she is."

"And what's that?"

"Nothing more than a whore. Sashaying 'round that ranch, shaking her tail in everybody's faces. I reckon half the hands there put their brand on her."

There was a coffeepot on the table. Asa poured himself a cup. "Maybe you too, huh? Maybe that's why you're so hot under the collar." He showed his gap-toothed grin.

Choctaw wasn't going to rise to that bait.

Ira said, "So he's gonna pay plenty to get her back."

Dec asked, "How much?"

"We left a note for her daddy. We asked for ten thousand dollars."

"Jesus Christ!"

"Lot of sugar. Even split three ways." Asa turned his grin in Choctaw's direction. "Sorry, boy. You ain't included in the deal."

"I don't want to be. I ain't in the business of kidnapping women."

A little silence descended. The twins started on their food. Then Choctaw asked nobody in particular, "How do you know Rawlins has that kind of money? Lot of ranchers, their wealth's on the hoof, in cattle and land. Not cash."

Ira answered, chewing bacon. "If he ain't got it, he can raise it. Even if he has to put his ranch up for sale. Anything for his precious Jade."

"Let's say you're right. Rawlins pays to get her back — and once he's got her, he'll pay out some more. For a bounty on your heads. He'll stir up the biggest manhunt this territory's ever seen. There won't be no place you can hide."

"It gets too hot 'round here, we'll head for Mexico."

"You think a little thing like a border will stop Rawlins? He'd chase you all the way to South America."

Ira smiled. "Well, maybe we'll head down there. Always fancied looking around them countries."

There was another pause, which Choctaw broke again. "Dec, can I talk to you? Private?"

"Sure."

The twins glanced at each other and smirked. It was a look Choctaw particularly disliked, but there wasn't much about either man that didn't rub him the wrong way.

Choctaw and Dec entered the room Choctaw shared with Rosa.

Closing the door, Choctaw said, "Dec, for

Christ's sake! You're tied in with murder now."

The Irishman's face became gloomy. "Sure."

"And kidnapping a woman! Surely kidnapping somebody's daughter ain't your style?"

"I know, but . . ." Dec gazed at the back of his hands. "I'm tired, *amigo.* Tired of being poor and hungry, living hand to mouth. And I ain't never been close to that much money before. Ten thousand dollars."

"Split three ways."

"Maybe."

The Irishman's face changed, taking on an expression Choctaw had never seen before. A look of cold and utter ruthlessness. As if he wasn't contemplating sharing the ten thousand dollars with the twins, or anybody . . . His face had no trace of the old warmth or humor, no softness at all. Choctaw wondered if he was seeing the real Declan Flynn for the first time. Inexplicably, he felt a touch of fear.

Dec said, "With that kind of money, I can quit all this. Live clean the rest of my life, some place far away."

"Live clean on money from a dirty business."

"It's a dirty world, *compadre.* I'll make

sure nothing happens to the girl, don't worry."

"I dunno. The way Ira talks about her . . . it ain't just the money with him. I figure he purely hates her. He's set on hurting her, whatever."

Dec's face became a ruthless mask once more. "If it comes to it, I'll take care of those two no-accounts. I'll see she gets back to her daddy safe."

There was a pause and then Dec said, "Well, I guess that's it."

He stepped towards the door. As he opened it Choctaw heard Ira say, "Wonder what's keeping the lovers."

Asa sniggered.

Choctaw felt a quick stab of anger. As he followed Dec into the main room, he kept to his rule about the Girds and their weapons. He figured the twins would have strapped on their gun belts, but to his surprise they still seemed to be unarmed.

Ira asked Dec, "Well — you in?"

"Sure."

Choctaw glanced at his friend. "Dec —"

Dec managed a small, tired smile. "You ain't gonna persuade me, boy. Ten thousand dollars buys off a lot of conscience."

Asa said, "That's settled then."

Ira said, "Almost settled, Asa. Still leaves

us with one conundrum." He gazed at Choctaw. "You don't seem so keen on our little enterprise."

Choctaw began to answer but Dec cut in first. "Don't matter if he is or not. He's just leaving."

A slight wildness came to Asa's eyes. "We let him ride out of here . . . How do we know he ain't gonna sic the law on us?"

Dec spoke to Choctaw. "You wouldn't do that, would you?"

"No."

Ira picked a sliver of meat from between his teeth. He asked Dec, "You believe him?"

"I believe him."

There was a little silence when Asa glanced over at Ira, for orders maybe. Ira did a little more tooth picking. "Well, he *is* your friend."

Dec told Choctaw, "You'd better get your things."

Choctaw went into his bedroom. Some of his saddlebags were lying on a chair. He filled the bags with his extra clothing and few possessions, draped this bundle over his shoulder, then returned to the main room. The twins were still unarmed; they didn't seem to have moved. Dec asked, "You got everything?"

Choctaw nodded slightly. The Irishman

went to the door and stepped outside.

Choctaw followed. He eased sidelong, not showing the Girds his back, keeping his eyes on them, most particularly on Asa. When he stepped into the doorway, he was still watching this man.

Which was a mistake.

Because it was Ira who moved.

CHAPTER FORTY-FIVE

In the tail of his eye Choctaw caught a flash of metal.

A knife had come from somewhere into Ira's right hand. He lunged at Choctaw's back.

Choctaw spun to his left and the blade thrust past his right hip, missing by inches. He grabbed the saddlebags over his shoulder and swung them.

The leather bundles smacked Ira hard across the face. He grunted and spun away, sprawling on his back across the long table.

He still held the knife.

Choctaw dropped the bags and grabbed both of Ira's wrists. He pivoted forward over Ira, his forearm barred across his opponent's chest, using his weight to keep the other man pinned down. The twin squirmed, trying to rise; his face reddened with effort.

Choctaw banged Ira's right wrist down on the edge of the table. Ira gasped and his fingers sprang open, the knife falling.

Choctaw lifted his eyes and saw Asa standing, staring at both combatants. He also noticed something he should have spotted before: a bulge under Asa's shirt, round about his belly button. Asa reached inside his shirt for this bulge and produced a handgun. He started to aim.

Dec said, "Hold it, Asa!"

Asa froze, staring. Choctaw glanced back and saw the Irishman in the doorway, his pistol in his hand.

Ira bucked off the table, jabbing his knee at Choctaw's groin. They swayed together, almost face to face. Choctaw let go of Ira's left wrist and jerked back. He swung a right hook to the point of Ira's chin. He put all his weight and strength behind it.

Ira's feet left the earth. He went back on to the table, his legs lifted and kicked at the air, then he somersaulted backwards, fetching up on all fours beyond the table. He lifted his head and stared at the world out of unfocused eyes.

By which time Choctaw had drawn his Starr double action. It hurt holding the gun, because his right hand ached from maybe the best punch he'd ever landed. His knuckles were bloody.

The twins were being covered by three

pistols: Dec covering Asa, Choctaw covering Ira, and Luz, at the door of her bedroom, aiming a Colt Navy at both brothers.

Asa stood braced like he was ready to charge, his eyes crazier than ever and fixed on Choctaw. "Let me take him, Ira."

Choctaw waited for that, but Ira shook his head slightly. His voice was muffled when he said, "Leave it."

He got unsteadily to his feet, one hand to his jaw.

Dec spoke in an easy voice. "Choctaw's gonna take his leave now. I suggest you Girds stay in the house till he's gone. Anybody pokes his nose outdoors is likely to get it shot off."

Ira scowled. "Don't push me, Flynn!"

"I ain't gonna push you, Ira." The Irishman smiled a little. "Not unless I have to." He addressed Choctaw. "You go ahead, *amigo.*"

Both men left the house and walked over to Choctaw's horse. Dec leaned on a hitching rail, watching his friend preparing to ride. He also watched the doorway of the main house, in case the twins decided to ignore his advice.

When he was ready to mount up, Choctaw said, "Say goodbye to Luz for me."

"Sure."

"And Rosa — wherever she is."

"She's ridden off somewhere. To spend Christmas with relatives, maybe. Who knows?"

"Looks like you saved me again, huh? With Asa. *Gracias, compadre.*"

"*De nada.*"

Choctaw flexed the fingers of his right hand, which ached like hell. That was some punch he'd landed! "The twins — you gonna be able to handle those two?"

"They need me. I'm the only one can think."

"I'd rather trust a pair of rattlesnakes."

"That's why I don't. Trust 'em."

"Another thing: You want to get out of this pass *pronto.* This is a bad place. All it needs is a posse at both ends and you'd be trapped in here."

Dec frowned. After a moment he said, "I'll be all right."

Choctaw nodded, although he was plenty doubtful. He tried to keep that from showing in his face as he swung up into the saddle.

The Irishman patted the buckskin on the side of its neck. "You watch out for yourself too. Once you get out of this pass, keep going."

"Sure."

"And one thing most especially."

"What's that?"

"Don't come back."

Dec's voice was cold. Choctaw glanced at him and he was looking into the hard face of the new Declan Flynn, the man he'd only seen for the first time today.

Choctaw smiled, although he knew it was a weak, forced effort. *"Adiós, amigo."*

For once Dec didn't smile in return. *"Adiós."*

Choctaw kicked his horse in the flanks. He rode away from Irishman's Wells, pointing east.

He rode for maybe a mile and then reined in. He sat his horse, listening for the sound of a rider or riders following him. Like maybe the Girds, looking to bushwhack him someplace.

He heard nothing.

Choctaw rode on. After another couple miles he came to the end of the pass. Here he reined in once more.

Free of the pass, of what might be a trap, he gave a deep sigh of relief. He gazed ahead. It was maybe thirty miles to New Mexico. Once he was across the territorial line it would be goodbye to the outlaw life, to Declan Flynn . . . providing he followed

Dec's advice.

Don't come back.

That would be the safest, most sensible thing to do, especially as posses would be swarming all over this neighborhood pretty soon. It would be the easiest way to keep his neck out of a noose, or to stay out of the path of a bullet. After all he didn't owe Jade Rawlins anything.

Of course, he had a pretty solid record when it came to choosing between doing the sensible or the crazy thing. Choctaw smiled bitterly to himself. Then he turned his horse and rode back into the pass.

CHAPTER FORTY-SIX

A quarter moon rode the night sky. By its spectral half-light, Choctaw could see the squat black shape of the tack shed, where they had Jade Rawlins. He was about thirty yards from the shed, hunkered down behind the only thing providing cover — a bone-dry horse trough. His rifle was in his hand, and his pistol belted on.

He'd been waiting here for a while — maybe only ten minutes, but it felt considerably longer. Listening for any out-of-place noise — something spooking the animals in the corral, riders approaching, a stirring in the main house, or any indication there was a guard outside the shack. Hearing only an icy pool of silence, save the odd horse noise.

He judged it was about an hour to dawn. Which meant now was the time to act. He'd already sneaked a horse out of the corral and saddled it, leaving it tethered nearby. Next, he had to enter the shack, get Jade free — he was a little hazy on how he might accomplish that — and get out of here.

A helpful rag of cloud appeared, settling over the moon's face.

For all that, fear was damp on the palms of his hands, in his cold belly and the tightness in his throat. He swallowed a rock-sized chunk of it and started forward.

He moved as quietly as Apaches had taught him, but his movements still seemed to fill the night with noise. As he neared the tack shed, he saw another building shaping out of the gloom to the left. This was a shed so small and narrow it was only used as an outhouse.

Choctaw paused, listening again. Mostly all he heard was his own breathing. He studied the darkness to the east. Was the absolute blackness there paling a fraction, as the first traces of false dawn showed?

His friend the cloud still wreathed the moon, leaving it dark enough to get the job done. He eased past the outhouse and towards the tack shed door.

He kicked something. It was metal and it rang. And then it hit something else that was also metal and also rang. He seemed to start off a whole orchestra of clanging and ringing instruments, loud enough to be heard in New Mexico. They pealed like church bells celebrating a victory. Or, in this case, his defeat.

He became aware that the earth before him was quilted with small patches of darkness. Then the cloud shifted and moonlight glinted and shone on what they were.

They were empty tin cans, mixed in with old bottles, strewn all over the ground before the tack shed.

Choctaw stepped back in alarm. His right foot came down on a bottle that rolled under him. He overbalanced, toppling backwards. He landed on his rump with enough force to jar his teeth; his hand came down on an opened tin and the jagged edge of the lid gashed the palm of his hand. He swore.

So did someone else. Behind him.

Glancing back over his left shoulder, Choctaw saw movement, a darkness bulging out of the outhouse. This darkness divided and became the shapes of two men. The light of the unclouded moon gleamed on metal: the guns they held, one a rifle, one a pistol, both trained on him.

The pistol-holding shape spoke in the voice of Dec. In weary resignation, the Irishman said, "I knew you'd come back."

The other faceless shape gestured with his rifle. "Lose your guns." Ira Gird.

Choctaw thought about how easily he'd been taken and his face warmed with embarrassment. But he obeyed, standing when ordered to do so.

He took one step forward, to get free of this treacherous stretch of earth. Ira leveled his rifle and said, "That's close enough."

Choctaw halted. But his captors kept moving, coming up on each side of him, moonlight catching their faces. Dec smiled bitterly and shook his head. "*Amigo,* I *told* you not to come back."

Choctaw said, "I was trying to stop you from getting —"

He was about to say, "Hung for a kidnapping." But he never spoke. Ira made a sound of anger and swung his rifle butt.

Choctaw started to dodge, too slow; the butt caught him alongside the right temple. There was a flash of pain and bright color.

And then he was falling.

Voices speaking, very far away. He listened and they grew louder.

Around him was a gray darkness he couldn't see into. Of all his senses, only his hearing seemed to be working. After some time, he decided he was listening to Dec and Ira. It sounded like they were arguing, but it was a while before he heard distinct words, Ira saying, "We might as well kill him now."

And then Dec replying. "No."

"Why not? He won't quit trying to get the woman loose. We're gonna have to kill him anyway."

"If that has to be done, I'll be the one to do it."

"Will you?"

"I said I will and I will. Now —"

Then the words faded out, or maybe they stopped talking. Choctaw felt hands under his armpits and the sensation of being lifted.

He rose through grayness, and it changed and darkened, becoming a night sky. From the look of it, still the gloom of false dawn, so maybe he hadn't been unconscious long. Maybe only a few minutes.

As his sight returned, so did other senses. His skull seemed to have a crack in it as deep as the Colorado River Canyon, at the base of which was a dagger point skewering his brain, sending waves of pain through his head, forcing him to screw his eyes shut.

He swayed and rocked in the arms of those carrying him, the jogging causing the dagger point to drill deeper. Then Ira said, "Old friend of yours."

Jade Rawlins asked, "Have you killed him?"

Reluctantly Choctaw forced his eyes open, although that brought more hurt. He was in a small dark place, the gloom only lit by a kerosene lamp. Jade Rawlins lay in one corner, on what looked like a bed of straw. She turned her startled face and wide eyes on him.

Those carrying him let him go. His knees hit the ground, then he slid forward on his face. He closed his eyes against pain once more.

He lay like that for a while. Maybe he slept. Next, his eyes were open and Jade was staring at him.

He lay on his face, his hands doubled behind him and firmly tied, his head aching like hell. He could feel the stickiness of blood on his face and forehead, thickest around his right temple. He and Jade were alone in the shack. She was maybe a dozen yards from him. She asked, "What are you doing here?"

It took him a couple of attempts to speak. "Long story."

"Obviously!"

He was puzzled about a lot of things, but it took him some time to work out one particularly confusing issue: that her hands didn't seem to be bound. He asked, "How have they got you tied?"

364

She lifted both legs. A black chain linked shackles around her ankles, and another short chain ran to a heavy block. "Just these leg chains."

"Where the hell did they get a crazy contraption like that?"

Jade gave him an angry glare. "I didn't bother to ask!"

He had to concede it was a stupid question. "Is there a lock on the door?"

"A padlock I think."

"Great." He shifted on to his back and lay with his eyes closed, groaning softly.

The girl made a sound of impatience. "Aren't you going to *do* something?"

"I'm gonna have to rest a spell. Ira fetched me a good one with a rifle butt."

"It's your job to get me out of here."

"You ain't the one with your skull broke."

As he spoke, Choctaw realized he hadn't asked about her and felt a little shame. "Are you all right? Did they . . . ?"

He paused, not knowing how to go on. Jade helped him out by coming back quickly. "No. The one with the eye patch, he keeps talking about me being valuable merchandise, they mustn't trifle. But I don't like the way the other one keeps looking at me." A note of anguish, desperation, or pure fear entered her voice, something he hadn't heard from her before. "I've never known such vile human beings. Those men are murderers; they killed Brazos!"

"I know."

He was trying to remember something important, but the pain behind his eyes stopped him from working out what it was. Maybe he drifted off because his next awareness was Luz standing there, and Ira. They were there, but not Dec . . . not his friend, Dec . . . Luz held some plates so he guessed she was bringing the captives food. Ira glared at him and spoke but the words got all mixed up and became bleary and formless.

Choctaw drifted in a gray and dark world and a voice was speaking, a persistent jabbering at him. Maybe it was Ira and then he realized it was Declan saying, "And one thing most especially . . . don't come back." And then he said something like, "If anyone has to kill him, I'll be the one to do it."

Choctaw felt a different kind of a pain. He said, "Thanks, friend." But what was a friend? He heard Dec again, saying, "There are no friends, boy. Surviving in this world — that's all that counts."

And then it was later, and Choctaw was alone with Jade once more. She asked, "Is that all you're going to do, lie there and moan?"

"All I can do, right now." All the same he decided that the pain in his head had eased a fair amount.

In a voice he was familiar with, she sneered, "My hero!"

"I surely am sorry to be such a disappointment to . . ."

Choctaw let the words trail off, because it came to him, what he'd been trying to remember before. He stretched out his right foot towards her. "Take my boot off."

In outraged surprise she asked, "What for? Has that crack on the head turned you into an idiot? An even bigger idiot, I should say."

"Do like I ask."

She swore.

A very small smile touched his lips. "You didn't learn language like that at Vassar. Or did you?"

"Why should I take your boot off?"

Choctaw bit down on his impatience. As calmly as he could, he answered. "Because there's a knife hidden in it."

CHAPTER FORTY-SEVEN

It took a while, Jade sawing away with the knife at Choctaw's bonds, and she cut him a few times, including a long gash in his left forearm. Naturally, she didn't apologize. But at last, he was free. He'd been tied so tight he'd started to lose all feeling in his hands, so he didn't figure he'd been cut loose any too soon. But what came next was even worse. As blood returned to these limbs, it brought exquisite pain. To add to that, his head began to ache again. A bruise was swelling to a lump the size of his fist on his right forehead, under a thick crust of blood, which was also sticky on his right cheek.

Jade asked, "What do we do now?"

"We can't go far with you in that ball-and-chain contraption. Let's hope one of those twins comes visiting. Then I can stick this knife up against his back and get him to dig out the keys and set you free."

"You think it'll be that simple?"

"Probably not."

Jade started to speak and there was a clanging outside, as someone kicked a tin.

They had sufficient warning to get into their positions: Choctaw with his back against the wall and his hands behind him, Jade lying on the straw. Choctaw squatted like a jack-in-the-box, pressed down on his hunkers, his rump resting on his back heels, ready to spring. He breathed long and slow, to steady his shot-to-pieces nerves.

A key turned in the padlock and Ira Gird entered.

He held a pistol, a long-barreled Remington Army .44. He gazed at both prisoners, but then concentrated his attention on Choctaw.

Ira said, "It's a funny thing." The bottom right side of his jaw was purple and swollen, and he spoke as if he was slowly chewing food. "Thought I heard something and I looked in here and somehow you'd got loose, boy. Tried to jump me. So, naturally, I had to defend myself." He turned the pistol in his hand. "I know Red said he'd take care of you if anybody had to, but he ain't gonna do it. You and him's too . . ." He sneered. ". . . *friendly.* So that unpleasant task falls to me."

He touched his jaw gingerly. Pain and then hatred gleamed in his good eye. "I owe you."

Choctaw braced himself.

Ira glanced at Jade. "As for you, bitch —"

Jade shrank back and her hands clutched fistfuls of straw.

Ira's hand moved from the bruise on his chin to the quirt mark below his eye. "I ain't forgot how —"

Choctaw sprang. As he leapt across the room, he brought his arms 'round and forward; he drove the knife in his right hand at Ira's throat.

Ira lashed out with the pistol. A wild swing, but lucky. He caught Choctaw's right forearm, numbing it. Choctaw let the knife fall. Ira sprang back and Choctaw sprawled facedown at the other man's feet. Ira raised his pistol, poised to strike down.

Jade lifted the bunches of dirty straw she'd grabbed. She flung them at Ira's face.

He swore and swept out an arm to deflect them. Which gave Choctaw time to scramble up. As Ira spun towards him, Choctaw struck the other man flush on the mouth.

It wasn't as good as the other punch but Ira reeled and went over. He hit on his back and slowly rolled backwards and fetched up against the wall.

Choctaw glimpsed his knife on the floor. He dropped on all fours and reached for it.

Ira reared to his feet. He stared out of eyes that didn't focus, shaking his head. Choctaw grabbed the knife and started to rise. Ira kicked out. His foot caught his enemy under the left-side ribs. Choctaw grunted as pain shot through his side. He flipped over, hitting the ground on his back.

Ira lifted his pistol.

Choctaw forgot the pain in his ribs. He drew back his arm.

Ira's lips twisted in a mirthless smile as he aimed.

Choctaw hurled the knife, putting all his strength into the throw.

The blade flashed in the air, turning, then the haft was standing out from Ira's throat. He slammed back against the wall. He clutched his neck and made strangled, choking noises. Blood spurted from the wound and his mouth. He dropped his gun and put both hands to the knife.

Hurt and winded from the kick, Choctaw couldn't move, only watch.

For a moment, it seemed Ira was pinned to the wall. But the knife in his throat — a slim piece of metal and its rawhide haft — might have been as heavy as a roof beam. Its terrible weight was forcing him down.

He sank to his knees, swayed, and then toppled onto his face.

Ira lay writhing while a great lake of blood spread around his head, a viscid darkness reaching across half the floor. He made some drowning-in-his-own blood and death-rattling noises that were hard to listen to.

Finally, he was silent. He no longer moved.

Choctaw stared at the dead man in something like horror, letting reaction do what it always did to him. He saw Jade had twisted away, doing everything she could not to look at the corpse.

Choctaw didn't like looking at him either. He rose, one hand to the pain in his side. He said, "I'm gonna have to turn him faceup to look for a key to them shackles. You might not want to see."

She kept her eyes averted as he went through the corpse's pockets. And got lucky: he found a key for the shackles in Ira's vest pocket. He also found his watch and a roll of greenbacks. He didn't count it, but it was clear Ira had died a wealthy man.

Choctaw unchained Jade. She sat, kneading her ankles, while he covered the dead man in a blanket. He tried to avoid getting too bloodstained, which was difficult given how much Ira had shed.

Jade said, "That was . . . horrible."

"Yeah. It sure was."

She went to the door of the shack and pushed it open a few inches. "Well, the door's unlocked." She peeked out. "It's close to sundown. Pretty soon they'll come looking for him, or that Mexican woman will bring food."

"I know."

"Then we need to move."

Choctaw closed his eyes and sat back against the wall. "My head's hurting again. I think Ira really busted it. How soon till dark?"

"Not long. Ten minutes, half an hour . . ."

"Right. We'll wait until the light goes."

"We can't wait! Any minute they could —"

"We'll have to risk that. Better we have cover of darkness. Soon as the light goes, you sneak a horse out of the corral."

"Me? What about you?"

"Way my head is, I don't think I can sit a horse. Not traveling hard."

"But —"

"So you get a horse. But . . . this is important . . . don't ride out. They'll hear. Lead your horse. At least half a mile. Then mount up and ride like hell."

"Which direction?"

"Doesn't matter."

"I don't want to go alone. Not with those two men after me. Especially that other twin." She made a noise like she was shuddering. "I want you with me."

"I didn't figure I was your idea of a hero."

"I still want you with me."

He sighed. "I'll just slow you down."

He saw fear in her eyes. The hard shield she normally wore seemed to have gone. Now she looked frightened, vulnerable, someone he could feel protective towards. Maybe even someone he could like.

He said, "All right. Just give me a minute and I'll see if I'm fit to move."

In alarm she asked, "You're not going to fall asleep again?"

"No."

But he nearly did, lying back with his eyes closed. He was drifting, and then Jade said, "It's pretty much full dark now."

Reluctantly, Choctaw opened his eyes. Slowly he got to his feet. The roaring in his head had calmed; now it was a solid dull ache. It was maybe on a level with the worse hangover he'd ever had. He took up his knife and Ira's pistol. He said, *"Ugashay."*

Jade gave him a bewildered look. "What?"

"That's Apache. Don't you speak it? I

figured you did, considering who you look like."

"What are you talking about?"

He smiled at the confusion and alarm in her face. She was probably thinking the blow on the head had rendered him an idiot after all. He stepped towards the door. "*Ugashay.* It means: let's go."

CHAPTER FORTY-EIGHT

Choctaw saddled his buckskin while Jade saddled another horse in the corral. Neither saddle contained anything in the way of weapons or food, but there was at least a full canteen of water draped on one. They led both animals away from Irishman's Wells.

It was a night of keen cold, but by the time he was out of sight of the buildings Choctaw was damp with sweat.

They weren't discovered.

He'd tried to figure out whether it was best to go east or west, without coming to a conclusion. Pretty much on a whim he pointed east. After what he judged was maybe half a mile, he whispered, "We can mount up."

But after only a mile or so he reined in.

Jade asked, "What is it?"

"We still need to keep our voices down."

Jade made a sound of anger. Nonetheless,

376

she lowered her voice. "Why are we stopping?"

"It's too dark in this pass. I can hardly see the trail in front of me. We keep on riding blind, pretty soon one of these horses will put their foot in a hole, break their leg or something. And we sure don't want to be set afoot. We need to find a place to roost, then we can get going again at first light."

"But they could be right behind us! That twin'll want to avenge his brother."

"Sure he will. But they can't ride blind either. The only thing we can do is find someplace to hole up tonight."

So they did.

Choctaw led Jade into a small canyon in the south wall of the pass. They followed its curving passage, climbing a long slope to a little plateau strewn with boulders. These giant rocks gave cover and shelter, while the slope was of loose gravel and shale that no enemy could cross without making considerable noise.

They sat against rocks and wrapped themselves in blankets. A night wind prowled, as cold against the flesh as the blade of a knife.

Jade said, "I'm hungry."

"Nothing we can do about that."

"I'm cold, hungry, and miserable."

"You've got to be alive to feel them things.

Unlike poor old Ira."

"Poor old Ira? He was an evil man!"

Choctaw ignored the outraged face she turned towards him. He saw, instead, Ira with his hands to the blood spurting from his throat. Ira lying facedown in a spreading lake of darkness. He heard the choking, strangling noises the man made as he died. "I figure the Almighty does the judging."

"Well, I don't believe in the Almighty and all that nonsense. You mean you do?"

Choctaw pulled the blanket tighter about his shoulders. "Try and sleep."

A sullen silence came between them. The night grew black as a bucket of tar and the cold sharpened. It felt like a film of ice was forming on his skin, burning his ears and nose, numbing his hands and feet.

Jade hadn't quit complaining. "I'm *so cold.*"

Choctaw began to say, "Come here" but she was ahead of him, moving to his side. He drew back his blanket and she pressed her body, still wrapped in her own blanket, against him, resting her head on his chest. Her hair brushed against his mouth as he pulled his blanket over her.

Slowly the warmth in each body began to warm both. He had no thoughts of lovemaking. Jade couldn't have either; from her breathing he judged she was falling asleep. Still, it sure felt nice to have a woman lying against him, even if she was as much of a handful as Jade Rawlins.

All over America there would be fellows his age, and younger, bedding down with their wives, thinking ahead to tomorrow and nothing more daunting ahead of them than organizing the doings for Christmas Day, any last presents to buy Ma or Grandma and the kids, and the last day's work on the farm or in the store, living lives of settled-down peace and order, no guns in their lives but the old squirrel rifle Grandpa left them for the one time in the month they went hunting, when they never killed anything bigger than a deer. Meanwhile, he was hiding in cover in the icy Arizona mountains, with desperate, lawless men on his heels, and a posse of the "law-abiding" too, good citizens crazy with hanging fever, eager to give him a taste of the rope. How had his life taken such peculiar turns that so many wanted him dead, that half the time his thoughts went back to a man drowning facedown in his own blood, a man Choctaw had himself killed?

While he was pondering such things, he fell asleep.

■ ■ ■ ■

The man sat his horse, his hands tied behind him, a noose around his neck and the rope climbing above his head. But his face was turned away; Choctaw couldn't see who it was. Rawlins asked, "Well, boy, what do you say?" and Choctaw heard himself answer. "Hang him." Then someone struck the horse's rump, the animal sprang ahead, and the body jerked into the air, kicking wildly . . . The rope creaked and the body turned, an endless river of piss streaming down one leg, and the face slowly twisted around towards him, the rope sunk deep into the neck, the tongue poking out of the lolling head, swollen and purple-black but at last recognizable.

It was Dec's face.

The Irishman's body turned and the rope creaked as Choctaw's own words beat in his ears like a covey of angry birds — "Hang him" "Hang him" "Hang him" — and Billy Keogh was striding towards him, down Main Street in Lobo Wells, a pistol in his hand, and Choctaw lifted his own pistol and aimed, but Keogh's soft face shifted; now it was Dec striding towards him, wearing his trademark crazy grin and his pistol aimed into Choctaw's right eye and his finger tightening on the trigger, and Choctaw trained the gold front sight at the middle of that crazy grin and squeezed the trigger but Jesus it was a hard, slow pull, then one gun, just one of the two pistols, banged . . .

Choctaw awoke with a start, jerking up.

He woke in the dark gray light that came just before dawn. The new sun was a line of orange turning red, peeking over the hard black edges of the mountains.

Jade lay on her side next to him, making small sleeping noises. Her head and shoulders were out from under the blanket. Moving carefully so as not to wake her, Choctaw slid out from under the blanket, then wrapped it around her.

Cold bit deep into his fingers and toes. He flexed these digits and gasped at the pain that brought. His ears smarted fiercely. He started to shiver and his teeth chattered.

He answered that by swearing slowly and meaningfully, standing, stamping his feet, rubbing his hands together, blowing steaming breath over them and walking around. All the time images from the dream stayed with him.

The air paled from dark to pure gray, so he stood in a mist-colored world. He walked through this strangeness to the horses and looked them over. Returning to where Jade lay, he inspected his only gun — Ira's Remington pistol — cleaning it as best he could. There were five bullets in the chamber and fourteen more in Ira's gun belt, which he'd strapped on. Not much firepower against two men with rifles, pistols, and plenty of ammunition.

By then it was daylight. Jade woke and copied him in the shivering and teeth chattering routine. He asked, "You still hungry?"

"If I ever thaw out, I might be. Aren't we going to get out of here?"

"Soon as we've warmed up some. We've got to get out of this pass. That's the main thing. Once we're out of this trap, we'll find a place where we can roost. Where we can risk making a fire. I might even take a chance and shoot a rabbit or something. Right now, I'll see if I can scare up something to eat."

"Like what?"

"Something like squaw cabbage maybe."

She gave him a look of pure contempt. "You expect me to eat like a squaw?"

Choctaw bit down on his temper once more. But this time it wouldn't be denied. "No, I tell you what we'll do." He held down his voice but spoke with slow anger. "We'll go find the nearest fancy restaurant.

There's bound to be one round here some-place. We can dine there! Christ's sake!"

Jade looked startled. For a moment the expression on her face was almost subdued. But then her lips pursed and her eyes narrowed as she glared her hatred.

He could try and match that. But he decided that in any hating contest she was likely to win. Instead, he smiled ruefully. "Way you act, you must have studied on Kate in *The Taming of the Shrew.*"

She snorted her contempt. "What would you know about Shakespeare?"

He rubbed his hands against his pants, warming them some more. " 'If I be wasp-ish, best beware my sting.' "

She raised her eyebrows in surprise, a look he enjoyed. Then he turned and walked away.

He was still enjoying that look as he churned his way down the gravel slope. Then it came to him he was making more noise than a buffalo in a hardware store. And that two dangerous men were looking for him, and might be within earshot now.

Choctaw moved off the slope and made his way down over a stretch of jutting rock ledges, making a staircase with deep steps. Slow and awkward going but quieter under-foot. He got busy looking for anything edible. All he could find were some mesquite beans, plus some prickly pear pads that would contain a fair amount of juice. And some squaw cabbage.

He headed back uphill. The path before him narrowed to a spine of bare rock about a yard wide, rising above thorny brush on either side. He chewed a few mesquite beans as he climbed, taking the edge off his hunger.

He couldn't shake the dream. Mostly he could still see the gun Dec pointed at him, and the one he pointed back. Would Dec be able to aim at him and pull the trigger? Could Choctaw shoot Dec, if it came to it? Then again, it *had* come to it.

Choctaw halted.

For a moment he wasn't sure why. And then he knew, and any shreds of the dream left him. He was all at once very alert, listening hard.

To a voice.

Coming from above and to the left, from where Jade had been. But this was a man, asking, "Where's your boyfriend?"

It was Asa Gird speaking.

CHAPTER FORTY-NINE

Choctaw remembered something about Asa Gird.

The first time he saw this man, he'd been wearing Apache moccasins.

How had Asa come across them? Just picked them up somewhere? That was possible. It was also possible Asa had known Apaches. Even been a scout against them. Had learned the arts of trail craft and sneaking around from them, just as Choctaw had.

Because Asa had sneaked up on him pretty good here.

On top of that Asa was totally amoral and borderline crazy. Which made him a very dangerous enemy.

Choctaw swallowed the fear in his throat. He went forward, moving as quietly as he could along the spine of rock. When he judged he was about level with where Asa's voice had come from, he got down on his belly. Using the barrel of his Remington, he parted wires of brush to his left and peeked through.

He'd ended up on a ledge overlooking the place where they'd rested last night. Down below, Jade was standing.

Asa Gird stood behind her.

He'd leaned his rifle against a boulder behind him, and had a pistol in his right hand. It looked like a Smith and Wesson, the barrel poked into the side of Jade's head. He had his left arm across her throat.

He moved slightly and Choctaw saw he wore his Apache moccasins.

Asa spoke in a fierce whisper. "Where is he?"

Jade was trying to squirm away from the pistol but he held her tight, careful to keep him in front of her as a shield.

Still whispering he said, "Just keep squirming. I can break your neck easy." Asa grinned. "Or maybe I'll start with your arm."

Choctaw couldn't risk a shot, too much chance of hitting Jade. He had to get closer . . . but remembering how Asa could roughhouse, not too close . . .

He edged back behind the screen of brush and thought a minute or so. Then he moved forward along the narrow ridge. His plan, in as far as he had one, was to come out behind Asa.

The ridge he was on — he christened it the East Ridge — ended a few yards ahead. There was another ridge angling off to the left — the North Ridge. If he moved along that, it would take him behind Asa.

The nearest end of the North Ridge was cloaked in brush. He couldn't see if there was firm purchase underneath. If he went there, maybe he'd find himself standing on nothing more substantial than a tangle of foliage . . .

But he decided to risk it. For Asa, the sensible thing to do would be to keep Jade safe for ransom. But Choctaw couldn't trust this man to be sensible. Not in the best of times, and certainly not now he had his brother to avenge. Any minute Asa might take it into his warped mind to hurt Jade, just to ease his own pain.

Choctaw wiped the fear-sweat on his hands against his pants. Then he moved forward, stepping onto the North Ridge.

His feet came down on something firm. He couldn't see through the tangle of cover but judged he was almost directly above the woman and her captor.

Another step and he was still on solid earth. More confidently he stepped ahead.

His left foot came down on rock.

But it was rock that shifted under him, sliding left and down. He brought his right foot down and that slid out from under him too. This ridge was covered with loose slates! He toppled to his right while his feet plunged to the left. He yelled in terror.

He fell.

Choctaw plummeted into brush that clawed and struck at him. He grabbed wildly, caught shrubs and roots and felt the yank of his arm in its socket as it jarred to full length. He hung by one hand. He grabbed out with the other hand, and the roots and shrubs he clutched broke loose from their moorings and he fell once again.

More brush ripped and raked him, and then he was through and dropping into space.

Asa and Jade were almost directly below him. Both glanced up; both mouths opened wide.

Choctaw struck against one or both of them. All three went down.

Choctaw didn't land as hard as he could have because someone under him broke his fall. He spilled sideways. Half of his wind had been driven out of him and he floundered dizzily.

After a time, he made it onto all fours, shaking his head. He was conscious of a prickling numbness in his left side and knee, pain in his left hip and elbow, many small cuts stinging with blood on his flesh. But he forgot all that when he realized two things:

He'd dropped his pistol.

And Asa was rising to his feet before him. He stared at Choctaw.

Choctaw had never seen such hatred in anyone's eyes.

Asa turned away, reaching for something behind him.

It came to Choctaw he couldn't just sit here and watch this. So he tried to rise. But he couldn't find the wind or strength to move.

Asa spun back and he was holding his Henry rifle. He lifted it, aiming.

Jade yelled something and flung herself against him, grabbing the rifle. They wrestled for it.

She was a strong girl but he was stronger. He swung the rifle butt; it caught her against the side of the head and she spun away, falling.

She'd bought Choctaw time to recover some of his wind. He came to a crouch and launched himself at the other man, grabbing the Henry.

Asa jabbed a knee at Choctaw's groin. Choctaw twisted so the knee rammed his thigh, and then fell onto his back. He yanked Asa towards him, kicking his feet into the other man's belly. He hooked Asa off the earth and pitched him ahead. Asa somersaulted forward and hit on his back.

They scrambled up. The Henry lay between them. Both got a hand to it simultaneously. But Asa was quicker. As his left hand grasped the barrel, he swung a right-handed punch. He clipped Choctaw's jaw and knocked him away.

Choctaw went sprawling. He lay dazed a moment. When he moved, something dug into his spine. He squirmed over and saw it was the Remington pistol.

Asa struggled to his feet. He lifted his rifle as Choctaw leveled the handgun.

Choctaw fired.

Asa jolted back on his rump. He still held the Henry.

He sat, his face gray with shock. His shirtfront was all bloody. In that instant Choctaw remembered Billy Keogh.

Asa started to lift his rifle and Choctaw fired again.

Then Choctaw's trigger finger couldn't be stopped. He kept firing until the pistol was empty.

CHAPTER FIFTY

Choctaw crouched over Jade Rawlins. At first, seeing her stillness, her closed eyes, fear ran cold through him. Then he noticed how her chest rose and fell; she made the small noises of a troubled sleeper, and he knew a wash of relief.

But her face was gray, and the darkness of a bruise was starting on her right temple, so it was only a qualified relief. You never knew about blows to the head. He decided not to move her, but rolled up a blanket and used it as a pillow for her, covering her up to the chin with another blanket.

Then he moved over to Asa Gird. Three of his shots had taken Asa in the face, leaving an unrecognizable mess of blood and bone. For the second time in little over twelve hours, Choctaw found himself going through the pockets of a dead Gird Brother, trying not to look at them, or get their blood all over him.

Asa also had a wad of greenbacks on him, less than Ira had carried. Choctaw also claimed the man's rifle, his revolver — a Smith and Wesson Model 3 — his full gun belt and his Apache moccasins.

Choctaw wrapped the corpse in a blanket and carried it maybe two hundred yards. He came to a little gully strewn with loose rocks. He had no means of burying Asa in the hard earth, so he piled rocks on the dead man. He covered the body as thoroughly as he could, although he didn't doubt wolves and coyotes would be able to dig Asa up eventually. But his main concern was to keep buzzards at bay, as these birds hovering would mark the place for all to see.

For Declan Flynn to see.

Choctaw returned to Jade. He frowned at how deeply she still slept. Then he went looking for Asa's horse.

As he searched around, he remembered to be hungry again, chewing the last of his store of mesquite beans.

He came across Asa's horse ground-hitched in a draw. An almost full canteen of water hung on the saddle. And the saddlebags were full of bounty: two cases of cartridges, one of rifle shells, one of pistol, a coffeepot, a sack of the grounds. A half-full bottle of sotol. A parfleche of pemmican, dried meat mixed with mesquite beans, piñon nuts, and berries. This was an Apache recipe, another indication Asa knew their ways.

Choctaw took a long drink of sotol. It wasn't the best liquor he'd ever drunk, or even the best sotol, but it did its job. Thus fortified against the cold, he took his plunder and returned to Jade. She slept on. Her color was better, although it worried him she hadn't awakened.

He posted himself back on the North Ridge. He sat with his legs hanging over the edge and his rifle across his knees, gazing through cover at the slope below. He chewed pemmican and drank water. He thought about the bag of coffee, deciding if they were still here this sundown, he'd risk making a fire, rather than endure another freezing night.

The day passed and shadows lengthened towards dusk. He descended from his perch to have a piss and look Jade over. Her color was normal, as were the sleeping noises she made. Still, she hadn't come 'round. He wondered if, as well as the blow on the head, she was sleeping off the full ordeal of the last few days, which must have been pretty terrible for her. At least she hadn't witnessed the killing of a second Gird

Brother; unconsciousness had spared her that.

There was noise, far below on the gravel slope.

Choctaw came instantly from his thoughts. He crouched down, gripping the Henry tightly in both hands. He listened hard.

There were more small sounds, and then it got quiet again.

If he was to call it, Choctaw would guess someone had started up the slope; then, realizing how noisy it was underfoot, they'd retreated, quiet as they could.

Choctaw moved forward to the boulders on the south side of this little plateau. He lodged behind one and peeked over it. At the bottom of the gravel slope was a scattering of rocks, the ground between them choked with brush. He studied that stretch in particular. After a little while he thought he made out a patch of red behind a screen of foliage.

Dec had a red shield front shirt.

Choctaw kept his focus on the red patch until it started to blur before his eyes; and then it shifted, and he saw a hat too. A sombrero. A man crouched back of a rock. And there was only one man this was likely to be.

Choctaw called, "I can see you, *amigo.* You'd better duck."

The voice he expected came, sounding happy as well as surprised. "Hey, Choctaw!"

"Dec."

The Irishman laughed, and despite himself, Choctaw felt a small smile work at his lips. Dec asked, "You seen Asa around?"

"He's around but he ain't going no place."

"You took care of him too, huh?" Dec whistled appreciatively. "No wonder you're a legend."

"I told you, I don't want to be no legend."

"Kind of late for that, ain't it? The way you put 'em in the ground? Pretty soon they'll be calling you the undertaker's best friend. Am I gonna be part of your legend too?"

Choctaw didn't know how to answer that. While he was thinking it over, Dec asked, "You got the girl with you? She safe?"

"Yeah."

There was a pause, which ended when Dec asked, "How's it come to this, *compadre?* We're friends."

Choctaw felt resentment about what Dec might be doing: reviving a friendship he'd dismissed in order to work on the other man. "So that's what we are, huh?"

"You know we are. And friends shouldn't

be trying to kill each other."

"It doesn't have to come to this. Not if you give it up."

"Give it up? Ten thousand dollars? The kind of money I've always dreamed of?"

"But it's a bad dream, *hombre.*"

"You're the one who should give it up. Leastwise give *her* up. I ain't gonna hurt her."

There was a silence while Choctaw thought. Finally, he said, "Can't do it."

"Come on, *compadre.* Best way for everybody. Rawlins gets what he wants, I get what I want, you get what you want."

"No, sir."

"Your preacher daddy again."

Choctaw felt the flick of temper. "Fuck you, Dec."

The Irishman laughed. "Fuck you too."

"Don't joke about this, Dec. Not this time. Our jokes aren't funny anymore."

"Sure they are."

"You've got a hanging posse on your heels, you crazy bastard. Best thing you can do is cut your losses and get the hell out of here."

"I intend to. Soon as I've got the girl."

"Dec —"

"So you just step aside and let me have her."

Choctaw felt anger at the words flying at him. Words Dec was so clever with. He couldn't seem to find any as skillful to use in reply. He hated how the words were a tangle around him, causing the confusion he felt. He found he was lifting his rifle; he fired a shot into the air.

That stopped the words for quite a time. A hard silence descended. He was the one who ended it. "You want her — come and get her."

Dec's voice was weary with regret. "That's it, then."

Choctaw guessed he felt the same. "I reckon."

Another silence. And then small noises intruded: gravel and brush stirring as Dec moved.

Choctaw took a quick glance over the top of the rock and saw the red patch had vanished.

He knew a sudden hope. Maybe Dec *had* called it quits. Faded back and taken off for safer territory. In which case Choctaw wouldn't have to point a gun at him after all . . .

He glanced behind him. Jade still appeared to be sleeping.

He returned his attention to the slope below. No red shirt, no sombrero, no gleam of metal or out-of-place movement.

He gave a hard sigh of relief.

In the same instant he noticed a piece of brush above and to the left, along what he'd nicknamed the East Ridge, stir more than it should in the low wind.

He started to duck and the shot came.

CHAPTER FIFTY-ONE

He felt the whip of the bullet in the air, the breath of it on the back of his neck. An instant later, he heard it keen.

Instinctively he pulled his rifle into his shoulder and fired back. He ripped off three shots, thrashing the brush along the East Ridge, before it came to him it was Dec he was shooting at.

There was silence. He waited to see a body come loose of the ridge, the dead man fall.

Nothing happened.

And then there was another shot. It whined overhead, not so close as Dec's first shot.

This time, Choctaw waited before returning fire. His rifle to his shoulder, his eye down before the sight, hunting for movement that would reveal his enemy . . . his enemy who had been his friend.

He gave the ridge hard scrutiny, seeing

nothing. But, after a minute, he heard a low rumbling.

It sounded like a small body of riders — three, four, five — approaching. Part of a posse, drawn by gunfire?

There was movement on the slope below. He heard running feet. Dec broke from cover and cut across and down the slope, his feet churning shale.

He must be pretty desperate to show himself like that, Choctaw thought. He made a fair target, plunging down the slant. Choctaw started to track the running figure . . .

Dec's feet skidded out before him; he crashed down on his rump. As he squirmed upright, Choctaw caught the middle of Dec's back in his front sight. It was an easy shot while the man floundered, all Choctaw had to do was squeeze the trigger . . . Dec crashed to his feet and went downslope, wading through loose stones that kept his progress slow. In that time Choctaw could have pumped four or five rounds through the fleeing man.

But he couldn't and didn't. He was still squinting down the sights, his finger laid against the trigger but not moving, when Dec reached the bottom of the slope. The Irishman even paused a moment, and half-glanced back, before lunging ahead, vanishing into cover.

Choctaw rested his forehead on the rock before him. His arms were shaking quite hard and he felt entirely drained.

A small noise behind him made him turn. Jade was sitting up, one hand to her head. He looked forward once more. In the draw, out of sight, there was the drum of hooves as a single horse ran. Then there was a gunshot, and another, and then the noise of other horses running after the first.

Jade called, "What's happening?"

"Wait here."

Choctaw moved past the boulders onto the slope. She called after him but he wasn't listening.

He went some way down the draw but saw nothing but settling dust. Hoofbeats still sounded, going away from him to the west, then fading out.

He returned to Jade, who sat with one hand to her right temple. He asked, "Are you all right?"

"I don't know."

He inspected her wound. Her color was fairly normal but the bruise on her right temple had become large, ugly, and purple-black. She said, "It hurts like hell and I'm dizzy."

"Not surprised. I've had the same, remember? Best thing you can do is sleep."

"What was that shooting?"

"Me and —" He almost said the name and paused. "— the other outlaw . . . we took a few shots at each other. But then a posse showed up and he took off."

"The posse's here?"

"No. They all went after the outlaw."

"What?"

"They couldn't have gone too far. If you want, I'll go after 'em, get 'em back here."

"But one of the kidnapper's is still out there? Is it the red-haired man?"

"Yeah. But don't worry about him. Right now, he's the one running for his life."

She glared. "Good. The sooner they catch him and hang him, the better."

There was a little silence before Choctaw said, "You want to eat something?" He offered the parfleche.

"What's this?"

If he told her what it was, he guessed she wouldn't eat it, so he lied. "I don't know. I found it in Asa's saddlebags. You don't have to eat it."

She sampled a little of the pemmican, pulled a face but kept eating. Choctaw sat, drank water, and tried not to think about the taste of tobacco.

Jade said, "I still don't understand what you're doing here." She chewed a moment. "That man, Ira . . . he said that you and the one they called Red were friends. And back at the ranch, everybody thought you were in with the Gird brothers. Were you?"

"If I'm in with the outlaws, why did I just kill two of 'em?"

"I don't know. Maybe you thought kidnapping a woman was going too far."

Now it was his turn to glare. But she concentrated on eating, not even looking at him. She finished the pemmican, which he took as a good sign, washing it down with water. Neither spoke until she said, "I'm sorry."

He glanced at her in surprise. "What for?"

"I haven't said a word of thanks to you. After everything you've done."

"Forget it."

She gave him an angry look. "I can scarcely do that."

After another testy silence he said, "Anyway, I got to thank you too. If you hadn't grabbed Asa's rifle, I'd've been done."

She ate; he looked around the little plateau, at nothing in particular. He decided he'd go look for the posse after all, and stood. She asked, "How do you know Shakespeare?"

The question surprised him. "My daddy used to spout it at me. He did it to brag on his book learning, but I guess some of it stuck. And winter before last I went prospecting with this old Englishman. Turns out he'd been an actor in his spare time. He used to ride his mule through the desert, declaiming Shakespeare."

Jade said, "I've seen Edwin Booth perform in New York City several times. I saw his Hamlet but I thought his Petruchio was better. I love poetry and poetic language."

"That old Englishman made me love words too." Choctaw smiled at his memories. "Unfortunate for him he also had a love of the bottle, which got in the way. Sometimes got his *Hamlet* mixed up with his *Romeo and Juliet.*"

A faint smile touched Jade's lips. Then she gave a slight laugh. He asked, "What's funny?"

"I'm just thinking how crazy this is. I'm stuck in the middle of the desert with outlaws and murderers after me and we're talking about Shakespeare."

Silence returned, not so unfriendly this time. Jade broke it, observing, "You're a strange person."

He nodded slightly. "Come to that conclusion myself."

"Before, what did you mean . . . you expected me to understand Apache?"

"Naturally, given who you look like."

"What?"

He spent a moment remembering. "That's who you remind me of. Nahlin, an Apache woman. Chiricahua Apache royalty. Niece of Cochise, no less."

He came out of his little reverie to see Jade had lost her smile and was back to glaring. In an icy voice she asked, "And how did you know her?"

Another occasion when he could lie. He considered that a moment, then said, defiantly, "In the Biblical sense."

She blinked. "That's what they said about you, but I didn't want to believe it."

"What they say?"

"That you'd learned what you know, how to kill people, from the Apaches. They called you an Indian lover."

He smiled bitterly. "I sure am. The only two women I ever loved were both Apaches."

She looked dazed. "I can't understand that. I can understand lust. I can even understand someone keeping a squaw over a winter, as a sort of blanket warmer. But . . . saying you *love* them."

"Why not? It's true."

"And I remind you of one of them?"

"I was paying you a compliment."

An ugly expression claimed her face, a mix of contempt and hatred. "A compliment?"

"Sure."

"To say I remind you of a *squaw*? I hate Apaches. Everybody I know hates them, including my daddy. My mother's brother was killed by Chiricahuas."

"What do you expect? A whole race of people . . . they've had everything taken from them. Their land . . . So they fought back."

She looked at him in something like horror. "You're justifying the murder of white people?"

"Apaches been murdered too. At Camp Walsh . . . they've been hunted like animals, bounty put on their scalps. We made treaties with them which we broke. When they've come in to talk peace, they've been arrested, poisoned, shot down . . ."

She shook her head slightly. "But they're . . . they're . . . savages."

He started to reply, but then he thought: What's the use? There was nothing he could say that would get past that one word.

Savages.

Choctaw felt drained again, tired into his bones. The friendship that warmed between

406

them had died as quickly as it was born. Killed by that word.

He stood and began walking. She asked, "Where are you going?"

Choctaw halted. "I'll go find that posse and get 'em back here."

"You're going to leave me alone?"

"There's only one outlaw left and last I saw he was running like a scalded cat away from here. Anyway, you got the rifle. And I know you can use it. You'll be all right."

She began to reply, and then her words fell away. He walked past the rocks and started down the slope.

CHAPTER FIFTY-TWO

Choctaw made his way to his horse and rode west.

He hugged the left side of the pass, in the shadow of the walls. He regretted leaving the rifle with Jade. If there was any more trouble, he'd only have a pistol to defend himself with.

Dusk was coming and the corridor ahead was filling with darkness. The sound of his horse's hooves rang eerily in the sounding board this pass made.

Then the buckskin lifted his head and his ears slanted forward. Choctaw knew he'd scented another horse and was swelling up to whinny. Choctaw laid his hand across the animal's nostrils. The buckskin shied, eyes walled in fear, then held still, knowing not to make any sound.

Choctaw waited, his hand on his pistol. More hooves knocked on hard rock. He judged two riders were approaching.

He was right: two shadowy figures turned a bend in the pass and rode their horses towards him.

Dry throated he called, "Hold up!"

Both newcomers reined in. They were a contrast: the left-hand rider appeared to be very tall and thin, the brim of his slouch hat shadowing his face. The man on the right was short and made up of square blocks piled on top of each other, including a square yellow-bearded face under a needle-crowned sombrero.

Longshanks asked, "Who are you?"

The man's voice had a nasal whine to it. Choctaw thought he recognized it. He fired the same question back.

A cold silence descended, as neither questioner answered the other. Shorty broke it. "We're part of the Eichmann's Crossing posse."

The very tall man said, "We still ain't heard who you are, friend."

Choctaw was working out how to answer when Shorty spoke again. "You with the Doan's Store posse?"

"Yeah."

Longshanks glanced at his fellow posse man in something like disgust. Then he regarded Choctaw with deep suspicion. He had a good face for doing that, long and narrow, with a long thin nose, flared nostrils and wild, close-set eyes. Choctaw was sure he'd seen him somewhere. Such a face, with its startled rabbit look, would be hard to forget.

Shorty was a contrast here too, as his face was open and cheerful. He asked, "Any sign of Jade Rawlins?"

"She's back there." Choctaw indicated behind him. "A mile maybe."

"What?"

"You catch any of the kidnappers?"

"The rest of the posse are chasing one of 'em."

Lengthy made an impatient sound. "Never mind him. What about the girl? She safe?"

"She's all right."

Shorty grinned, "Hey!"

Lengthy said, "Well, thank God for that. You better take us to her."

Choctaw said, "You'll find her easy. Like I said, she's just back there."

The tall man glared. "You still better take us to her."

There was an uneasy pause. Shorty started to look suspicious too, for all his friendliness. Choctaw said, "Sure."

He turned his horse and rode and the posse men followed.

Lengthy came alongside Choctaw. "I know

you from someplace?"

"Don't think so."

Choctaw was lying. Now he remembered: this was the deputy from the Eichmann's Crossing jail.

Choctaw reined in. "She's just up ahead. In those rocks, top of that slope."

Both posse men commenced hollering. "Miss Rawlins! Jade Rawlins. This is a posse here!"

After a minute, Jade's voice came. "I'm up here!"

Shorty laughed delightedly. "Jesus Christ!"

Lengthy called, "We'll be up there directly, Miss Jade!"

Shorty asked Choctaw, "You the feller found her?"

"Yeah."

"Pretty good Christmas present for you, huh? Rawlins has upped the reward for anybody finds his daughter to a thousand dollars. The same money he's put on each of the kidnappers."

"I don't want no reward."

The posse men stared in astonishment. Choctaw told them, "You can have it."

Shorty asked, "You crazy?" He addressed the tall man. "You hear that?"

Lengthy told Choctaw, "You gotta be plumb *loco* boy, turning down that kind of

411

money."

"It's yours."

The short man said, "Well, it's your loss. If you —"

Jade's voice came again. "What are you waiting for?"

Lengthy called, "Coming, Miss Jade!" He spurred his horse, and rode up the slope. Shorty followed. They seemed to be racing each other. But after only a hundred yards or so their horses were struggling, sliding about in the gravel, raising dust.

Choctaw didn't watch any more. He turned his horse and rode back the way he'd come.

Darkness fell. But there was a full moon, bathing the pass in a silver-blue mockery of daylight. So Choctaw could see where he was going, most of the way. Until he hit a stretch where the rock walls pinched close and deep shadows pooled on the ground ahead. When a voice called out of this darkness, he almost jumped out of his skin.

A man ordered, "Hold up!"

Choctaw reined in so suddenly the buckskin whinnied and half-reared.

The disembodied voice came again. "Who's out there? Speak up or duck!"

Choctaw gulped down the fear that was in

his throat once more. "I'm one of the Doan's Store posse."

The invisible speaker considered that. After what seemed a long period of considering, he called, "Come ahead. Nice and easy."

Choctaw kneed his frightened horse gently in the flanks and moved him forward at little more than a walk. Only a hundred yards or so along, two shapes formed out of the gloom, becoming men with rifles in their hands. Moonlight caught the face of the nearest man. He looked to have been in a fair few fights and to have lost most of them. His nose had been flattened and pushed half sideways into his right cheek; when he grinned, most of his front upper teeth seemed to be missing.

Choctaw reined in so close to this man his horse almost snorted its steaming breath into his face. Flat Nose rested his rifle on his shoulder. He asked, "You wanna be in at the kill, that it?"

"Huh?"

"We got one of them kidnappers trapped back there." He indicated behind him. Choctaw saw a break in the pass to the north, a gap maybe thirty yards wide. "Fellow called Flynn. We run him up a box canyon."

413

The second man also stepped into the moonlight.

Choctaw's stomach tightened as he gazed at this ghostly apparition, at home in this moonlit darkness. A gaunt figure with lined and ashen face, gray chest-length hair and drooping silver mustache.

Sheriff Blackstone.

Blackstone gave Choctaw a fierce look, which reminded the younger man of an eagle glaring at its prey while it flexed its talons. "What's your name, boy?"

"Calvin Taylor."

As soon as he spoke, Choctaw regretted it. He'd forgotten that Blackstone would have been asking about him in Eichmann's Crossing, where he might have identified himself to somebody.

But maybe he hadn't, as Blackstone didn't react to the name. Instead, he asked, "Any word on the Rawlins girl?"

Briefly Choctaw told how Jade had been found safely.

Blackstone said, "Thank God for that. We better tell the others."

Blackstone turned away, walking up the canyon.

Flat Nose followed him.

Choctaw dismounted. Leading his horse, he strode after Flat Nose. Coming alongside him, he asked, "You say you've got one of 'em trapped?"

Flat Nose grinned wolfishly. "Sure. Killed his horse and he took off up the canyon afoots. But he ain't going no place."

"No?"

"We've got him backed up against the cliff face. Which is a straight up climb. A mountain goat couldn't get up that, let alone a wounded man."

Choctaw felt alarm. "That fellow's wounded?"

"Hit bad, maybe. He's left a fair blood trail."

The canyon widened out. They came to a campfire, where two men sat or stood about.

Someone gave Choctaw a cup of coffee, which he drank gratefully while Blackstone told the posse about Jade. That caused a considerable commotion.

Choctaw asked Blackstone, "This your entire posse?"

"We got a fellow watching the horses and another watching Mr. Flynn. We had a bunch more, but they decided they wanted to be home with their families right now."

Choctaw was puzzled by that, but before he could ask about it the sheriff said, "Still, there's enough of us left here to get the job done. What about you? Are you staying with us?"

"Sure. A thousand dollars is a lot of money."

Dislike flickered for an instant in Blackstone's eyes. Then he spoke to all the posse men. "I think we better chow now. Bed down here tonight. Come sunup, we'll roust out Mr. Declan Flynn." He scowled. "That red-haired laughing bastard."

Choctaw asked, "What if he tries to sneak out past us in the night?"

"Afoot and wounded?" Blackstone snorted. "No, as long as we have a man keeping watch on him and the horses, we've got him treed. And come morning . . ." The sheriff let the words trail off. For a few seconds he stared bleakly; there was an expression almost of pain on his face. Choctaw wondered at that.

Flat Nose showed his broken grin again. He made a gesture like he was tightening a noose around his own neck. "He won't be laughing then!"

Food was dished up, prairie chicken washed down with black coffee. It was a grim, almost silent meal. After eating, men moved quickly to their blankets, wrapping themselves against the bitter cold.

Choctaw lay with his blanket pulled up to

his chin, watching stars in the icy blackness of the night. He thought about tomorrow, and what he was going to try to do. To himself he said, "Goddamn you, Dec."

CHAPTER FIFTY-THREE

Choctaw didn't intend to sleep that night.

He huddled in his blankets against the piercing cold and waited as the hours crawled by.

The blue full moon gave enough light to read his watch. When it told him it was 4 a.m., he slipped out of his blankets and made his way out of camp. He used every piece of skill he'd learned to do it without waking other sleepers.

He carried a full canteen on its long strap and a spool of rope; the Smith and Wesson he'd inherited from a dead man was holstered in his gun belt. He walked in the same man's Apache moccasins.

The next tricky bit was getting past the night guard, the fellow assigned to watch over Declan Flynn.

This turned out to be his friend Flat Nose. But Flat Nose was easy to sneak up on. He was sitting with his back to a rock, his rifle laid across his knees. And he was in a fairly sound sleep, judging from his snores.

Choctaw eased past Flat Nose and came to a long slope, pale blue in the moonlight. Atop the slope was a line of rocks, black blotches on gray darkness. Presumably Dec was up there.

Choctaw studied the slope. It was of deep sand, ground he could cross fairly noiselessly, even if he hadn't been wearing Apache mocs.

For all that, fear and tension gripped him like a fist. He didn't like the situation at all.

He was caught between two guns.

A man with a rifle behind him, and another armed man on the slope above.

If either spotted him, he could be shot to doll rags trying to climb that slope, naked of cover, cruelly revealed in blue half-light, in the baleful eye of the moon. It didn't mean anything that the man above had once been his friend. A bullet from a former friend would kill just as easily as a bullet from an outright enemy . . .

Still, he had no choice. He willed himself to find the courage to move forward.

He began to climb the slope . . .

After a hundred yards or so, he paused.

Despite the keen cold, his hands were damp with sweat. He rubbed that off on his pants. He crouched down, dizzy and harsh throated with fear, thinking grim thoughts, thinking what a crazy risk this was. As he did so, the sun appeared, a golden eye blazing on the black horizon. Darkness began to fade.

And this slope was no place to be once full light came.

To his left, parallel with the slope, Choctaw saw a long, steep incline. A gully made a groove down the middle of it, flanked with thorny shrub and stunted, wind-bent trees. If he climbed the gully, rather than the slope, he'd have cover on his right side, screening him from Flat Nose at least. He guessed the gully would take him parallel to, and past, Dec.

So when he started uphill again he angled to the left, off the slope and up the gully.

He felt relief at being off the slope. It was still a stiff climb. In places he pulled himself up hand over hand, clutching knots of brush and the stubby branches of the trees. But eventually he was out of the gully, lying on the flat place above it.

This was a little table, squarish, maybe twenty yards across.

Lying on his left side, not wanting to raise his head, Choctaw took his pistol out and checked for any dust in the mechanism. In his chest was the burn of high altitude, in his ears the lonely sear of wind.

Where was Dec?

There was a harsh cough, below and to the right. And very close.

Close enough to get Choctaw's heart leaping into his mouth.

Very warily he moved towards that sound, dragging his belly along the earth like a lizard, using his knees and elbows. He came to the edge and risked a quick glance over.

There was a stretch of flat ground maybe twenty feet below. Here Dec lay, sprawled on his face.

He was still, and Choctaw remembered the Irishman was wounded. Maybe he'd passed out from loss of blood. He might even be dead . . .

Then Dec moved. He raised his head and eased forward along the ground. He came to a scatter of rocks and peeked over them, gazing at the slope beyond, running down into the canyon. He held a Henry rifle.

Choctaw's fingers tightened on the grip of his pistol. It would be easy to shoot Dec now, drill him through the center of the back, and claim the thousand dollars reward. After all, the last time they'd met, they'd been trying to kill each other . . . and there are no friends . . .

Choctaw eased back from the edge and scouted around for a way down from this little table. He found one, an easy slope of deep sand he descended almost noiselessly. This brought him out behind Dec, with an angle of rock jutting between them.

Choctaw gripped the Smith and Wesson tightly. He waited until he had any fear under control, took a deep swallow, and moved, sliding around this corner of rock.

The Irishman seemed to be stretched out in exactly the same position as before, still pointing his rifle. There was a pistol lying at his side.

Choctaw aimed his Smith and Wesson and cocked it. He said, "Got you covered, *amigo.*"

Dec glanced back over his right shoulder. Seeing Choctaw spoke the truth, he held very still. But his face, as much as Choctaw could see it in profile, almost instantly lost its surprise. He grinned. "Hey, Choc!"

Choctaw guessed almost nothing would put a dent in this man's grin. Despite everything, a small smile worked at his lips in response. But things were too hard; he couldn't keep smiling more than an instant. He said, "Throw the rifle clear. Easy."

"You gonna shoot me?" Dec's voice rasped with thirst.

"Do like I say."

Dec tossed the Henry onto the ground maybe four yards away.

Choctaw said, "And the pistol."

"Don't worry about the handgun."

"Get rid of it anyway."

Dec appeared to shrug slightly. He lifted the pistol off the earth and threw it after the rifle.

"Now get your hands up."

The Irishman raised his hands, palms forward. He slewed around, resting his back against the rock, facing the other man. He was still smiling.

Choctaw said, "Move away from those guns."

"Don't think I can. Can't hardly move."

Choctaw walked over to the other man, keeping the Smith and Wesson trained on him. He picked up Dec's pistol, a Remington Conversion, and laid it next to the Henry.

Choctaw passed Dec his canteen. The Irishman drank hungrily, his face gray with exhaustion. His right pants leg was black with blood, and there was a large pool of it on the earth by him. A bullet hole showed near the top of his right thigh. Bright red jets of blood came out of the hole in regular spurts. Choctaw knew what that could mean and frowned.

He took his bandanna and tied a tourniquet around the top of Dec's leg. A couple of times the Irishman hissed with pain. Dec said, "Just think what you can do with a thousand dollars, *amigo.*"

"How do you know about that?"

"A couple of those bastards down there shouted up about it. Telling me how I was going to make 'em rich. Well, now I can make you rich."

"I don't want any fucking reward!"

"No? Then why are you here?"

"We've got to figure a way to get you out of this."

Dec gave a small, bitter laugh. "Can't be done. Posse's in front of us, and behind us —" He pointed.

Choctaw turned and looked. Behind them the cliff face reared sixty, seventy feet into the sky, the angry red rock of the Mogollon Rim country.

Dec said, "I been studying on that cliff. No way up there. It's so sheer I doubt an ant could climb it, let alone a feller with a busted leg."

Choctaw studied the rock wall. After a minute or so he had to admit Dec was right. Despair filled him.

The Irishman said, "No, I figure this is as

far as I go. Mr. Blackstone and company'll be along pretty soon. What happened to my pa and my brother . . ."

"I ain't gonna let 'em lynch you."

"Huh! You think you can stop 'em? You gonna stand guard over me all the way back to the Crossing? You got to sleep, you know."

Choctaw felt his despair turn to anger. "Can't you quit talking for once and let me think?"

"I know what the best thing is, *compadre*. For both of us. You just pull the trigger now."

"What?"

"You get the reward and I go the way I want. Better a bullet than a rope."

"You crazy?"

A plea came into the wounded man's voice. And fear too. "I don't want to die like my father, Calvin."

Choctaw scowled. There was a pause. In the silence he thought he heard small noises in the canyon below, like feet moving on loose soil.

Dec sighed. "No, you can't do that, can you, Choc? Even though it's the kindest thing. If you really were my friend, you would."

"Can't you shut up? I think I hear 'em coming."

"Then get it done, boy. Do it now!"

Choctaw didn't move, he didn't speak.

Dec took a slow drink from the canteen. "All right. If you can't do it, let me."

"Huh?"

"Let me have a gun. I won't use it on you, I swear. Leastways I'll go out shooting. Up to the last bullet, anyhow."

Choctaw rested his forehead on the back of his right hand. "There's got to be another way."

"There ain't."

There was the rustle of stones, below and to the right. Both men turned towards this noise. Dec pressed himself against the rocks, gazing downslope. He said, "They're coming, all right."

Choctaw stepped past him, to get a better view.

He was focusing on that, and not on Dec. In the tail of his eye, he glimpsed Dec move.

Spinning back towards him, swinging his arm.

There was the whip of the strap, then the full canteen struck Choctaw in the mouth like a solid punch. He staggered and fell, sprawling on his back.

Dec flung himself headlong towards his weapons. He landed facedown on sand, grunting with pain. His rifle was under his right arm. But Dec did a funny thing: he ignored this gun, reaching for his pistol instead. He stretched along the earth, getting a hand to the grip of the Remington.

There was fire in Choctaw's lips and blood in his mouth. He scrambled to his knees, still holding the Smith and Wesson.

Dec rolled over onto his back. He sat up, lifting the Remington, aiming at Choctaw.

Choctaw caught the other man's chest in his sights. He called, "Dec! Don't —"

But words couldn't stop this; Dec's pistol was pointing into his face, the Irishman's thumb worked at the hammer.

Choctaw fired. The shot went high, creasing the top of Dec's right shoulder. Dec jerked and swayed but he was still pointing, aiming. Choctaw squeezed the trigger again but he knew he was too late; he heard the click as the Remington's hammer fell. Then the pistol bucked in Choctaw's hand and Dec slammed back against the earth.

Choctaw got to his feet. As in a dream he approached the figure lying there, the prone shape that couldn't be Dec, and sank to his knees beside it.

There was a small hole in the center of the Irishman's chest and blood all over the front of him. But he was still smiling, his eyes bright with humor as well as pain. His lips moved, but the words were faint. Choctaw lowered his head to listen.

Dec tried again. As he strained to form words, a line of blood ran from each side of his mouth. He said, *"Gracias, amigo."*

In a strangled voice, Choctaw called, "You crazy bastard! Why did you make me — ?"

Dec's smile stretched towards a grin. He began to answer, his mouth filled with blood, and he died.

Choctaw sat, not moving. For how long, he didn't know.

He remembered something strange. He glanced around for Dec's pistol. It lay a few yards away and he picked it up.

The Remington had been pointing into his face and he'd heard the hammer click as it fell, but there had been no shot and he wasn't dead, which didn't make sense. He spun the cylinder to inspect the loads and what he saw didn't make sense either. So he looked again, only this time he couldn't see. Then he wiped his forearm across his eyes and he could.

He was sitting, staring numbly at the gun in his hand, as posse men came and stood around him. Blackstone said, "You wanted the reward all for yourself, huh?"

"That's right."

The sheriff gave him a look of contempt.

After a moment that vanished. "Well, you took the risk, you earned your money. You can collect it at the Crossing."

"All right."

Flat Nose gazed at Dec. He made a sound that was half wonder and half disgust. "This son of a bitch is dead and he's *still* grinning." He regarded Choctaw with angry resentment. "We had a rope ready for him, boy. I figure you cheated us."

Blackstone spoke with considerable weariness. He told this man, "Leave it."

Two men lifted the corpse and carried it somewhere. There was more talk, more angry and hostile looks directed Choctaw's way, but he ignored the posse and what they were doing. He sat, Dec's pistol in his hand, slowly turning the cylinder.

Blackstone declared, "Let's go home, boys."

The posse men descended the slope. Only the sheriff and Choctaw remained. The latter told Blackstone, "I'll follow you down."

The sheriff nodded. He turned and took a few paces downslope, then paused. He said, "Oh. There I was, forgetting what day it is."

"Huh?"

The very barest smile touched Blackstone's stark face. "Merry Christmas."

CHAPTER FIFTY-FOUR

Somewhere along the way, as Blackstone's posse rode west through the pass, Choctaw managed to lag behind. When the sound of their hooves had faded, he turned his horse and rode east.

He rode across the territorial line and into New Mexico. He kept to the wild places, camping on the trail, until he came to a little pueblo tucked up against a bend of the Rio Grande.

This turned out to be a Mexican settlement called Los Lunas. Choctaw was practically the only Anglo there, but that was all right by him. He could speak their language and people were friendly enough if you were friendly to them. They had a free-and-easy approach to life he approved of, hence their saying: "God made time, only man made haste."

He figured to lay up in Los Lunas a few weeks, as long as his money lasted. "His" money being the greenbacks he'd taken off dead Gird brothers. He saw 1874 in there. And then the weeks stretched out to over two months. His money lasted longer than he thought it would, and there was always somebody to get drunk with in the *cantinas.* There were also a few *señoritas* happy to help a lonesome young drifter forget his pain.

The winter passed this way, and then the land was waking into spring; he started to feel the same restlessness as the world around him. With most of the rest of his money he outfitted, then prospected the nearest mountains for a few weeks. He managed to pan out enough color to last him another month or so, which was as far ahead as he cared to look.

Still restless for pastures new, he made his way to Albuquerque and cashed in his findings at an assay office. He slept in a good hotel, the best Albuquerque had to offer, anyway, and spent a leisurely few days.

One afternoon in the middle of April, Choctaw was sitting in a saloon on the outskirts of town. He was the only customer, save for the barkeep, who leaned on the bar and ran a cleaning rag over dusty glasses.

Choctaw studied the glass of mescal in his hand. He felt more rested than he had in . . .

how long? The slow time of doing nothing and the solitary days he'd spent prospecting in the mountains seemed to have brought him some peace and calm at last.

But maybe he was ready to move on now, to be doing something after all this aimlessness. Being idle left him too much time to think, to remember . . .

Tomorrow, he decided, he'd point south to the nearest military post and sign up for another hitch as an Apache scout. Although things were becoming so quiet, Indian-wise, he might have to find another line of work.

A man entered the saloon. As was now his instinct, Choctaw glanced at the newcomer, looking first not at his face or his clothes, but at whether he wore a gun.

This man did, a pistol in a cross-draw holster. So Choctaw looked at the rest of him. He saw a medium-sized, dark-haired man in his forties, in pinstripe shirt, dark gray pants, and vest.

This man strode over to Choctaw's table and addressed him. "Are you Calvin Taylor?"

Choctaw looked the stranger up and down warily. "That's me."

"I'm Thaddeus Johnson. I'd like to speak to you, Mr. Taylor. Business proposition."

Choctaw indicated the vacant chair on the

other side of the table. "Sit down, Mr. John-son."

"Thank you."

Johnson sat. "Buy you a drink?"

Choctaw nodded. The older man ordered two mescals. While they were coming, he made himself more comfortable in the chair.

Choctaw's first impression of Johnson was of tension. His lips were pursed tightly and his eyes were a little too brilliant, too star-ing. It was a stern face, more given to frown-ing than smiling, emphasized by the heavy handlebar mustache and the dashes of gray at the temples.

Johnson said, "I have a ranch southwest of here. Cattle and horses." His voice was clipped, New England Yankee maybe. "I know Zack Rawlins."

"Yeah?"

"He says you took care of a horse thief problem for him."

"It wasn't just me."

"He reckons it was mostly you. And then there was that other business . . . with his daughter. You took care of that too."

That pushed Choctaw into doing what he was trying not to do: remembering. He frowned.

Johnson went on: "Though I have to admit, you seem a lot younger than I expected." The rancher took off his Plainsman hat and turned it on his lap. "Still, Rawlins reckons you'll get the job done."

"What job is that, Mr. Johnson?"

Johnson started to answer, then paused as the drinks came. Once the barkeep was back at the bar, Johnson lifted his glass. "Your health."

Both men drank. Choctaw asked, "What job are you talking about?"

"I've got the same problem as Rawlins. Thieves into my herds. Not a month goes by I don't lose stock."

"What's the law doing about it?"

"Huh! There isn't any — nothing nearer than Silver City. On the rare occasions the law shows up in my neighborhood, the thieves make themselves scarce. Soon as the authorities have gone back home, I'm being robbed again. I've even got my suspicions that these so-called 'lawmen' are tied in with the thieves." Johnson sat back in his chair. "So that's the situation. And I'm sick of it."

"What's that got to do with me?"

"Isn't it obvious?"

"I'd rather you put it into words."

Johnson thought a moment. "I want to hire you . . . officially as a cowhand. But you won't be spending much time punching cows. Stopping the thieving, that'll be your business." The rancher fingered one wing of his long mustache. "All right, that might be dangerous work. But you'll be paid accordingly, don't worry."

"And just how do I stop this thieving?"

"Any way you see fit."

"Up to and including killing?"

Johnson didn't seem to want to answer that. He placed his glass on the table and turned it, studying it as it revolved.

Choctaw asked, "You just want a hired gun, don't you, Mr. Johnson?"

"I've heard the term 'range detective' used."

"And what does that mean, exactly?"

The rancher gave the younger man a hard look, impatience putting a crease between his eyes. "Whatever you want it to mean."

It was Choctaw's turn to study the glass in his hand. He seemed to remember Rawlins telling him something. Warning him of something. Rawlins, or was it MacNee? Or maybe Swenson.

The rancher put his hat back on. "Well, I haven't got all day. I've got a ranch to run."

Choctaw pushed his memories away. Memories were useless. As useless as an empty gun.

Johnson stood. "What do you say? You want the job or not?"

Choctaw lifted his glass and drank. "Why not?"

ABOUT THE AUTHOR

Andrew McBride's previously published westerns — *Coyote's People, Canyon of the Dead, Death Wears a Star, Death Song, The Arizona Kid, Shadow Man,* and *The Peacemaker* — have won acclaim. All have the same central character — Calvin Taylor — as *Cimarrón.* Pulitzer Prize–nominated author Ralph Cotton describes Andrew Mc-Bride as "among the top Old West storytellers." Praise for *Coyote's People* (published by Five Star Publishing) from: Lucia Robson (Winner of the Spur Award and *New York Times* best-selling author), "An outstanding novel"; Robert Vaughan (Pulitzer Prize–nominated author), "Wonderful"; Kathleen Morris (Winner of the Peacemaker Award), "Masterful"; Richard Prosch (Winner of the Spur Award), "Highly recommended," Wayne D. Dundee (Winner of the Peacemaker Award), "Western fiction at its best!" Other reviewers: "Classic," "A superb western adventure." Andrew McBride lives in Brighton, England.